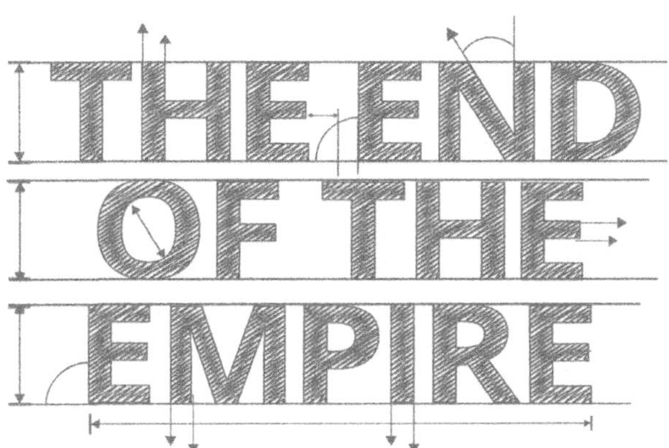

BY KEITH LOVELAND

ISBN 978-1-956573-02-2

This book is a work of fiction. Any references to historical events, real people, or real places are used fictitiously. Other names, characters, places, and events are the products of the author's imagination, and any resemblance to actual events or places or persons, living or dead, is entirely coincidental.

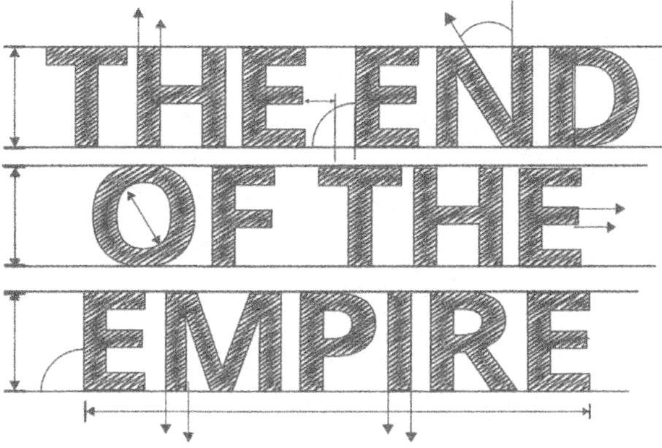
THE END
OF THE
EMPIRE

THREE: THE SLIDE

FOUR: THE FALL

ONE:
The Rise

WE WON THE WAR AND MADE THE WORLD SAFE FOR DEMOCRACY

The USS Wakefield pulled into New York Harbor in November 1945, filled with returning United States servicemen. They had won the war, VE Day had come and gone, VJ Day had also come and gone, and now they were free. Cameron MacAlpine and Harold Bergen rode the train home west to Saint Paul, Minnesota, Harold's hometown. Cameron grew up in Big Piney, Wyoming, an orphan who had enlisted as soon as war was declared. The two young men were paratroopers together in the 101st Airborne Division and best friends.

Now Harold had an idea. He was tired of destroying things, he wanted to create home, build houses and create home. He could imagine communities being developed and he wanted to be part of that. He wanted to be a builder.

"You know, Harold, that's brilliant," Cameron told him on the long ride. "I have nothing waiting for me in Wyoming. I would love to build with you. Let's do that together."

Cameron MacAlpine, though totally alone in the world, was a man of enterprise, a seeker, willing to roll the dice to get what he wanted. The idea of starting a business with a solid, hard-working guy like Harold was a dream to him. He could already see their success.

They could've claimed twenty dollars a week for fifty-two weeks as veterans, but instead they chose to work as carpenters for Bud Cronkite near the University of Minnesota. Bud had been too old to go to war, and he liked helping Cameron and Harold get started in this new life. They were go-getters. Get-it-done kind of guys. They learned soffits, plates, structure, measurements, squaring, tools, mudding, painting, roofing, and tacking, literally everything they needed to know to build houses from the basement up. But they didn't want to work for wages forever. They wanted to have something of their own, be in charge. Neither Cameron nor Harold wanted a boss. They wanted to be the boss. The Army had taught them that.

But first they wanted women in their lives. Harold Bergen had been a hard-working warrior, but he was also a totally romantic man. Right after he returned from the war, he walked into Nordquist Bakery, saw the beautiful woman running the cash register, and fell in love. Sunny, whose parents owned the bakery and an entire farm outside of the city, told the story for years, how this tall, lean soldier in his Army uniform with his fresh haircut and sassy talk, curly hair and blue eyes came in looking for the address to a bakery that sold great Danish. They were married six months later and had their first child, Lars, a year after that. His sister Ellie Mae came along a year later just before Christmas 1948, and Lena in early 1950.

Cameron married Sunny's best friend, Susie, on her eighteenth birthday, a year after the Bergens. Although she was young, Susie was not naive and understood Cameron's wolfish grin. She believed she could handle him just fine. Perhaps they weren't as romantic as their friends, but they shared a desire to succeed in life and each knew the other would contribute well to that end. They had two boys in two years—Cameron Junior and Andrew, who were like little bears, playing and screaming and having a ball—healthy, happy, all-American boys rolling around and having fun.

Both Harold and Cameron bought homes on the GI Bill in a neighborhood close to the University of Minnesota and kept thinking about the company they wanted to create. In 1951, they put out a sign announcing Alpine Homes. They purchased a pickup truck, a Ford F-1, and painted the name of the company on both doors. This was a big day for them. This is what they fought for, the American way of life. Two guys owning their own business, doing good work, and going home to wives and kids. Harold and Cameron were happy men. They bought television sets, watched the Saturday night fights, and rode the wave of building that followed the war. They built good homes at good prices and everything was gorgeous and wonderful.

In 1952, the Bergens and MacAlpines all voted for Ike. They liked that he had helped to win the war and was steady, not flashy, and that both the Republican and Democratic parties had courted him to be their candidate. It wasn't that they didn't like Adlai Stevenson, but they preferred Ike. They did not particularly like Ike's vice-presidential pick Richard Nixon, or as Cameron continually complained, "I just don't trust him—that's the thing." But they all overlooked that in order to have Eisenhower as their president.

When Sunny's parents died in 1953, she inherited several hundreds of acres of farmland just south of Minneapolis and that's when the Bergens and MacAlpines decided they would expand from being simply a building partnership into a land development and building corporation. All four of them owned the development corporation and were now in total control of the land, the models for houses, and building them. This changed everything. They could leverage the land they owned to buy more land and build more homes and create more communities. Within five years they had completed Birchwood Acres, Nordic Woods, Alpine Village, Alpine Farm, and Bergen Shores, totaling 872 homes.

Sunny and Susie created award-winning model home designs with room to expand upstairs and downstairs. Early on, they persuaded their husbands to install windows which were larger than most pre-war houses, giving the interiors an open, airy, spacious feeling. All of their designs utilized traffic patterns which maximized space and minimized the chopped-up feeling of many older houses, and the variety of models from which to choose caused potential buyers to feel as though the houses could be custom-built. Sunny and Susie also paid careful attention to landscaping details, giving their models immediate curb appeal, creating a welcoming feeling which turned drive-by lookers into walk-in home buyers.

Susie and Sunny were integral to the huge success of their company and with all four adults working together, it wasn't hard for them to gain enormous wealth. They took the risk at a time when the population was increasing, demand for home ownership was increasing, credit was available with easy terms, and the economy was expanding. It was the virtuous cycle in the aftermath of war.

It was only right that it would be the American Century following World War II and that the country would be an undisputed superpower. America's shores had not been attacked—other than Pearl Harbor. So of course, the World Bank would be here. Of course, the United Nations would be in America. And of course, the dollar would be the world currency, as good as gold and backed by the same.

It was also only right that the country would generate great wealth. This was the American Dream and the MacAlpines and Bergens could not think of it any other way. They didn't see luck as an element in their success and, as time went on, their children would not consider the element of luck either.

THE COWBOY CODE

Gene Autry had come along in the 1930s and continued to entertain through and after the war. He was known to be honest, brave, and true and in his movies, radio shows, and comic books, he set forth his code of good behavior for all his followers, mostly boys who wore braid-trimmed felt hats and toted pretend pistols on their hips. Lars Bergen, Cameron Junior, and Andrew MacAlpine loved Gene Autry. They learned the code, recited the code, and tried to live it in their own way.

1. *The Cowboy must never shoot first, hit a smaller man, or take unfair advantage.*
2. *He must never go back on his word, or a trust confided in him.*
3. *He must always tell the truth.*
4. *He must be gentle with children, the elderly, and animals.*
5. *He must not advocate or possess racially or religiously intolerant ideas.*
6. *He must help people in distress.*
7. *He must be a good worker.*
8. *He must keep himself clean in thought, speech, action, and personal habits.*
9. *He must respect women, parents, and his nation's laws.*
10. *The Cowboy is a patriot.*

By 1958, the Bergen and MacAlpine boys had formed a tight bond, informed by Gene Autry's commandments. They especially liked number seven: a cowboy must be a good worker. To that end they began a business, using Lars's bicycle to pull Cameron Junior's red wagon hauling a barrel of fertilizer that could help all their neighbors have more beautiful lawns. It worked, and everyone loved their lawns. Soon it was the real deal and they added mowing, raking, and clipping to their lawn care services. They called their business Lars Mows Best.

They thought they would be friends all their lives like their fathers.

But what did children know? Their parents were multimillionaires with very little strife and the boys thought this is the way life was meant to be, the way life had to be. You followed Gene Autry's Cowboy Code and you were rewarded.

IN GOD WE TRUST

One thing Cameron MacAlpine lost in the war was his faith. He did not believe that God would permit what he had seen in World War II. Still he thought it important to take his children to church for what it could teach them about community, service, humility, and the practical lessons of love and kindness. He may not have paid attention to what the minister was saying, but nonetheless he was good at repeating the church's lessons to his children—God is in your heart, God is love. That's where God is.

But then God came into the *Pledge of Allegiance.* In 1954, Congress added "under God" to the pledge—one nation, under God, indivisible, with liberty and justice for all. Cameron noticed this in the newspaper, of course, but he was busy and didn't mention it to his children. When they were very young, he had taught them to stand straight with their hands over their hearts and recite the pledge at parades and ball games and any other time the nation stood to honor.

Andrew MacAlpine started kindergarten on a Tuesday in September 1954. Miss Ward began the day with the Pledge of Allegiance and Andrew noticed immediately that everyone was saying it wrong, adding words. Miss Ward corrected Andrew with the prod, "one nation, under God, Andrew." To make her point, she had the class say it again, and when they were done, Andrew informed her that, "God is in your heart. This is school." Miss Ward escorted him to the principal's office, described his sins to Miss Taylor, and returned to her classroom. Miss Taylor explained to young Andrew that the pledge had changed during the summer and he had to learn the new words.

Andrew stubbornly repeated, "God is in your heart and in love. This is school,"at which time Miss Taylor wrote a lengthy note to Andrew's parents and told Andrew to give it to them when he got home. During lunch, he wrote his own note to his parents. "Dear Mom and Dad," he penned in his precocious fat printing. "I have a note from the principal because the president changed the pledge of allegiance this summer and put God into it and nobody told me and I said God is in my heart and now you have to sign her note and I have to bring it back and if I don't change my attitude I will grow up a delinquent. That was my first day of school. Love, Andrew." He was an unusually bright child. His parents signed the principal's note and had a good laugh over their morning cup of coffee.

The next summer Cameron Junior and Andrew enrolled in Pastor Lindquist's vacation Bible School, a two-week immersion into scripture and songs. The church was on the bluffs overlooking the Mississippi River. The morning of the second day went pretty well right up until Mrs. Lindquist told the children about Jonah and the whale. Several children could not understand how a whale could swallow a man without the man dying. Andrew piped up, "It's just a story. It probably never happened."

Mrs. Lindquist held her Bible to her bosom with her left hand, slapped the pulpit with her right hand, and said, "This is the Holy Bible. The very word of God." At which point, Cameron Junior, who was just as advanced in his thinking as his brother, piped up to say, "I think what Andrew meant is that the whale story is a parable. We're supposed to think about it and decide what it means." Mrs. Lindquist went to get Pastor to settle this theological point but during her absence one of the church ladies announced it was time for lunch. All the children went downstairs except Cameron Junior and Andrew, who walked out the side door, down the steep bluffs to the river, and began skipping rocks. And walking toward the arch bridge. And skipping more rocks. After lunch was over and the children were reassembled in the pews, neither Mrs. Lindquist nor Pastor Lindquist knew where the MacAlpine boys were, until Linda Horton, who always knew everything, said she'd seen them climbing the bluffs as she was going to lunch. The parents were called and then, hours later, the boys came back to the church just as study classes were ending for the day. Pastor and Mrs. Lindquist drove the boys home and informed Mrs. MacAlpine that they were no longer welcome at vacation Bible School.

This did not bother their father in the slightest. He sat his boys down to explain how things were in the world. "The reason that people are putting God everywhere and hanging on to the literal word of the Bible is because we're in a war with godless Communism," he said seriously.

"What are you talking about?" Andrew asked. He really did want to know.

And that's when Cameron showed them the Soviet Union on the map. "They are atheists over there," he said. "People are afraid, really afraid."

"Why?"

"Everyone wants God on their side," their father answered and left it at that.

THE RED SCARE

The year before Cameron MacAlpine explained the fear of godlessness to his children, Edward R. Murrow called out Wisconsin Senator McCarthy on his *See It Now* television show which aired on CBS, Tuesday evening, March 9, 1954. This "Report on Senator Joe McCarthy" revealed the senator's own words. McCarthy labeled anyone who opposed him treasonous, declared that only Republicans were honorable, that the Democrats were tools of Communism, and that even Eisenhower might now be a tool of Communism. Anyone who did not believe the senator was stupid, arrogant, or witless. For thirty minutes the television viewers saw clips of McCarthy speaking with Murrow's brief rebuttals interspersed. Murrow reminded his viewers that "we must not confuse dissent with disloyalty." He hoped the television audience was listening.

This made an impression on the MacAlpines and Bergens, who found Senator McCarthy to be a demagogue. "Dammit, that man is terrible, he sounds like a Nazi. He's a Fascist is what he is," Harold told his wife. "What did we fight the damn war for, Cameron?" he asked his friend.

Cameron wanted to make sure his sons were very clear about the meaning of all this. "In the world of ideas," he carefully explained, "any idea needs to stand or fall on its own merits, including ideas like Communism, Socialism and Democracy. One of the reasons people are so upset by this Joe McCarthy is that he's not a fair debater. He exploits people's fears. He pours gasoline on fire."

Cameron looked at each of his sons and asked, "Do you know what I mean?" And they both nodded, because in fact they did know what he meant.

It was a moment that shaped Andrew MacAlpine. He thought he'd like to be someone who saved the world from bad ideas.

In October of 1957, Andrew's third-grade class practiced hiding under their desks in case of a nuclear attack. His teacher, Mrs. Oakes, had thirty-six students to keep in line and she didn't like them very much. Clapping loudly, she'd holler, "Children, it's time to do our drill now." Andrew was not convinced that his desk would protect him from anything, let alone a bomb like the ones he'd seen in *Life* and *Look* magazines. To him it was all just a bunch of cheery baloney.

Andrew was sensing a problem with Mrs. Oakes with her grey hair and calm but extra-large presence in the classroom. What was she always saying to him? "Didn't you hear me, young man? I called on you to recite." She pointed at a paragraph. "Recite this if you can."

Andrew read it to her without difficulty, then focused past the flowerpots on the classroom window shelf and far out the window. He could see the sun shining on the playground outside, just next to the banks of the Mississippi River. He thought she'd gone on to others in the class, determined that everyone should recite some paragraph of her choosing. But then suddenly there she was again, looming above him. "Show and tell, Andrew," she announced. All around him the kids seemed anxious.

"What is it you want?" He asked this clearly, unafraid. Adults didn't bother him because his parents always treated him like an adult. Expected him to think like an adult, actually. Which he did.

"It's your turn to say something about yourself to the class. It's your turn today," she said sharply.

Andrew stood straight and spoke with precision. "I like to read," he said and pulled a small book from his back pocket. "I have a book you all might like. It's by Aesop and the stories are great. I'll share them with anyone who is interested." That said, he sat back down in the desk that would never protect him from a nuclear bomb.

"Well," Mrs. Oakes said. "I'm sure we're all glad to hear about that." She wiped her palms against the crocheted hanky she usually kept up her sleeve and called on the next student.

Andrew's attention stayed with her for a minute or two, but then his gaze returned to Aesop, who was telling him stories just outside the window while basking in a shaft of warm yellow sunlight. Old teachers and Communists were nowhere in sight. At least not just then.

ALL FOR ONE & ONE FOR ALL

In 1958, Andrew was not quite old enough to join his brother and Lars in Boy Scout Troop # 177, but he was such a good kid they let him in anyway. "I've already done everything with the Cub Scouts. I did their pinewood derby and learned how to tie knots," Andrew told everyone who would listen to him. "And I know the Cowboy Code. I'll be a great Boy Scout. I want to go camping with Cameron and Lars. I'm ready," he said, and the truth was, he'd always been ready to be a Boy Scout. The scoutmaster agreed, as did his parents.

The boys had developed into a group of their own, a kind of three musketeers, a book they read and reenacted. Lars was the tallest, a blond Nordic boy, handsome and sure of himself. Cameron Junior and his brother, Andrew, had the same wavy hair and athletic build, but Andrew had darker hair, his eyes very blue and steady, whereas Cameron's gray eyes were always darting from one thing to another.

Using wooden sticks, they whacked each other in sword fights and swore an oath to protect one another forever. They took their pocketknives and made small slices in their thumbs, rubbed their thumbs together, and became blood brothers. All for one and one for all.

One Friday afternoon, Harold drove the boys to their campsite near Stillwater and promised to pick them up at noon on Sunday. All the Scouts assembled and were assigned to their tents. Lars, Cameron Junior, and Andrew were assigned to the same tent, which they had to put up as a team before they went for dinner. Some of the boys had never put up tents before but Lars, Cameron Junior, and Andrew had done tents so many times, they were the first ones done and then set off to help the others because no one could go to dinner until all the tents were up. "Looks like you need some help," Lars said to the other Scouts with obvious loftiness. He also was the one that noticed boys who had no bug spray or repellants. First-timers, he thought. "What did you think was going to happen when the mosquitoes came out?" he asked a few of the kids, but then he shared his own bug dope with them to make up for his annoying superiority.

After their dinner of beans and franks with soggy buns and a round of singing at the campfire, the scoutmaster said, "Lights out, boys! We're going to rise and shine early in the morning." But Lars, Cameron Junior, and Andrew all had flashlights and comic books. So they did not do lights out, but read and reread, exchanging their comics in the tent. They tended to favor Superman and Batman because they fought bad guys and believed in truth and justice. That made so much sense to them.

Finally though, Cameron Junior said, "I'm going to sleep. Turn off your flashlights," which Andrew did, of course. Lars, however, pulled his sleeping bag over his head and continued reading. He was eleven years old and had a mind of his own. Also, it was important to note that Lars was one of the tallest boys for his age. This gave him a certain angle on things.

The scoutmaster was true to his word. Just after dawn he circled the campsite, playing the only bugle tune he knew over and over as he walked around the tents. Soon the scouts were up and dressed. The scoutmaster managed to get the whole troop lined up facing the flagpole. They all saluted the flag and recited the *Pledge of Allegiance.* Lars poked Andrew in the ribs and whispered "Communist" when he noticed Andrew skip over the words "under God." Cameron Junior poked Lars in the chest. "Mind your own business," he said. Lars poked back. Cameron Junior didn't respond.

After a breakfast of scrambled eggs and sausages, the scoutmaster announced, "An outdoor tournament, boys! This morning we're going to have games of strength, speed, and skill. Line up and count off red, white, blue. Let's go!"

The scoutmaster separated the reds, whites, and blues into three teams of eight scouts each and proceeded to give instructions. "Each team line up according to height, shortest scout to tallest. First game is footrace. Winner earns his team three points, second place earns two points, and third place earns one point."

The scouts ran their races and the scoutmaster added up each team's points. Lars, Cameron Junior, and Andrew were on different teams, didn't race against one another, and all won three points for their respective teams.

The field was filled with noisy, sweaty boys after the races were run. The scoutmaster rounded up the scouts for more competitions. They threw a softball for distance, kicked a football for distance and accuracy, and then had a terrible lunch of leftover sausages with soggy buns.

After lunch they returned to the field for more competition. The scoutmaster said, "The red team, white team, and blue team are very close in points, boys! The championship will be decided by the results in the next two events. First, line up by height for the wrestling matches!"

Lars and Cameron Junior faced each other, ready to do battle. Lars smiling confidently, a half inch taller. Cameron Junior, five pounds heavier, crouching like his dad had taught him, low with no smile.

"Watch out," Lars said.

They circled each other slowly inside the larger circle of Scouts, neither wanting to make the first move. Lars reached in to grab Cameron Junior's arm, and Cameron Junior quickly dove at his friend's knees, knocking him on his back. Cameron Junior pounced on his friend, pushing his shoulders to the ground. The scoutmaster slapped the ground, yelled "You're pinned!" The scouts filled the field with shouts and cheers. Cameron Junior stood and offered a hand up to Lars, who refused. "I'll get you later," Lars said.

King-of-the-Hill was the final game of the tournament. Three large washtubs were placed upside down on the grass in the shape of a triangle, eight feet on a side. A scout was assigned to a particular washtub, his "hill," and tried to pull the two other scouts off of their hill by pulling on a long rope which had been tied into an encompassing circle.

Lars, Cameron Junior, and a husky kid named Duane mounted their washtubs, grabbed the rope, and waited for the scoutmaster's signal to begin. Upon hearing the whistle, Lars yanked hard on the rope and Duane tumbled to the grass. Cameron Junior turned to face Lars, balanced on his washtub. He held the rope in both hands with a loose grip. Lars stared, said, "I'll get you now!" and gave a sharp pull on the rope. Cameron Junior watched the slack go out of his rope, leaned forward, and with a mighty tug, pulled Lars off his washtub. The Scouts cheered as Lars fell onto the grass. Cameron Junior offered a hand up to Lars, who only nodded in a royal sort of way and left for a swim in the lake.

The next day at noon, Harold picked up the boys and on the drive home asked them how the weekend went for them. Lars said, "We learned a lot. Cameron's team won the tournament."

"You weren't all on the same team?"

Andrew sat forward in the back seat. "We are now, Mr. Bergen."

IN THIS TOGETHER

Although Susie MacAlpine married on her eighteenth birthday, she was not immature. Her sisters had taught her to take care of herself and to not expect coddling because she was the baby in the family. After they left to start their own families, Susie ran the household for her widowed father. She was a responsible daughter, managed the money through the war years, and learned how to stretch a dollar, keep the house spick-and-span and herself stylish and modern. Unlike her contemporaries, she let her hair flow without primping and so had a look all her own.

She graduated high school and had been out and about on her own when she met and married Cameron. Having a husband and children and a home fulfilled her dream. But she still had ideas of her own. When she watched Edward R. Murrow's program on Senator Joseph McCarthy, Susie was glad that he was showing the nation the vile poison that dripped from the senator's lips. She thought McCarthy was a traitor. She thought he would ruin the unity that had prevailed during the war, the weeks without meat, not using cars, the unity of that sacrifice. He was threatening it all with his divisions of US and THEM. Susie believed that in the mix of ideas, the better ideas would prevail. She'd learned that in school and she felt it to her core.

She was, at a very young age, a free thinker and a patriot. Her sister Ebba's husband, Patrick, had been killed in Holland in 1943. Ebba had worn black through the remainder of the war and had not remarried, would in fact never remarry, and this was the family's personal sacrifice for freedom and courage and unity. So when talking about the country—to her friends or children or others in the family—Susie would always emphasize that this was the UNITED States of America. United. That's what she would say.

Susie lived her life as a realist. She chose the practical path in running her household and, more important, in raising her children. In this she differed almost completely from her lifelong best friend, Sunny Bergen. When Sunny discovered any new childrearing tip or technique, it caused no end of trouble for the two of them. Sunny would say, "I just want my kids to like me. I think they'll mind me better if they like me better." She had just read about negotiating techniques with children. How to bargain. How to all get along using these ideas.

"I already have my friends, Sunny. You're my friend. I want my kids to be good citizens. If they misbehave, they know it. I don't care if they don't like me for punishing them or spanking them."

"Dr. Spock doesn't believe in spanking, Susie, you know that."

"Is he raising my boys or am I raising my boys?"

She didn't mean to be harsh and she wasn't harsh. She set the rules and enforced the rules and her boys understood and loved the clarity. And they loved their mother for being constant and caring in her own consistent manner. Whereas everything was a bargain at the Bergens' house, at the MacAlpines' they marched to the same tune and seemed the better for it.

Weeks after Cameron Junior, Andrew, and Lars had been to camp, they decided to have a sleepover at the Bergens'. This was something they had never done before, this sleeping over at a friend's, and Susie gave her boys instructions on how to behave. "When you're over there, you need to do things the way they do things—just like in our house we do things the way your dad and I want them done."

"What are their rules, Mom?" Andrew asked.

"No rules," Susie answered. "There are no rules over there. They bargain."

And that is exactly what happened. Dinner was lovely except that Sunny had to beg Lars, Ellie Mae, and Lena to come to the table. Cameron Junior and Andrew were, of course, seated as soon as they were told that dinner was ready. Ellie Mae whined, "I just want to finish this game," which surprised Cameron Junior since the girls were playing Monopoly and might need to keep playing that all night. Harold came to the table and meekly announced, "Children, children, your mom has dinner ready."

Then Cameron called to Lars to come and eat and he did, and soon so did Ellie Mae and Lena.

After dinner Andrew asked, "Do you want me and Cameron to help you with the dishes, Mrs. Bergen?" Sunny assured them that they were so sweet but they didn't have to do that. "We do it at home," Cameron argued, "and we're really fast." So, the MacAlpine boys dried and put away the dishes for Sunny while the Bergen girls returned to their Monopoly game, Lars curled up with a book of poetry, and Harold sat in his chair to read a magazine.

Later, after the boys had played catch in the yard and the sun began to set, Sunny told her daughters, "Maybe you girls should think about going to bed now."

Ellie responded, "In a little bit, Mom."

And Lena said, "In a little bit, Mom."

Fifteen minutes later, Sunny again suggested to her daughters that it was bedtime.

"We're not done yet, Mom,"Lena answered, and Ellie Mae ignored her completely.

The boys had been reading comic books in Lars's bedroom, lying on the floor and passing the books among themselves when Cameron said he thought it was time to go to bed. He and Andrew went out into the living room to thank Mr. and Mrs. Bergen for dinner. Sunny said, "I'll wake you in the morning for breakfast." Everyone stood during this exchange, making it rather formal and important.

Lying on his cot next to his brother, Andrew heard the Bergen girls arguing about rental properties. Who owned Boardwalk was his last conscious thought.

When Susie asked her sons how they liked doing a sleepover, Cameron said it was fun and he hoped they weren't too much trouble for the Bergens. But later Andrew hung around Susie to say, "Would you ever let us play Monopoly until midnight?" He was just curious.

"What do you think?" Susie answered.

THE EPIC CAMPAIGN

In junior high school, Lars Bergen began pulling in his own direction. He loved libraries, reading, and especially poetry. He loved the order of the English poets and the elusiveness of crazy Walt Whitman with his sense of self. But when it came to ideas, Lars favored the conservativism of the political right.

When Vice President Nixon ran against John F. Kennedy for president in 1960, Lars was all for Nixon. He listened to the two candidates debate on the radio, happy that his man had clearly won. When the newspapers reported a Kennedy win, "impressed with the junior senator from Massachusetts," Lars was stunned. On television, he learned, his candidate had been dull and sweaty, while Kennedy had been confident, vigorous—and tall.

The 1960 campaign launched the next three presidents of the country. Thirteen-year-old Lars could not know this. Nobody could. Lars only knew that he chose Nixon. He was also quite certain that he knew more than the rest of his family and all the MacAlpines as well in their collective enthusiasm for an ill-equipped Irish Catholic with too much hair.

On Friday, October 14, the seventh-grade social studies class sat to discuss the television debate between Nixon and Kennedy that had occurred the night before. Mr. Volker asked the class who had followed his assignment and watched or listened to the debate. Almost everyone had, though a couple of boys had stuck with the seventh game of the World Series between the Pittsburgh Pirates and the New York Yankees instead.

"I thought Vice President Nixon made some excellent points about national defense," Lars said to kick off the discussion. His classmates turned toward him and stared. "Plus he's got eight years of experience in the White House. And he was a senator before that. And he was in the House of Representatives before that."

Linda Horton, sitting directly across from him, did not agree. "I just don't believe Nixon. He's a good debater, I'll give you that. But I don't trust anything he says." Linda was a mature girl who had lost both her parents and her brother when their car crashed through the ice on Lake Mille Lacs. So the other kids in class gave her respect. And she was very smart.

"Thank you," Mr. Volker said to both Lars and Linda. "Anyone else?"

"Well you can sure trust Bill Mazeroski," Duane Lewis called out, chuckling and squirming around to look at his baseball-loving buddies for approval.

"Yeah, well Bobby Richardson was the MVP," another boy yelled.

Mr. Volker nodded. "So did you watch the debate on television and listen to the ball game on the radio?"

"Or did you even know there was a debate?" Lars said to the boys, who laughed without shame. "Anyway," Lars continued not even raising his hand for permission, "Nixon will win."

But, it turned out, Nixon did not win. After all the popular votes were counted, Kennedy had 34,220,984 and Nixon 34,108,157 for a percentage split of 49.72% to 49.55%. Lars liked to remind his family that Nixon had won twenty-six states while the junior senator had won only twenty-two. "You're a sore loser, Lars," was all they had to say.

Thanksgiving came and went and Christmas came and went and the New Year came and went. Then just before the JFK inaugural, President Eisenhower gave his official farewell address, in which he warned the country that the military industrial complex put the United States at increased risk instead of guaranteeing its safety. Lars, though, favored the idea of increasing military heft so that no other country would ever even think of messing with the United States.

Lars aside, it was an eye-opening idea that Eisenhower presented and one that fractured the country. But this took a while. Not everyone had truly heard him and many others did not understand what he meant. War was important to the economics of the country and to protect the world from Communism. And so the country went along.

It wasn't that Eisenhower had softened. At the time of his speech and the time of Kennedy's ascent to the presidency, Eisenhower was more interested in spies than battles. More interested in using technology to keep an eye on our foes, more interested in sending up surveillance planes than sending troops into the jungle. More interested in intelligence than physical force. When the Soviets rumbled tanks into Red Square, Eisenhower dismissed them as petty tyrants. "That's not what we do in a democracy," he assessed.

But the nation's attention pivoted quickly to the young president's inaugural speech and the world focused on Kennedy's stirring challenge to move the country forward into a daring new future. Though Lars still thought Kennedy an incompetent, he sat listening to Robert Frost recite the poem he'd written just days before in celebration of democracy. "The land was ours before we were the land's," Frost read, his voice faltering as his eyeglasses fogged in the cold.

"You know, Lars," his mother told him, "you may not like Kennedy, but he invited a poet to read at his inauguration. He wants to bring the arts into the affairs of state. No president has ever done that before."

Robert Frost didn't tend to be a favorite of Lars's, but he loved hearing the old poet read. And after that, Lars began to recite Frost. He had a thought just then at the age of thirteen that there may be a way to make a life out of words. It was an inkling. The beginning of what might be.

The last year of his presidency Eisenhower had sent 3,500 military advisors to Vietnam to assist in that country's fight for independence. In the spring of 1961, Kennedy sent Vice President Lyndon Johnson to Asia to meet with South Vietnam's President Diem and let him know that in the minds of this White House, Diem was the Churchill of Southeast Asia, and he could expect America's support. Diem wanted US money for his army and the US Army to back up his army. Four months later, Kennedy asked his staff what it would take to win in Vietnam. The joint chiefs told him it would take 40,000 combat troops with another 100,000 at the border. The new president responded by sending 18,000 men to Vietnam within a month. In December of 1961, the first Huey helicopters landed in Saigon with US personnel.

At home, Lars and his date won the dance competition at their eighth-grade holiday mixer and the toy company Mattel introduced Ken as a companion to Barbie.

GO-GO GROWTH

When the new president gave federal government employees the right to unionize in January 1962, more than one out of five persons in the labor force were union members. And home buyers. The Camelot years were a good time for American workers and accelerated the growth of Alpine Homes. The men who worked for Cameron and Harold had "a chicken in every pot and a car in every garage," as the saying went. The unions were trusted partners in providing qualified carpenters, plumbers, and electricians who had been well-trained and apprenticed. In return, Alpine Homes paid union wages and complied with union standards. Unions provided stability. When Harold and Cameron were young and starting out working for Bud Cronkite, they certainly joined the union. They could not imagine it any other way.

The fortunes of Alpine Homes rose as did the fortunes of America, each positioned to succeed in the go-go 1960s. Every Monday morning the Bergens and MacAlpines would meet around the kitchen table at one of their homes, drink coffee, and confer on the workings of their company. There was always much to discuss—the women on the interiors of the homes, Harold on the building process, and Cameron on the business end. Early on they had divided the responsibilities in this way and it worked for them all. They trusted one another, continued to be best friends, and relaxed most weekends square-dancing together.

On a closer look, Cameron had the better end in this division of labor, remaining in the office all day with his feet up on his desk, keeping the company's relationships with their suppliers and insurers, their banker, lawyers, and the rest. Harold, on the other hand, tended to work very hard to manage the building projects. All day he would drive from one site to the next, inquiring "what do you need, are you on track," sometimes coaching a new employee on carpentry skills. Then he'd hop in his truck, drink another cup of coffee, eat another donut, and zip off to the next project. When Harold got home at night, he was too tired to do more than eat dinner and page through a *Field and Stream* or *Reader's Digest*. Both Cameron and Harold were born in 1922, but the years had taken a harder toll on Harold who had gained almost forty pounds since his days as a soldier and lost most of his hair as well.

That said, both men truly loved the lives they'd created. They wanted for nothing and had even purchased *Encyclopedia Britannica* sets for their families, a true sign of material success. Like so many Americans of that era, they benefited from the increase in worker productivity, low inflation, and the growth in wages. A whole bag of groceries cost no more than four dollars.

"Jack Kennedy is good for this country," Cameron announced at one of the weekly company meetings. "We're doing better every year."

"He keeps our taxes low," Susie said.

"Not to mention closing the missile gap with the Soviets," Sunny added.

They all loved Kennedy, but Sunny truly loved him the most. Even when she couldn't think of a good reason, she loved him the most. "He's got my girls doing sit-ups at school now."

They all laughed. Harold patted his stomach. "Maybe I should be doing those sit-ups too!"

THE BEAUTY SHOP

The weekend had been too long, too sad, too unthinkable. Now on Tuesday morning, Susie MacAlpine and Sunny Bergen came to Barbara Dahline's beauty shop early just to be together and talk and try to find some sense in the crazy world. They had watched television for four days straight, transfixed by the terrible spectacle of the assassination, grieved at the sudden loss of the young president being shot and killed. The ladies loved to sit at the shop, where two Red Flyer wagons held a half-dozen geranium plants, moved throughout the day to follow the sun.

After Barbie Doll, as they called her, had poured them each a cup of coffee and they'd all lit another cigarette, Susie sighed. "I'm just not sure that Lee Harvey Oswald was the only person involved."

"What are you saying? Who else would it be?" Sunny Bergen was startled to hear her friend say this.

"I don't know, but one guy and all those bullets and people ducking everywhere on that plaza, shots and screaming and people looking every which way and it's one guy in a window?" Susie took a deep drag on her Pall Mall. "I just don't buy it. Cameron says as a trained sharpshooter in the Army, he couldn't have done that no way, no how. I mean, the car was moving, and three bullets hit two men in twenty seconds? Really?"

"But he was a Communist, Susie."

Barbie said, "That don't make him a sharpshooter, Sunny." She leaned forward toward her friends, "I say it was the Mafia. Oswald was just a patsy."

"Oh good Lord, Barbie, that's the most ridiculous thing I ever heard. Why would Italian criminals kill a Catholic president?" Sunny was incensed.

She could see that her friends were going to blow this all out of proportion. Wasn't it bad enough that they'd lost the president, without coming up with all kinds of stories that didn't even make sense. "Are you telling me that all the news is wrong and it wasn't that kook who killed Kennedy, but some murderers from New York?"

"Not just them, Sunny," Barbie said. "I say what if it's the whole damn bunch."

"What bunch?"

"What if the rest of the government didn't love Kennedy the way we all do? You know? You ever hear of the Deep State?" Barbie read lots of the magazines in her down time at the shop. "What about the CIA? Or the Secret Service and FBI?"

This made Sunny angry. She got out of her chair and circled the room before saying, "Why would the CIA or FBI want to kill Kennedy? What do they have against him?"

"None of them liked the Kennedys. Think about it. The Kennedys have power, they have money, everyone loves them, they look good on television. Eight years of JFK then eight years of RFK and then eight years of Teddy. It's a dynasty. These other guys are lost. They can't compete with the Kennedys."

"How do you compete with hair like that?" Barbie laughed. "I got guys with three strands coming in here wanting to look like Jack Kennedy."

"Well, now that's over," Sunny responded and, very suddenly, started to cry. Her grief was immense and now her friends were painting a picture of undercurrents beyond her belief.

Barbie lit another cigarette, possibly the eighth that hour. "We still have Bobby though," she reassured.

I'LL TELL YOU SOMETHING I THINK YOU'LL UNDERSTAND

Lars, Cameron Junior, Ellie Mae, Andrew, and Lena watched John, Paul, George, and Ringo sing on *The Ed Sullivan Show* on February 9, 1964. It was the Beatles' first performance in America and the Bergen and MacAlpine sons and daughters thought a new world order had arrived—a world where things came true if you closed your eyes and wished very hard. A world of wishes come true without delayed gratification, without sacrifice, without unfair suffering. Oh, they wanted to believe that they could have it all—the victory in WW II without the dead and wounded and walking wounded and walking dead above the neck and without the pain and suffering and enormous loss of innocence. Without the price, they wanted glory and goodness and victory and satisfaction and ecstasy and privilege and power and, above all, insight and knowledge and respect and the right to flaunt old rules and the right to establish a new world order because they were so very smart and so very certain of everything of which they were certain.

It was a time when the children of the war warriors took the mantle upon themselves without having spilled all the blood of WW II and claimed the high moral ground without engaging in any national referendum.

Oh such a time it was.

SOMETHING IS HAPPENING HERE

In the late spring of 1965, Sunny Bergen sat with a magazine to wait her turn at Barbie Doll's beauty shop. Rhonda Hill, a recently divorced exotic dancer getting her hair done, wondered where she could get a publicity photo.

Barbie pointed a stubby finger at Sunny and said, "Her little man could do it for you. A regular award winner with his camera, right, Sunny?"

It was true. That same year Lars had won awards at a local art fair for two of his photographs. They were beautiful. One, a black-and-white photograph of a small tree, the sun coming through the branches. The other was a color time-lapse photograph of the Milky Way.

The Bergens had bought him a 35-millimeter camera, converted a sewing room into a darkroom for him, and generally supported this new and expensive hobby. And that's how Lars began doing glamour shots for some of the women at the Roaring Twenties strip club downtown. It was just before his eighteenth birthday and Lars was going through some changes.

He had made a scene at the Spring Fling school dance. He kept cutting in on Roger Lund, wanting to dance with Roger's girlfriend. His parents had to be called.

Then he told Harold and Sunny he wanted to quit school.

His dad was pretty sure Lars was sneaking cigarettes.

His mom had seen *Playboy* magazines in the sweater drawer of his dresser.

His sisters were complaining that he tickled them too often, and too vigorously.

Harold and Sunny were surprised, confused. Sunny read articles about juvenile delinquency and its causes.

Meanwhile, Minnesota's own Bob Dylan was singing:

You try so hard but you don't understand
Just what you will say when you get home
Because something is happening here but you don't know what it is
Do you, Mr. Jones?

MAKE LOVE, NOT WAR

Ellie Mae and Lena had always been as close as sisters can be, sharing secrets, clothes, and a room. They continued that closeness when Lena pledged to Ellie Mae's sorority, again sharing secrets, clothes, and a room.

In the spring 1967, Lena enrolled in an honors seminar. Her thesis topic was The Pill. The story of The Pill. Opponents of The Pill. The birth-control movement. Feminism. She read somewhere that with the pill women could have sex, the more the better. Sex without marriage. Sex without children. Sex redesigned, reengineered, made safe, made limitless, for the pleasure of women.

She also read somewhere that a counterforce existed that was against any drive for female progress and sexual equality, and held to the social scripts of the 1950s, which insisted that, if a woman "had desires of her own—be they sexual, professional, or personal—she was expected to hold them in check, to wipe them out the same way she wiped germs from the kitchen counter."

Lena thought long and hard about these and other questions. She reflected on her experiences with boys and young men. Kisses, hugs, touching, and how it made her feel. She thought about feminism and the complexity of female sexuality. Was there a correlation between the pill and more divorce, sexually transmitted infections, and the objectification of women? Was sexual intercourse only for procreation? Was thinking or acting otherwise a sin?

Lena was coming of age when everything was changing and there she was, part of it all, a college girl who planned her own independent life and liked boys, and wanted to get married, but also wanted to be a professor. And maybe a poet too. Lena thought deeply in general, and was certain women should be able to have sex without shame and consequence.

Her sister, Ellie Mae, who was a true Nordic beauty, tall and blonde, blue-eyed, and stunningly curved, flirted with boys mercilessly. She didn't think about marriage or a career. She wanted to be a butterfly and land here and land there and make love and be free. She could not help herself.

Ellie Mae went out with one boy after another, hooked up all the time, and if she ever had any difficulty, it was with boys who felt entitled to be with her a second night. So how could Ellie Mae understand Lena's fascination with this topic of feminism? "You've got books everywhere in this room, Lena. What on earth?"

"It's the movement. Feminism. It's changing everything, El."

"Like what?"

"You can have sex whenever you want without worrying about getting pregnant—and it's the norm, it's easy, it's our freedom."

Ellie Mae lifted her gorgeous chin and laughed. "I have never worried a minute about any of that." She raised her eyebrows. "There are ways." She flopped down on her bed opposite Lena. "Women have always been in power. That's the thing. Who runs the show at home, Lena? There's Mom with her work and her friends and us and Dad hopping around to do whatever she says. Mom has freedom. Susie MacAlpine has freedom. We all have freedom."

"That's too obvious, Ellie," Lena replied in her most intellectual tone. "You're stating an anecdote. It means nothing in the full picture of women's lives around the country—or the world even. The pill changes everything that women can expect for themselves whether they have a nice husband like Daddy who makes tons of money or whether they live in poverty with abuse and chauvinism and rape and—" Lena was getting herself very wound up trying to explain a simple reality to her sister who basically held life in the palm of her hand to toss or squish as she wished.

"It's boring, Lena. I have a date tonight with one of the Gopher football players, did I tell you?"

"No, I guess you didn't."

"Well now you know." Ellie Mae grinned. "That's all the freedom I need for today."

At the same time, the war for freedom in Vietnam—if anyone called it a war—appeared to be going well by all reports. Whenever America lost four soldiers, it would hear that the enemy body count was in the hundreds. The country seemed to be winning with fighter jets and Huey helicopters and the most powerful force in the world. There seemed nothing to worry about.

Then came 1968.

In January, the Marine Corps base at Khe Sanh in South Vietnam came under siege by North Vietnamese troops, which must have snuck up the Ho Chi Minh Trail to attack the base. This battle lasted for months and resulted in a psychological victory for the North Vietnamese. They did not let up and they did not give in and they made it clear that they would rather die than submit.

On the Lunar New Year, all forces ceased fire. And then came a massive attack by 80,000 North Vietnam soldiers in 136 cities including Saigon. The war was shown on television every night, reported live, the fire and smoke and even the losses. World War II soldiers like Cameron MacAlpine and Harold Bergen watched this and saw that their side was not doing well at all, that it didn't seem America was winning as everyone had believed. To get pinned down in a rice paddy with people you couldn't see shooting at you from all angles began to seem to the MacAlpines and the Bergens and much of the American people that something was wrong, some part of the story that the military and government were telling was very wrong.

Martin Luther King added the war to his emotional speeches on civil rights, widening his message to the moral imperative of stopping the war. At this time, some people in the country were even talking about the possibility of King as a candidate for the presidency and, in backlash, Alabama Governor George Wallace decided to mount his candidacy on the American Independent Party ticket, campaigning in favor of racial segregation.

And then on April 4th, Martin Luther King was assassinated.

Across the country the killing of Martin Luther King unleashed an outrage such that the country had not seen since the Civil War. Buildings were burned in 100 cities across the country, including 1,200 in Washington, DC. Thirteen thousand troops were dispatched, marines mounted machine guns on the steps of the Capitol, and the economy of that city was ultimately gutted.

The Bergen girls painted Make Love, Not War in lipstick on their mirror.

But at this point in the spring of 1968, that somehow did not seem enough.

BLACK AND WHITE

Cameron and Andrew MacAlpine, Lars Bergen, and some friends were living in a big house close to the university that spring. Classes were in session but the buzz was all about the assassination of Martin Luther King, LBJ's decision to leave the White House at the end of his term, and what would happen next.

Andrew thought that Bobby Kennedy would now be selected as the nominee for the Democratic Party at the convention in Chicago. He told Cameron Junior and Lars, "Kennedy'll bring together the Eugene McCarthy supporters and the Martin Luther King supporters and win in November."

Lars was still a Nixon man. "Well, on the right side, Nixon will easily beat Rockefeller and Reagan and win the Republican Party nomination. Then he'll win in November."

Cameron interjected, "How's he going to do that, Lars? He lost to one Kennedy in 1960. He couldn't even get elected governor of California. Who wants to buy a used war from him?"

Lars responded quickly. "Easy. He'll run as the law-and-order candidate, reminding voters about the long hot summer of riots we had last year. He'll scare the hell out of Southern voters, traditionally Democratic voters. After he's in the White House, he'll win the war in Vietnam and get reelected in 1972 in a landslide."

Andrew disagreed. "The country is dying for a candidate who has a moral vision of the future. Bobby Kennedy has that vision. Nixon only cares about himself. Voters will see that Kennedy is the one and that he will honor the message of King. He even said so."

Lars was not sympathetic. "He was trying to push the country too fast," he told them. "People's attitudes don't change overnight. It's still a white country and likely to stay that way."

Andrew flipped. "I can't believe what I'm hearing, Lars. This is the country where a person is supposed to be judged by character, not color.

Didn't you hear King say that?"

Cameron did not enter the discussion. He did not really care about the broader events of the day. He was white, protected, and rich. He just wanted to take his business classes, get out of school, and go run the family business. This irked his brother, Andrew. "It's your country too, Cam," he said. And Cameron nodded. Yes, it was.

Earlier President Johnson had established a national commission to examine the root causes of the 1967 riots. The Kerner Commission, as it was known, reported its blunt conclusion in early 1968. "Our nation is moving toward two societies, one black, one white—separate and unequal."

Andrew read the entire 426-page report which recommended government programs to provide needed services, to hire more diverse and sensitive police forces and, most notably, to invest billions in housing programs aimed at breaking up residential segregation. Lars had no interest in the report and continued to have nothing positive to say about the mix of black and white people in the country. And Cameron did not know that the report existed.

Lars correctly predicted Nixon's Republican Party nomination, however, the assassination of Bobby Kennedy the evening of the hotly contested California Democratic Party primary ignited state-wide protests. Vice President Hubert Humphrey edged out Minnesota Senator Eugene McCarthy and ran a close second on November 5, 1968. The final tally was 43.4% for Nixon, 42.7% for Humphrey, and 13.5% for the segregationist Wallace.

Richard Nixon and Spiro Agnew were elected and Lars was ecstatic.

SUMMER SCHOOL

Andrew had always loved Lena Bergen. Loved her without saying so, and almost always at a distance. They had gone to some parties together, more as friends, and shared the closeness of those whose childhoods are spent together. He had never asked Lena on a date. And he couldn't even say why.

But he was happy to see her at his door one evening before classes were to begin the summer of 1969. "Hi, Andrew, can I come in?" She smiled as she always did and sat next to him on the couch.

"What are you up to?"

"I decided to take French this summer, just want to add another language, and I thought maybe we could do some conversations together. I mean, you speak French right?" Everyone in the MacAlpine and Bergen families knew that Andrew had a way with languages.

Andrew brightened thinking that one of his skills would be helpful to Lena, who needed no help academically. "Yes, of course. Sounds like fun."

And so it happened that Lena and Andrew got to spend time together during the summer of 1969. He would soon turn twenty, and she was nineteen. They had known each other all their lives and time passed comfortably between them.

In mid-July Andrew and Lena were deep into one of their French conversations when the radio reported a terrible accident and tragedy on Chappaquiddick Island, a part of the town of Edgartown, Massachusetts, on the eastern end of Martha's Vineyard. Senator Ted Kennedy's car had gone off a bridge and a young woman, who was also in the car, had drowned. The announcers speculated on the negative impact this accident would have on the senator's presidential ambitions. Andrew loved the Kennedys, was drawn to their charisma and idealism, so when he heard this story, he felt heartbroken. There had been three brothers. Two had been killed and now the third—young Ted with his rakish personality and movie star looks—was involved in such a sordid event. Talk of his drinking. Talk of his not saving the girl. Talk, talk, talk.

Just days later the commotion over Senator Kennedy was overshadowed by Apollo 11 landing on the moon. Neil Armstrong and Edwin "Buzz" Aldrin landed the lunar module on the moon's surface in the Sea of Tranquility on Sunday, July 20. Lena and Andrew brought blankets to the deck on the roof of his house and stared at the moon. They had no telescope or binoculars but in Andrew's mind that didn't matter, because they were together. Maybe she'd kiss him and they'd get nicely tangled in the blanket and each other. But she pulled her knees to her chest and lit a cigarette. "They're there, Andrew. They're right up there on the moon."

"They are," he agreed, wishing he had something more profound to add.

Six hours later Neil Armstrong stepped onto the surface of the moon and made his historic declaration, "That's one small step for man, one giant leap for mankind."

Andrew barely had time to dwell on this good news when the president announced the Nixon Doctrine, declaring that the United States would "henceforth expect its Asian allies to take care of their own military defense." On July 30th, President Nixon traveled to South Vietnam for a man-to-man talk with President Nguyen Van Thieu to communicate his "doctrine." Andrew knew that there were more than a half-million US military personnel in Vietnam and that the losses as of that spring had been higher than in the entire Korean War. That was what Andrew was thinking about—the Nixon Doctrine and its ramifications. His brother, living in the room next to him, only picked up on the fact of Woodstock.

Cameron Junior loved any reason to throw a party, so after hearing radio reports of long lines and superstar performers at Max Yasgur's farm, he organized an impromptu Woodstock party, chose the albums, and got ready to canoodle on the couch with whomever while friends came and went. Everyone in Cameron's world was there. Ellie Mae came and danced all night. Jimmy Nelson and his brother Richie stopped in for a beer and left early to go to another party somewhere on campus. Annette Freeman, the only black student at the party, had come along with Linda

Horton to meet people. A Greek student named Connie Demopoulos brought a bottle of Retsina and offered a taste to anyone who cared to imbibe. And Tommy Buffalo and Lewis Wright smoked a special blend in a ceremonial peace pipe.

Cameron Junior danced a few dances with Linda Horton, who had been his girlfriend for two weeks in high school and was attending Macalester, but she mostly wanted to argue politics and philosophy, which was not what Cameron had on his mind. He had just finished reading *The Fountainhead* for his literature class and, though he thought Ayn Rand's emphasis on self-interest was the cat's pajamas, he didn't really want to do Woodstock yakking about ideas. But Linda wanted to discuss Ayn Rand and was quite clear about her disdain for the Objectivist movement. "It's not a real philosophy, Cameron," she said, "although it might persuade some weak-minded would-be's to think they are Libertarians." Cameron nodded absently and winked at Ellie Mae across the room.

Andrew came to the party, but when he didn't see Lena there, he went back to his room. And several weeks later summer school ended. With the start of the academic year, Andrew and Lena no longer had time to hang around talking French. But they continued to meet for coffee and long conversations about the state of the world. They thought so much alike. It was a wonder how much they thought alike.

NEVER MIND GWENDOLYN BROOKS

Cameron's Woodstock party had challenged Lars Bergen. He knew he was smarter than the others in his circle, he was used to getting whatever it was he wanted—he always got exactly what he wanted—and understood at a deep level that he came from a position of privilege and power. So when he walked into the party, planning to have a beer and leave, he was not prepared for his immediate reaction to Annette Freeman standing near him talking to Linda Horton about art. He had never seen anyone so beautiful in his life. His chest tightened and he thought his legs would not move again.

"Do you know Annette Freeman?" Linda Horton had asked, seeing Lars frozen next to them. "Annette's my roommate at Macalester and we were just talking about Fragonard's *The Swing*. You know that piece, Lars? Lars is a poet," Linda said to her friend. "Oh, there's Andrew," she noticed and left so suddenly that the other two had nothing to say for a minute.

"What kind of poetry do you write, Lars?" this stunning young woman asked him. But he couldn't think, he just couldn't think.

"Can I get you something to drink?" he asked instead, before seeing that she was holding a can of soda. "So where are you from?"

"I grew up in Mississippi." She smiled, her teeth white, her dark eyes humored. "My father is a professor at Tougaloo College. He teaches literature. Do you like African poetry, Lars? Gwendolyn Brooks or Langston Hughes?"

He had not read Gwendolyn Brooks and did not particularly like Langston Hughes. "Do you want to dance?"

"Not really my kind of music," she said with a glance around at the kids flapping wildly.

"Should we go for a drive? I have a car right outside. Maybe you could find some music you like on the radio."

Without answering, Annette put her hand on his arm, they turned away from the party, and walked out without saying goodbye. And from there they had a night of talking and kissing one another with an intensity that Lars had never known.

Annette Freeman was a brilliant, beautiful, black woman from the South. Lars had no experience with someone this confident and understated. He was matching wits with someone beyond his equal but more than that, it seemed to him that he caught on fire just looking at her. And he couldn't pull away from that and he couldn't make sense of it and he did not know what on earth to do about it.

And he wanted nobody in his life to know.

GOOD FRIENDS

Linda Horton had been randomly assigned to be Annette Freeman's roommate in their first year at Macalester. They were both there on scholarship and instantly recognized one another as fellow travelers. But while Annette had a family in Mississippi who supported her every move in life, Linda had always been very much alone since the fatal accident that took away her family. She hadn't wanted to go ice fishing with them that day, preferring to sit in the warm dry air of the library amidst the books she loved so well. Her grandmother had given her the bleak news, that her entire family had fallen through the ice in their big Cadillac with electric windows. Everyone in town blamed the accident on those windows, newfangled things that trapped the family inside.

But Linda did not blame the windows. She blamed her father, a blustery arrogant man who, she knew, would have paid no attention if her mother had suggested they walk out on the ice to fish. He loved his car and he loved his own ideas and he had taken his family right to the bottom of Lake Mille Lacs. From then on she had lived with her mother's mother in a small corner house with no heat in the bedrooms. And all her striving had been on her own behalf. She simply loved learning and nobody in any of her classes could ever match her, not even Lars Bergen who had begun to annoy her by high school, nor Andrew MacAlpine who she considered one of her best friends.

Linda had always been what the kids and their parents called a Tomboy. She liked to play kickball, race her bike around town, and whack a baseball. She wasn't a spectator type. She wanted to be in on the action, a skinny girl with red hair and a sprinkling of freckles, who loved to laugh even after she'd experienced the most awful grief. She was wholly likable except to those boys who resented her natural authority and independence.

Annette Freeman had become the sister Linda never had. She just loved Annette and thought they were alike in almost every way. So it was a surprise to her when Annette confessed her steamy times with Lars Bergen, of all people. Not only was Linda surprised that her dear friend would be falling in love with such a self-absorbed person as Lars was, she was also surprised at her own deep jealousy. It seemed to stir something she had not expected. A different kind of feeling, maybe possession or maybe absorption or maybe just a new sort of love. It was something to think about.

It also was exactly the kind of thinking that came naturally to Linda Horton. She observed people and she thought very much about what made them tick. It was about that time in college when she knew she would become a psychologist. It was one of the easiest decisions of her life.

What she should do about her love for Annette Freeman, on the other hand, was one of the most difficult.

TUNED IN

More than any of their siblings, Andrew and Lena were political and sensitized to world events and the war, the Buddhist monks immolating, and all the atrocities on the nightly news. They were the most tuned in to current affairs. So when Lena heard that anti-war activists on campuses around the country were organizing The Moratorium to End the War in Vietnam, she asked Andrew to march with her. On Wednesday, October 15, they joined five thousand students at the University of Minnesota marching hand in hand across campus, singing songs of peace and hope.

In response to the October 15 Moratorium, Nixon went on national television on the evening of Monday, November 3, 1969. He asked for the support of the "silent majority" of Americans for his Vietnam War policy. He argued that the United States had to win in Vietnam. That we had to keep the war going until the government of North Vietnam ceased trying to overthrow the government of South Vietnam.

Almost one month later, anti-war activists paraded silently down Pennsylvania Avenue to the White House, walking single file, each bearing a candle and a placard with the name of a dead American soldier or a destroyed Vietnamese village. The White House tried to count how many people were participating, eventually reaching the figure of 325,000. Nixon joked that he should send helicopters to blow out the candles.

After the Moratorium, Andrew and Lena met every day for coffee at the student union, chairs close and eyes focused on one another. There was so much to discuss and so much to do and they both felt the same way about everything. As the youngest in their families, they had spent years trailing their older siblings, put together for competitions and Bergen-MacAlpine events.

Andrew loved Lena's quiet intensity and she loved how he completely focused on whomever he was with. Andrew was so present. In these days, their bond deepened and the connection they'd felt all their lives turned into something so particular that it became more important than anything else.

TWO:
The ride

THE LOTTERY

December 1, 1969, was the first Monday after a relatively late Thanksgiving that year. Minneapolis was cool and fair, just above freezing in daytime and just below at night. The Vikings had shut out the Lions 27-0 and were on their way to the NFL Championship and an ill-fated Super Bowl IV.

Andrew was living with Cameron, Lars, and some other guys in an old mansion close by the university, one of those rundown, partly furnished places that students lived in back then. The others in the house were a real motley crew—Nelson Coleman, Bobby Kovacs, Jimmy Nelson, Lewis Wright, Tommy Buffalo, and their friend from Greece, Konstantinos Demopoulos Economides. They all called him Connie.

Lars was the ladies' man in those days, always chasing the girls. He looked like a wild Viking with his blond hair, fair skin, and reddish beard. He was taking graduate courses in the creative writing department, a poet, a real brain. He felt above them all, Lars did.

Bobby Kovacs and Jimmy Nelson were guys from the Iron Range. Bobby had been a super star hockey player until he busted his knee. His friend Jimmy was the best looking of them all. One of those blond guys with no goals and barely a thought in his head. Women would be attracted to him, realize he wasn't that smart, but he came from money and had his own car.

Cameron Junior was at that phase of life where it was all about him, the power of one kind of guy. He thought he was in love with Ellie Mae and she thought she was in love with him. Cameron came home lottery night and left again, staying just long enough to shave and shower. He borrowed some money from Andrew so he could fill up the beautiful old Ford he drove in those days.

Nelson Coleman came from Detroit and was at the University of Minnesota to play basketball, until he had an injury that cost him his scholarship. He stuck around anyway and enrolled in the university's divinity school to become a reverend. Nelson was memorable, kind, gregarious, tall, and thin, with skin the color of black coffee.

The lottery that night was about to define their futures. They were all sitting around the living room of that old house studying—except for Jimmy who never studied. None of them had ever seen him open a book. He was listening to his music, and Andrew had settled in the big chair that faced the front door, his backpack on his left next to an acoustic guitar and on his right, a table holding the ashtray of Marlboro cigarette butts. That's when Bobby turned on the television.

Jimmy thought they were about to watch reruns of *It Takes A Thief* and squawked when Bobby turned the channel to CBS and the newscaster Roger Mudd.

"I don't wanna watch this," Jimmy protested.

"Don't you want to know if you're going to Nam?" one of the other guys said.

"I ain't going, man," Jimmy said.

Bobby pointed to the television screen. "Quiet guys, I want to hear what he's saying. Give me some paper, Connie. I'm gonna write down our birthdays."

Connie picked up a spiral-bound notebook and a ballpoint pen from the large dining room table where half the guys were sitting and handed it to Bobby. Then one by one they listed their birthdays:

June 22nd for Cameron
October 18th for Andrew
April 24th for Bobby
September 14th for Lars
The list went on.

CBS had preempted the regularly scheduled broadcast of *Mayberry R.F.D.* to show a live feed from the Selective Service headquarters in Virginia. Three hundred sixty-six plastic capsules, each with one day of the year, were dumped into a large glass container. To pick a lottery number, a capsule was pulled out of the container, the piece of paper with the birth date was unrolled, the birth date read aloud and assigned a number beginning with 001. The slip of paper was then fastened to a wide board with the heading Random Service Selection 1970.

They were all quiet as Roger Mudd read out the numbers, five at a time:
September 14
April 24
December 30
February 14
October 18

"I guess I'm a big winner," Lars said without expression.

"Me too," said Bobby. "April 24th." He grabbed a bottle of beer.

Andrew was a winner too. And though he'd been protesting the war for months, he didn't believe he was a conscientious objector.

When the drawing was over, they sat considering their varying fates. Those with lower numbers had a choice to make. Did they stay in school and maintain their student deferment or enlist immediately, take control of the decision, and get it over with?

In the next week, Bobby and Andrew joined the Navy. Andrew's aptitude tests were above 98 percent and he could speak a number of languages, so he was sent to the Office of Naval Intelligence. Bobby asked for a deferment so he could finish that year of college and they gave it to him.

Lars enlisted in the Army. Cameron lucked out. And Jimmy, as he had told them, "wasn't going."

Andrew thought about Lena and knew he had to talk to her soon about his lottery number and the decision he had made. When he saw her to study for quarter finals, he told her, "I didn't get a good number in the lottery, so I went to the Navy office and enlisted."

Her face changed in an instant. "I thought you were opposed to killing, all killing. How could you do this, Andrew?"

He explained that he couldn't in all honesty claim to be a conscientious objector, and this is what he had to do. He asked that maybe she could write to him and that he could write to her about what was really happening. Nothing he said persuaded Lena.

"You'll be helping to kill people, Andrew, even if you are on some big ship. I can't believe what you're doing. I don't want anything to do with it—or you," she added.

"And what would you do, Lena, if you were a guy and—what would your number have been?"

"I know my number. It's thirty."

"So what then, what would you do?"

"I wouldn't go. I would never go."

She picked up her backpack and walked out.

* * * *

But Lena did not leave Andrew without regret. She'd made him a card and in her best calligraphy had written a favorite quote from Martin Luther King Jr. which said, "Our scientific power has outrun our spiritual power. We have guided missiles and misguided men." Then she'd added her own quote:

Change the way you look at people and the people you look at change.

She'd hoped this gesture would bring them closer, that after reading it Andrew would kiss her and they'd leave their studying for later.

That's what Lena had hoped.

* * * *

Andrew was stunned. Lena was just so certain anti-war was the only thing and it wasn't acceptable or okay for anyone to do anything different. That was the problem. There wasn't going to be any relationship if he didn't agree with her. So did she love him? What was love anyway? What was the place of love? Was love just time spent, attention shown, affections freely shared? He knew he loved democracy. He had always loved his country. But what else? Who else?

Vietnam was the story no one wanted to talk about. Slogans yes. Posters yes. But America was so divided that They (the real Americans) did not speak the same language as They (the other real Americans). Love-It-or-Leave-It patriots and End-the-War-Honorably patriots could not see eye to eye. Andrew couldn't figure out what Gene Autry really wanted young men to do when he said the cowboy is a patriot. Andrew wanted to be sure. He wanted to have certainty about the war and certainty about the path forward to an honorable result. He believed his intellect would provide the solution.

At the National Maritime Intelligence Center in Suitland, Maryland, where Andrew had been assigned to Officer Candidate School, they watched the war each and every evening on the news. It was a horror show. They could hear the screams, see bullets hitting people and bodies dropping into the tall buffalo grass. It was all there. So in a way it was really simple. Fight some more or stop fighting. And Andrew was going through the training to be Naval Intelligence, learning small arms, disguises, map reading, hand-to-hand combat, flight school for small planes, scuba, long-distance swimming, and photography. He was polishing his language skills to have native accents—all to prep him for keeping high-grade drug smuggling off the Navy ships, especially in the dangerous ports of Pearl Harbor, Manila, and Hong Kong, not to mention New York and San Francisco. Andrew was getting ready to be deep undercover.

All these things trained him to do what he did, to sniff out Navy servicemen who were bringing heroin to our troops in Vietnam. He grew a beard and let his hair grow long. A dream it was for him, those days. Like a midnight memory, not sleeping enough, always being someone else. He had no doubt that he was doing the right thing. He wrote home and when his mother wrote back, she let him know that Lars had been in OCS at Camp Gordon, Georgia, and his sisters were still at the university. In one letter, she told him that Cameron Junior was about to graduate and work with Dad. He was always meant to be in business of course, she wrote. You're more academic, she assured. He did not, could not tell her what he was being trained to do. He said things were going well. She accepted that and continued to write her cheerful, hopeful notes of home.

When he was assigned, Andrew wrote to say he'd be out of contact for a while, knowing she'd continue to write to him anyway. After a long run in 1971, he returned to base to find stacks of mail. There were the words, "Cameron Junior and Ellie Mae are engaged and will be married June 18th. We hope you'll be able to come, dear." This was nicely tucked into her report that she and Dad had gone to the Guthrie to see a play, that Dad was trying to lose a few pounds, and that Sunny had decided to change her hair color.

Andrew was not surprised that Cameron Junior would want to marry Ellie Mae who was so beautiful. He'd would be a fool not to have her if he could. But that Ellie Mae would choose Cameron knowing his immaturity and wandering eye troubled Andrew. He did not go to the wedding. He was in Manila Harbor on that day in June doing what he did. He had sent a card earlier saying, "Congratulations. I wish you all the best." That was all he could say.

* * * *

On June 22 that year, just four days after his wedding, Cameron Junior turned twenty-three. Andrew was in the field so he didn't send his brother a birthday card. Many days earlier, he had thought about breaking the rules of tradecraft and getting him a card, but there were too many risks, and Andrew followed the rules.

He was on assignment, in disguise and waiting at the Honolulu airport, watching the inbound passengers disembark. And then, coming toward him, he saw Ellie Mae and Cameron Junior. Andrew did not move, secure that his disguise was perfect and they would not recognize him in his short grey beard and shaggy hair. Their heads were together, talking intimately, on their honeymoon, he supposed. They walked off the tarmac into the main terminal and right past him.

And then his target came into view, carrying the suitcase Naval Intelligence suspected was filled with enough cocaine to get a thousand servicemen high for a week. Andrew kept his nose in a slim volume of poetry and his eyes locked on the target. He stayed still until the target and his suitcase were ten steps past him, then turned and casually followed the man out of the terminal.

He had correctly forecasted that the target would be on this flight, be alone, have the goods with him, and travel with those goods to the historic hotel where Andrew was a guest. It was supposed to be another monthly delivery of the rich, white powder. Naval Intelligence had successfully sniffed out this run.

Andrew watched at a safe distance while two plainclothes officers cuffed the target and took him away in unmarked sedans. Two more plainclothes officers arrested an accomplice of the smuggler at the hotel before he could raise an alarm. Quiet, orderly, professional, and all done in a minute. No need to have uniformed shore patrol officers involved with that arrest. It was always better that way, Andrew thought. Better to leave drug runners to the plainclothes force.

The target talked, gave up the names he knew. A small part of a much larger drug ring was exposed and a few more arrests followed. But not Mister Big. Not the brains of the outfit. Only mules and runners and small fry, just like always, it seemed.

But even so the Office of Naval Intelligence (ONI) was impressed that they got all that cocaine out of circulation and Andrew was given a commendation and promotion for the role he played. It was two years before President Nixon created the Drug Enforcement Administration, so everyone was involved in the government's drug control activities, including Andrew and his colleagues at ONI.

He stayed in Pearl for a while, then got assigned to investigate some hooch huts and girlie clubs near Subic Bay. He stayed there just long enough to help make the nightlife scene a little safer for the servicemen. Nothing permanent, just a temporary clean-up operation. HQ then sent Andrew on similar missions to the Bay Area and Virginia Beach in the USA. He picked up more commendations and another promotion.

The next summer, word came that there had been a burglary at the Democratic National Committee's headquarters in the Watergate complex near Washington, DC. Andrew's co-workers at ONI laughed. They would never have been caught!

* * * *

Andrew had less than a year to go on his enlistment when one of his superior officers at ONI told him that he'd been detailed to the Pentagon. He was told he would be partnered with the Central Intelligence Agency. "You'll be with the Company, MacAlpine, not the Pentagon. You better not expect the CIA to be regular military. You're not going there to have a regular job with regular hours and a regular home base, got it?"

"Yes, Sir," was the required answer and that's all he said. That, plus a crisp salute. He did his same undercover intelligence gathering—but for different bosses and in different environs. It was his investigative skills the CIA most needed.

The months went by quickly. When Andrew's enlistment obligation ended, he applied for, and received, a position with the State Department, and occasionally did work for the CIA. He got a place to live and started to feel at home in the DC area. He became so adept at his daytime duties that he suddenly had hours of free time. He treated himself to a serious regimen of reading, focused mostly on graduate textbooks and course-work in world history, international diplomacy, and geopolitical strategy, and he reached out to catch up with his old friends from the university.

Andrew learned that Bobby Kovacs had gotten wounded in combat, seriously enough to end his military career. He went to the VA Hospital in Minneapolis and was back in school. In the four years since the lottery, Nelson Coleman had become a minister and got his own congregation in North Minneapolis. Jimmy Nelson was selling insurance, making a ton of money and messing around with the idea of starting a savings and loan someday with his brother Richie. "I don't know anything about much, Andrew, but I know money." He was clearly excited about this idea.

Lars was out of the Army. He told Andrew that his published book, *Scenes from the Jungle,* was doing very well and was up for some prestigious literary award. The way Andrew heard the story, Lars had used the letters he wrote home from Vietnam and put them into a book along with some of his photos in country then interspersed pithy quotations from all sorts of places. When Andrew mentioned this to his mother, she said, "Oh that Lars. He had Lena editing and rewriting those things for him for almost a year after he was out. Drove Sunny crazy, using his sister that way."

Andrew bought the book, but he didn't see any acknowledgment to Lena for her part in it. He did recognize her voice in the writing. She was off at Saint Hilda's College, Oxford University on a fellowship studying western literature. Andrew heard she was getting noticed, which made him happy for her. He hoped she'd gotten over being angry with him and regretted not having heard from her all those years. He regretted it deeply.

LENA'S LETTER

In June of 1971, a C-135 Stratolifter left Pago Pago to observe a French bomb site in the Pacific. On this flight, scheduled to land at Hickam Air Force Base adjacent to Pearl Harbor, were twelve civilians, twelve military officers, and many bags of military mail, including one long and meaningful letter from Lena Bergen to Andrew MacAlpine.

Dear Andrew,

Ellie and I have moved home to get ready for her wedding. I'm maid of honor, of course. Connie will be the best man, Linda Horton and Ruth Ann Kovacs are the other bridesmaids, and Nelson and Jimmy are the other groomsmen. The wedding color, if you'd like to know, is powder blue. Our dads look great in their identical tuxedos and they've bought brand new Florsheims—but not to match.

So it's a lot of fun you're missing here, Andrew. Bridal showers, shopping, fittings, invitations, arrangements, engagement parties. I would never have thought people our age would go to this kind of trouble to get married. But Ellie Mae loves a party, so here we are.

Except you aren't. Your mom told me you're on assignment and wherever you are, we can't know about it. My dad says while it's sad that you and Lars aren't here, you have a greater mission and he's proud of what you're doing. The Cowboy Code, he says, whatever that means. You know our dads' World War II injuries have started to take a toll. They're only forty-nine years old and the business is doing so well, but they did go together last week to the VA to have their disabilities reevaluated. I guess that's part of the Cowboy Code too. My dad has put on too much weight and continues to smoke no matter what we say. I don't know if that has to do with being a soldier or not.

I'm sorry I was so mean about the war the last time I saw you. I just couldn't be with you once you said you'd enlisted. It drove me crazy. I realize now you're doing what you believe a patriot must do. Listening to our dads talk about you and Lars has opened my eyes, Andrew. It's not an either-or, not black and white, and not as simple as I made it appear. I understand that now. Your calm demeanor the last time we talked was not indifference to my feelings, but acceptance of your duty as you saw it. I hope you will forgive me.

I would like a second chance, Andrew. I've probably loved you for years, since we all used to swim in the neighborhood and go exploring on our bikes. You've been part of my life like family, but I've always had more than a family feeling for you. Call it a crush. But more than a crush. You're such a good person and so deep. I loved when we would go to the protests together and talk for hours afterward. You don't think like other people think and I miss that so much—I miss you so much.

I'm not going back to the commune at the university and I have no interest in being with other men. I've dated but I don't sleep with men, Andrew. It's important to me that you know that. When you get out of the Navy, I'm hoping we can be together, that we can have a chance to be together—our ideas and closeness, all the good times we've had together. We both feel the same way about everything. I want to keep that going. Maybe that's bold, but I'm not shy, you know that. I know what I want and I want to be with you.

I'll be living at home until I graduate next June. And then I'll probably do graduate work, but for now this is where I'll be. I'm sending the address just in case you don't know it by heart (that's a joke) and my phone number too. Please call me, Andrew, and let me know that you are okay and write me your thoughts and whatever else you are at liberty to share.

It's June, I know, but anyway—be my Valentine. I love you.

Lena

Approximately seventy miles from its destination, the plane carrying Lena's letter to Andrew disappeared forever. And though ships and divers searched for it, no wreckage was ever found.

HAROLD'S FUNERAL

The war had worked out for Lars Bergen exactly as he had hoped. He had lived, he had experiences, been there and done it, had stars and bars and could talk about it. He returned to the university, had "some help" editing his letters, though as he would say, "They were my letters home and they were my photos." Lars was not deeply emotional about anyone. He'd let his passionate relationship with Annette drift and had not felt drawn to anyone else in that way because he was so very self-contained and happy with himself. He enjoyed sex and indulged himself whenever he could, but there were no real connections. Other than his parents and sister Lena, he wrote few letters those years he was away, not even to old friends.

Scenes from the Jungle thrust him further onto his own plane. Everywhere he went he was acknowledged for his wonderful book and his service to his country and it was always, always about Lars. What he wanted was a literary career and the book vaulted him into that. His book was good, he had family wealth, and he got what he wanted.

There were vets at the university in their fatigues still trying to unwind from the war, trying to find their way. But that wasn't Lars. Being in Vietnam didn't rip his guts out like it did for others. While some came back angry that they had been put into that situation, doing what soldiers had to do, Lars was out and about enjoying his successes. There weren't any scars. When people asked him about being in Vietnam, he would say, "Read the book, it's all in the book."

In March of 1975, the president of South Vietnam ordered the Central Highlands evacuated which turned into a mass exodus of both civilians and troops, a harbinger for the end of the war to follow. Operation Frequent Wind carried Americans and their allies out of South Vietnam by helicopter. Saigon fell the next day, on April 30, 1975, and Lars used this as an opportunity to sell more books. His publicist scheduled readings for him in major cities across the country and he went on a marvelous spree, reading and signing his books and bedding any fan who was interested.

While Lars was roaming the country, his father—working at his home office—had a massive heart attack and fell over onto his desk. Sunny came in to say she was heading over to Susie MacAlpine's for a bit and there he was. Reluctantly Lars canceled two readings and flew home for the funeral. Lena came back from England and Andrew returned from DC to pay his respects to the man who had been a second father to him. Harold had treated Andrew and Cameron Junior the same as his son, Lars—drove them to camp in the summer, picked them up later and listened to them as though they were all men. Four men. Andrew did not know why his own father had always been too busy with work and meetings, but he knew he had a caring male adult in his life when he was with Harold Bergen. He was deeply sad to have to say goodbye.

It was the first time in five years that many of the men and women from the university days were together. Linda Horton now had a PhD in psychology, Annette Freeman was doing her residency in pediatrics, and they continued to live together as they always had. And always would, as it turned out. When Lars saw them, his heart rate spiked as it did in the months when he had Annette all to himself in 1969, parked together near the mighty Mississippi. He chose not to remember her eventual cooling and her contentment to continue living with a know-it-all like Linda Horton. And so he avoided them and the memory.

Jimmy and Richie Nelson arrived at the funeral scrubbed and polished in their Brooks Brothers attire with a bit too much aftershave slapped on to their handsome faces. If Harold had been alive to see them, he would have said, "Those boys have more dollars than sense."

Cameron Junior and Ellie Mae were the only married couple of their old friends. Ellie had bought a little suit and tie for their three-year-old son, Cameron III, and a baby version for infant Jack, whom Ellie was still nursing. After the funeral, waiting for the luncheon to be served, she snuck away to the anteroom with her children to let the baby nurse. Andrew stumbled in, not knowing, uncomfortable.

"Oh, excuse me, Ellie."

"This is John Andrew MacAlpine," she said smiling at Andrew. "We named him after you."

"That's so nice, thank you," he responded and averted his eyes from the mother and child to Cameron III. "You're a handsome little boy," Andrew said and the minute he said it his brain exploded with the truth. The toddler looked exactly like Connie Demopoulos.

"What, Andrew?" Ellie Mae saw the look on Andrew's face.

But Andrew chose to say nothing. He only smiled. And Ellie understood.

"Have you talked to my sister? You know she was sitting with Bobby Kovacs during the funeral."

"Yes, I noticed."

"It's not too late, Andrew."

Maybe it wasn't. But Andrew had long since left behind whoever he once had been. He was still present for those in his life, but his training, experiences, and maturity caused him to perceive history and situations very differently than when he was younger. His high intelligence had not been blunted by the undercover life he'd led. On the contrary, nowadays, Andrew was even more capable of creative, synthetic, and intuitive thinking.

"I'm sorry about your dad, Ellie. I loved him."

"I know, Andrew. We've all loved each other for a long time." The baby had finished nursing and she was adjusting her clothing. Andrew nodded, took one more long look at Cameron III, and left to see about lunch.

In the noisy basement of The Church of the Faithful Shepard, he made his way to the table where his brother was talking with the Nelsons. "What's going on?"

Jimmy slapped Andrew on the back. "We're just talking about joining forces in an insurance business."

"Geez, Andrew," Jimmy said then, "you should work with us too.

Whatever you're doing in DC over there can't be as exciting as this, right, Cam?"

Andrew laughed. "You're all better off without me in that equation."

"Brothers together," Jimmy continued. "Just like old times."

Andrew said nothing. Across the room he saw Lena Bergen talking with friends of the family. He needed to share his sympathies with her, he knew he did. But what could he say? The last thing he remembered her telling him was that she didn't want to have anything to do with him again. Where could he go from there?

Instead he gravitated toward Lars who appeared to be holding court with fans at his father's funeral.

"Congratulations on your book," Andrew said. "I hear Lena helped you out quite a bit. Nice to have another poet in the family, right?"

"Yeah. The book is doing really well. They want me to go back on tour as soon as I'm done with all this here. Maybe you'll see me on TV."

"Well, I'll be sure to look for you there, Lars. I'm glad you made it back from Nam in one piece."

"You look good, too, Andrew. I never did hear what it was you were doing. I suppose you could tell me, but then maybe you'd have to kill me, right?" He laughed heartily at his own joke.

Lena showed up at that moment. "Still at war, are you?"

"I got out in January and I'm at the State Department now."

Lena seemed unimpressed or uninterested or distracted, Andrew could not tell. "I'm so sorry for your loss, Lena," he said. "I loved your dad. He did so much with us boys and I'll always remember him."

She nodded, and starting to cry, she moved away.

Susie stayed close to Sunny all through the day, making sure she had tissue or a plate of food at the luncheon, more coffee, another cigarette. Her devotion to her friend heightened knowing that Sunny would no longer have Harold coming home at the end of the day.

Cameron Junior touched Andrew's arm. "So what do you think?"

"About what, Cam?"

"Jimmy's offer to sell insurance, no?" Cameron's laugh had an edge.

"How are you doing, Cameron?"

"It's all good, Andrew. The boys are good. So sad about Harold. Looking great one day and dead the next. Go figure. Lena is still in shock. At least Sunny will be taken care of."

"Taken care of?"

"Dad and Harold had an attorney draft a buy–sell agreement funded by life insurance. You know, a business buys life insurance policies on the lives of each owner. When one of the owners dies, like Harold did, the company gets the death benefit from the insurance policy and uses the money to buy out that deceased partner's interest."

"So Sunny gets the money from Harold's interest in the company?" Andrew asked.

"Most of the proceeds do go to her," Cameron Junior said. "Lars, Ellie Mae, and Lena get some too. Harold set up trust accounts for them. Dad told me yesterday. I'm not boring you with these business details, am I?"

"Is this something I should know about?" Andrew asked.

"I think so, Andrew. Dad owns forty shares, just like Harold did. The women have ten shares each." Cameron nodded toward their mother and Sunny. "The business redeemed Harold's forty shares, so there are sixty shares outstanding. Dad owns two-thirds of the shares now. Understand?"

Andrew nodded and said, “I understand. Anything else?”

Cameron Junior continued, “If Dad dies, the buy-sell works the same as Harold’s did. Mom gets most of the insurance proceeds and the rest goes into trust for you and me.”

“So, then, Mom and Sunny would own the business?” Andrew asked.

“Yep, that’s right. Assuming no one sells any stock and assuming Dad dies first, then Mom and Sunny will own the whole damn thing.”

“I thought you were going to get the business. Wasn’t that always the plan?”

“I thought so, too, Andrew. I’m going to ask Dad for some stock as soon as Harold’s estate is settled. Can’t have five years of my work go down the drain, can we? God helps those who help themselves. Right?”

“Well, Cameron, I hope you get whatever you deserve.”

I MADE IT BIG

Cameron Senior and Harold had long ago diversified from buying land and building homes into buying and managing apartment buildings. Harold had always managed the building crews, hired and fired, and maintained good relationships with all the building trades. He had been a real people person and could swing a hammer until the end. Workers admired Harold. As soon as they heard of his death, they worried about who would be able to take his place. Who would be the boss?

Cameron Senior wondered the same thing. He knew that his son with his razor haircut and buffed nails would not be accepted by the crews. Father and son went for breakfast to discuss the future. "Well, son, who do you think should manage the crews?"

Cameron Junior looked out the window and said, "You know it's been almost ten years since I ran back and forth getting tools out of the chest." He shrugged. "My degree in business never prepared me to be a supervisor of workers in the field. Maybe we could hire somebody from another company. Or maybe you'd like to get back out in the field again, Dad. At least you know these guys."

"I suppose I could promote one of the crew chiefs. I could talk to Jake and Dave, interview them, see what they could handle."

"Sure, Dad. Sounds good. So since we're talking about changes, maybe this is a good time to figure out when I get my stock in the company. Maybe we could leverage what we own at the bank and buy some more apartment buildings. Then maybe I could help you more and get some stock." He made this sound very reasonable. "I took courses at the university. This is what businesses do, Dad, they leverage their assets."

"You know I built this business with a minimum of borrowing from the bank. I don't care about debt, Cam. If you want to own more of the business, then you can do as I suggested five years ago and take half your salary in stock. You think things just happen overnight? You think I didn't have to scrimp and work my balls off to have what I have now? We drove used cars for years and reinvested every penny in this business to live in a big house in a nice neighborhood—and you live there already. Something to think about, Cam."

His son didn't know enough history to remind his father that building a business after the war was a no-fail venture, that times had changed, that big begot big. Cameron Senior rode the wave of productivity that had now come and gone. The United States had adopted a policy after World War II which laid the foundation for home ownership through the GI Bill of Rights—the large families, the low interest rates, and the government policy that allowed long-term credit to those with honorable discharge papers and a decent reputation. Jobs were plentiful. Women returned to the home to have children, clothe and feed those children, and furnish the homes. Businesses manufactured all the products that young families needed and also supplied the world with what it needed after the decimation of the war.

A unified Congress wanted to change the dynamic, to shift the equation so that the great wealth concentrations of the early twentieth century could be dispersed more democratically to the country's population at large. Eisenhower proposed the National Defense Highway Improvement Act, which was approved by Congress and enabled people to travel to the city and to the suburbs and someone, someone needed to build those homes and make money on building those homes. Neither Cameron nor his son completely understood that.

Instead, Cameron Junior said, "My job isn't just putting entries into the general ledger. I do a lot to maintain relationships with the bank and I know the bankers want us to take on more debt and expand. They don't think we're over-leveraged. I get the buildings insured and visit with the onsite property managers. So I'm already doing a lot of what you used to do. I mean, I don't even know what all you do anymore." This was a challenge, but he didn't really mean it that way.

His father finished his cup of coffee before saying, "I know lots of builders and developers who've gone belly-up listening to their bankers. They want the interest, Cam. I'm not about to let that happen. And what I do with my time is my business. I don't answer to you. This is my company. I own this company."

Cameron Junior was not understanding why he wasn't getting what he wanted. Why was it so hard? In his mind, his father was being stubborn and unreasonable. "Don't you want the business to stay in the family?"

"Nobody ever handed me a business on a silver platter. You've had a college education. A job right out of school. No military. Big salary. So. Subject closed, Cam."

But the subject was not closed to Cameron Junior. "Mom's a stockholder too, Dad. Doesn't she want me to continue the family business after you're gone?"

His father did not answer. He slapped the bills on the table to pay for their breakfast and went back to the office to think about all he had accomplished in his life that never would have happened without his grit and drive. That's all he wanted to think about that day.

THE BEST TRANQUILIZER

The tennis ball whizzed by Ellie Mae for the winning point. She said, "Nice shot, Merrilee. You guys win. Do we have time for a glass of wine today?"

Merrilee called across the net, "Soon as I've had a shower and quick trip to the sauna."

Carol and Diane nodded their agreement, zipped their racquets into their monogrammed tote bags, and headed toward the women's showers. Carol shouted a quick "Hello, Molly" to the trim blonde woman who was walking onto their court with the tennis pro, obviously about to get a lesson.

The four women were alone in the sauna, oversize white towels wrapped loosely around their bodies and smaller white towels on their heads. Carol and Ellie Mae were seated on the highest bench, Merrilee and Diane just below them, an intimate gathering of sorority sisters, best friends from their university days.

Carol said, "Did you see how good Molly looked out there? My cousin's hairdresser, Mister Richard—you know, Mister Richard's shop in the Skyway—told my cousin's best friend that after Molly got ditched by that jerk husband, she went to a plastic surgeon and had lots of work done."

Ellie Mae said, "Whatever they did, she sure looks good."

Carol continued, "Well, Amy told my cousin Mandy that Molly had everything done. She had her tummy tucked, got implants, had the skin under her chin tightened, even got a little tweak on her beak."

Merrilee, who preferred the straight and narrow in life, said, "Oh my!"

Carol continued, "That's what I heard. She's fifty-three and looks thirty-five. Can you believe it? Mister Richard said she got the house and a million dollars in the divorce."

Diane laughed, "I'll bet she doesn't have any trouble getting dates."

Merrilee chuckled. "She's sitting on a gold mine."

Carol took a deep breath. "There's way more to the story. The divorce? Yeah, well, the reason it went so well for Molly was because she caught her jerk husband on camera in a very compromising situation." Carol stretched out the words "very compromising situation" and licked her lips. "She'd hired some ex-cop private investigator to follow him. It paid off big for her."

Ellie Mae said, "Her ex must have been pretty stupid to cheat on her."

Carol had more to say. "I'm not taking his side, El, but two years ago, Missus Molly wasn't that trim blonde you saw hanging on to her tennis coach, if that's what you want to call him. Mister Richard said she looked old and gray and lumpy before her hubby went looking for greener pastures."

Diane laughed again, "I'll bet she's getting lots of sex now. My sister, the one with the migraines, she told me sex is the safest tranquilizer in the world. Ten times more effective than Valium. I've heard that the more sex you have, the more you'll be offered. It's because a sexually active body gives off greater quantities of pheromones, which are really just natural sex perfumes."

"Who told you that?" Merrilee reacted with total surprise, clearly offended.

Diane continued, "My sister read it, Merilee, and she's very smart. She says sex relieves her headaches. That's what she said. Something about lovemaking releases the tension that restricts blood vessels in the brain."

"I can see where that might be true," Merrilee answered. "I haven't had a migraine since high school." They all roared.

When their merriment ended, Diane asked, "Did her ex marry the woman who broke up their marriage?"

Carol snorted, "Are you kidding? Why would he?"

Diane stood up, adjusted her towel, and said, "Let's get dressed and have that glass of wine."

Later, as the four friends sat at a table sipping wine, Diane said, "You remember that my fiancé Daniel is in New York now, right? He's down on Wall Street for his four-month stockbroker apprenticeship. Well, I had Lars do a glamour shot of me so that Daniel could see what he's missing." Diane paused, poked Ellie Mae's arm and said, "Your brother is a regular devil, El. Completely incorrigible. Completely," she repeated.

Before Ellie Mae could respond, Carol added, "That's the truth," and Merrilee said, "He's very cute."

"Oh, you guys," Ellie Mae said, "he'll stop if you just say so."

Diane winked and added, "Who said I wanted him to stop?"

"You didn't! Did you?" Merrilee gasped.

Diane paused, "Bachelors do it all the time. I say, what's good for the goose is good for the gander."

"You're right, Diane," said Carol, "and it isn't just bachelors out there swinging. Husbands and wives go to parties and swap spouses. Do you know that? My cousin's best friend said Mister Richard has some magazines, right out in the open, that are all about 'The Lifestyle.' You know, open marriage, wife swapping, threesomes, and right here in the Twin Cities too."

"Oh my gosh," Merrilee shuddered.

Ellie Mae waved to the bartender to bring another round.

The bartender brought more wine and the women told more stories, the kind sorority sisters tell after two glasses of wine, a sauna, a rousing tennis match, and no breakfast or lunch because they're dieting.

Ellie Mae listened and nodded and occasionally threw in an, "Oh my," but mostly she was in her own head. She had been feeling empty lately, lonely and unloved. At three and a half years old, Cameron III liked spending time with the nanny and the grandmas and that was good, but he didn't need her as he once had. She had stopped nursing Jack and started him on a bottle and that had been good, too, she thought. She wasn't as tied down as she had been right after Jack's birth, but she didn't feel free or happy or loved.

Cameron Junior worked long hours and had joined a sports club. He looked trim and fit and seemed to enjoy being out of the house. He was always too tired to spend intimate time with her. More and more lately, especially in these weeks after her dad's unexpected death, Ellie Mae had daydreams of her sorority days. She had so loved all her boyfriends then. She had been exuberant and intense with each of them for as long as the relationship lasted, even if it was only a weekend. Now she loved her husband. And she wasn't quite sure he loved her in return.

"Hello. Hello. Earth to Ellie Mae. Come in, Ellie Mae," said Carol. The others were all looking at her.

"What? What'd I miss?" Ellie Mae's fingers tightly clasped her empty wine glass.

"Do you want a ride home?" Carol repeated. "Or do you want to walk?"

Ellie Mae let go of her wine glass and said, "A ride would be great."

After the bill was paid, the goodbyes said, and Ellie Mae was seated in her friend's Corvette, Carol asked, "A penny for your thoughts? Something's on your mind, El."

"It's nothing."

"You'll feel better once you get it off your chest."

"I don't know, Carol. Something doesn't feel right. I didn't expect my life to be this way. Cameron's never home and he never seems interested in me. He's not acting like he did before we got married, that's for sure. I couldn't keep him off me back then. He's never played much with Cameron III, you know that whole story about me and Connie, but now he doesn't even come home in time to play with little Jack." Ellie Mae's eyes teared. "I don't know what to do, Carol."

"I'm sorry. I had no idea. We all thought you were just down in the dumps because of your dad dying."

"That certainly didn't help."

"Why don't you send the boys to your mom's house for the weekend and make his favorite dinner, with you as dessert?"

Ellie Mae laughed, "Thanks, Carol. 'The way to a man's heart is through his stomach, right?"

"Or, buy a sexy negligee, chill some champagne, and greet him at the door with a kiss. You could do that, El. He'd melt in a minute. Don't worry. He'd be a fool to stray when he's got you at home."

"You don't think he needs some spice, something new and exciting, like what we were talking about over wine?"

Carol paused, looked at Ellie Mae, and said, "Well, what if he does, El? How do you want to play it if he does?"

She pulled to the curb and parked her car in front of Ellie Mae's Kenwood house. Ellie Mae put her hand on Carol's arm and said, "I don't think I could do it, Carol. I don't want to share him and I don't want to go to that kind of party just looking for sex. I only want Cameron and I want him to be satisfied with me, just me. Like my mom and dad, that's what I want."

Carol looked across the car at her stunningly beautiful friend. "I hope you get what you want, El. I really hope that you do."

THE BOARD MEETING

Lucille Shea began working with Cameron and Harold when she was quite young. She was a vibrant and attractive woman who still held her own. She dressed well and dyed and styled her hair so that it framed her face just as it did all those years ago. In 1953, she took a leave for a time saying that she had gone to San Diego to marry a marine who was then immediately killed in Korea. But that wasn't altogether true.

She was imperious, drank exactly four cups of coffee a day, and smoked at least twelve cigarettes in a morning. She lived alone in one of the suburban apartment buildings owned by Alpine Homes and worked in the company's main office at the other end of that same building. Each Christmas she would take ten days to visit with her sister and niece in Duluth, but in general said nothing about herself. She was friendly, but generally kept her distance and every man in the business knew if she approved of him or would prefer to eat him for lunch.

For the first board meeting after Harold's death, she organized her files and arrived early to take her place just to the left of where Cameron would sit at the large oak table. Next to her she set her rolling file cabinet, all her files color-coordinated for easy access. Sunny arrived first, with Susie and Cameron just behind. After their polite greetings, Cameron began.

"Here we are," he said, presenting the financials. "The insurance proceeds have been taken care of—the lawyers tell me that the money has been deposited in your account, Sunny, and in the trust accounts for your three children. Now we have to think about who can take Harold's position." He paused. "Also I had a conversation with Cameron Junior who wants more stock in the company. But he's not too interested in cutting back on his salary to do it."

"We could have him give us a proposal, dear," Susie said.

Cameron stared at her for a minute. "What kind of proposal would that be, do you think?"

Susie looked uncomfortable and Sunny nodded to be agreeable.

"What do you say, Lucille?" Cameron asked, moving his attention from his wife to her.

"A proposal can't hurt. Then we'd understand what Junior wants." Lucille always called Cameron's son just Junior. She folded her hands in her lap.

Then for nearly an hour they discussed other details of the business and all agreed that they would offer Jake Bachman a promotion to become the field crew boss, stepping into Harold's shoes. They would entertain a proposal from Cameron Junior and plan to decide on that the next time they met. At the end of a long hour, Sunny asked the others if they would like to buy her home or exchange it in a real estate swap for an Alpine Homes duplex.

This was a bombshell to Cameron.

"Geez, Sunny, don't you want to give it some time. They say people shouldn't make major decisions until at least a year after a death."

"I don't want to live there without Harold. I don't know if I can make it a whole year alone in that house. Just those trees scraping against the roof keep me up at night. I can hardly sleep."

Susie said, "We have extra space in our house, Sunny. Why don't you move in with us?" She looked across the table to her husband. "That would be great, don't you agree, dear?"

Then she laughed. "It would save me a lot of driving!"

Sunny jumped in. "My gosh, that would be so wonderful."

"You can have the wing where the boys used to live. Plenty of privacy. And your own fireplace."

"You won't even know I'm there."

"Good plan, ladies," Lucille interjected. "I can have one of Jake's men drive by your house a couple times a day to check on things for you." She gave a peremptory nod. "We have the cash to buy Sunny's house, Cameron, and in today's market, homes are selling so quickly, we can make our money back in a flash."

There was nothing Cameron could argue. Sunny would move in and Susie would take her further under wing and Cameron would come and go as he always did. "I'm going to get the books ready to bring to the accountants now, so why don't you two take off," he said to his wife and Sunny, "and Mrs. Shea can drop me off at home later."

The door closed behind the two women. "What do you think, Lucy? Do you have a drink for me?"

He watched her file her folders from the meeting into her rolling file cabinet and followed her out of the conference room. He had never ceased to be amazed at this woman's efficiency. She had set up the office so that their business had operated smoothly for the past twenty plus years. He fell in love with her over and over again.

And he had always loved that her apartment was just down the hall.

JUST ONE LINE

The next thing Cameron Junior knew he was being asked who was the president and did he know where he was. He and Jimmy Nelson had only snorted one line each when Cameron passed out. Jimmy thought Cameron was dead, that's what he thought. Cassandra Block and Janet Mueller, their dates for the evening, dressed quickly and helped drag Cameron Junior out of Jimmy's apartment. They propped him into Jimmy's Mustang and all four of them roared over to Hennepin County Emergency Room in a complete panic. Jimmy couldn't even feel Cameron's heartbeat.

An ER doctor rushed to them immediately, found a pulse, and brought him back to consciousness, though his heart continued to flutter. The young nurse helping him had just moved from Duluth where she had obtained her degree from the College of Saint Scholastica. She was serious and pretty and determined to do well.

Jimmy said, "We should call Ellie Mae."

"Tell the girls to leave, Jimmy," Cameron answered and as soon as Cassandra and Janet were out of the room, he called his wife to say he'd passed out while swimming at his sports club and was in the ER, but not to worry. He'd be fine soon.

Ellie's first reaction was high concern. "Are they going to keep you? Are you coming home? Should I be there?" But the more he talked the less sense his story made. He was a wonderful swimmer. The whole thing sounded suspicious to her. She felt she hardly knew her husband anymore. "Who are you with, Cameron? How did you get to the ER?"

"Jimmy brought me, but he's got to leave. I'm okay. Don't worry." He didn't like seeing Jimmy and the girls leave him to face his situation and his wife and the long night ahead.

Ellie arrived at the ER within the hour. The first thing she saw walking into the space was the young nurse attending to his medications. She looked so much like Cameron Junior, she could have been his twin.

"Hello?" Ellie stood stunned. "Do I know you?"

The young woman smiled. "I just moved down here from Duluth, so I really don't know anyone. Except my aunt. She's always lived here."

"Really? Where does she live then?"

"Oh, she's in the suburbs, in Minnetonka. It's real pretty." The nurse turned again to Cameron Junior's care.

"Hi, El," her husband called from the bed, pale and sweaty, his eyes pinpricks. "How're the boys?"

"The boys are with the nanny and they're fine." She leaned in closer. "Excuse me," she said to the nurse. "Did my husband almost drown? Cam for Christ's sake you're high as a kite. Oh my God. He's high as a kite. My husband is stoned. Did you OD, for God's sake?" She spun to the nurse. "Why do you look like my husband? Do you know why? Are you a relative? Jesus, Cam." She flopped into the chair near the bed wanting a cigarette. "You're never home and you give me some baloney story about drowning—drowning, Cam, really—and I walk in here to find a nurse that looks like you! What the hell!"

She huffed in silence while Cameron tried to think of some better story.

The nurse said nothing. She knew the name MacAlpine. Her aunt worked for a man named MacAlpine. In the flurry of this man's arrival, she hadn't even looked at his name on the chart, but his wife's rampage made her very curious. She supposed she did look something like the brown-haired, gray-eyed patient. But why that would be, she did not know.

"Can I get something for you, Mrs. MacAlpine?"

Ellie Mae didn't even hear her. For God's sake, what was happening to her. She had no father now and maybe she had no husband worth a damn and the nurse hanging around her was some kind of long-lost connection to someone.

And none of this was what she wanted.

WHAT SHE WANTS

Just as the autumn grew colder and grayer, Cameron Junior and Ellie Mae lost whatever fragment of energy, passion, and illumination that was left in their relationship. Cameron promised, "no more coke," but continued to have late evenings of swimming, bowling, billiards, and poker while his wife stayed home smoking cigarettes and drinking coffee, pacing and waiting.

Then came the morning following a night when Ellie Mae had waited for Cameron Junior to come home. Around seven a.m. she was toasting a bagel when he breezed through with, "No time for breakfast, El, got to head off to a meeting with Dad." In less than a minute he was gone again, not allowing her the chance to ask him where he had been and why he so seldom came home.

She could not swallow her coffee and did not hear her porcelain cup shatter in the sink, nor did she know why it happened. Sliding to the floor, unaware of the cold tile, she watched the ceiling descend with a great weight on top of her. She could hear animal sounds, shrill and strange, like some creature caught in a trap was trying to chew its legs off to escape. She felt something damp around her and the ceiling continued to push down against her, squeezing the air out of her.

Upstairs Cameron III sang the alphabet song with the nanny, the phrasing predictable, nursery rhymes in a morning ritual of hands clapping and joyful chases in and around the nursery furniture. The pale light through the kitchen window cast no warmth on Ellie Mae. Squirrels ran frantically and the last of the leaves swirled in the morning wind. Maybe there was a crow. She thought she knew the sound of the crow and she felt so very cold, as if the sun were dying and there may never be sun again.

It was near lunch time when the nanny came down to get a bottle for baby Jack. Luckily she'd left the children upstairs so they didn't have to see their mother sprawled on the tiled floor without movement or obvious consciousness. She called 911 and tried to reach Cameron Junior, but nobody seemed to know where he was or how to find him. She ran back and forth between the nursery and the kitchen to keep watch on all the

MacAlpine family until the medical people arrived. It wasn't until Ellie Mae's haggard body was wrapped in a blanket, lifted onto the stretcher and into the ambulance that the nanny searched the family address book to call Ellie's mother, poor Mrs. Bergen, who had just lost her husband and now this. That's all the nanny could think of really. Poor Mrs. Bergen.

She didn't feel sympathy for Ellie Mae, though she'd always liked her in a general sort of way. But for a mother to be so busy, to be so distant from her children, and to allow herself to fall unconscious on the kitchen floor in the middle of a weekday morning—this was nothing the nanny understood or approved. It was not the way she was raised, though clearly these people who employed her had been raised in some other way. They only thought about what they wanted. They only wanted to get their own.

The nanny could not know that Ellie Mae had lost her organizing principle, lost track of where she was and who she was. Ellie Mae's fragmentation was like atoms shooting off into space, no longer held together into a mind and whole person. It would soon be important for Ellie Mae to know she was on the third floor of a medical facility in the city of Minneapolis in the United States of America on the planet Earth in the solar system that was part of the Milky Way. She would figure that out again. But it was going to take time.

WHEN ELLIE MAE WENT AWAY

If anyone in Ellie Mae's life had opened the journal she'd been keeping, they would have found this note to herself:

> Every day it was the same little things: tennis and lunch, or shopping and lunch, or just lunch for a heart-to-heart chat. And the chats always heartless gabs. Endless whining tales, those chats—can't find the right stove and how much should a good stove cost to buy, can't find the right couch and how much should a good couch cost to buy.
>
> Can't find the right nanny or maid or cook or tennis coach or pool boy—can't get no satisfaction from the money I got.
>
> Can't buy me Love. Every day like every other day.
>
> Little things every day; always the same things and always little. No chatting about big things. Honest to God we never spoke about truth and beauty, peace and love, duty and honor, time and memory, the meaning and importance of person and place, the courage of one's convictions.
>
> Not ever, not once.
>
> I cannot go back to being the kind of person who would live a life like that.
>
> I can't go back to that. And so—that person just went away.
>
> Did you just ask me how I ended up in this place?
>
> Didn't I just tell you that story?
>
> I was raised to negotiate every condition in my favor and I got to be good at getting my way. I've lived almost completely on my own terms from an early age. Only a few missteps along the way, but everyone told me I was a woman before such a person could've fairly formed. Are you surprised I went off the rails?

My brittle self suddenly broke apart, evaporating one morning like dawn's mist, and what had been called Ellie Mae disappeared onto the cold floor of that spacious kitchen. Some were surprised I had cared so much about what my husband did after my youthful years doing what I had done.

I am no longer earthbound.

I have ascended to the stars and my concerns are now global and galactic.

Which is why I no longer worry about Cameron Junior or his boys. They're all fine. And my mother is with Susie, so she's fine. And Lena is always fine. As is my sexually inappropriate egomaniac brother. All fine.

They would be better off thinking I died that day.

Whatever has once been me—that Ellie Mae you keep asking about—melted down, and will be forever after unseen in this earthly realm.

Aren't you the shrink I saw yesterday? The doctor who told me I'd had too much self, and much too soon—not really a full self, though, and certainly not myself.

Wasn't it you who told me a restored Ellie Mae could return home soon, very soon—with proper medications and continuing therapy working a miracle of rebirth?

So you said, but Ellie Mae will never return to play wife and mother, daughter and sorority sister.

She's moved on.

COME WALK WITH ME

It was 1976 and Lena Bergen, barely 26 years old, had finished the coursework for her PhD. All she needed to do was write her dissertation. If a man comes into a room and a woman is talking—does anyone still hear her? That was the essence of what Lena had pursued throughout her matriculation.

During her fellowship at Saint Hilda's College, Oxford, Lena had written a summary of her years of thinking, a brilliant series of feminine insights she entitled *Letters to American Women,* which she sent to an agent, who immediately fell in love with it. Lena had crafted twenty letters, one for every decade, supposedly written by English women to their American sisters. The book's positive reviews, sales success, and award nomination immediately led to Lena being invited to regional radio stations and television studios all around the country to talk about *Letters to American Women.*

Two hundred years had passed since the Declaration of Independence, and 1976 was turning out to be a good year for Lena Bergen's book. Spurred by the bicentennial fever, *Letters to American Women* was in its second reprint in less than a year, providing glimpses into the problems the new nation had faced, and critiques of how previous problems had been dealt with and left to fester, unresolved. Critics were favorably comparing Lena's book with the writings of Betty Friedan, Germaine Greer, and Gloria Steinem.

The book was more often discussed than read, however, so many interviewers began by asking Lena what the book was about. She had developed a series of answers, some short, some longer, to help move the interviews along. A number of the questions related to the Equal Rights Amendment, which had been passed by the United States Congress and sent to the states for ratification in 1972. Many interviewers were personally involved in the ERA battle, pro or con, and some of the questions were quite pointed. In a recent phone interview, the radio host asked if Lena was married and hearing the negative response, followed up with, "Okay, I think we now understand what your book is all about." Lena terminated that interview by hanging up.

Now, as she sat in a local television studio hoping today's hosts wouldn't make her want to spit the bit and walk off the stage, all the people in her life were gathering to see what she had to say.

Sunny and Susie waited in the big kitchen of the MacAlpine home in Kenwood, drinking coffee and making nervous small talk before watching Lena's interview on television. Sunny had told Lars who had said he'd try to tune in if he had the time, but he did not. He decided it much more important to work on his own book that morning.

Ellie Mae, now out of the hospital, was living with Lena in Sunny's old home, which Sunny sold to her daughters on a contract for deed. Ellie Mae had recovered sufficiently to be alone and sat riveted to the television set drinking her beloved coffee. She liked being alone. Whenever Lena was gone and Ellie had the house to herself, she did very little, but thought very much and breathed in deep meditative beats she had not known before.

Cameron Senior was watching the show with Lucy Shea, of course. Cameron Junior chose to sit and watch in the nursery with the nanny, whom he rather liked these days, and his children who played on the carpeted floor with their toys, completely unaware that their mother's younger sister was a local celebrity.

Jimmy Nelson had his feet on the desk in his office and the television volume on loud, which was the way he liked things. He'd always found Lena Bergen so beautiful and interesting, even though he wasn't sure he understood what she was talking about half the time. But it was fun just listening. He'd known her most of his life and often imagined how he could impress her, take her to an opera or a play and buy her a fancy dinner. He had a lot to offer, he thought. Money, ease, and some good laughs. But the two or three times he'd asked her out, she'd just laughed, like it was a good joke between them. And there were so many other women available. Still, he watched her interview with something of a renewed fervor, he had to admit.

Bobby Kovacs also watched, daydreaming about what he wished had happened between him and Lena. She was kind to him but always said no, "We're never going to happen, Bobby, you should find someone else." Even so, he thought she liked him more than the other young men she knew. He just had a feeling about it. And now she was front and center, the author and super-feminist, being interviewed in her hometown and watched by everyone in her life.

Surprisingly Lena felt exposed. Did her family and friends realize what she had been thinking and studying all these years? Maybe they wouldn't like what she was about to say and would drift away from her. Her book was a critique on women's roles in the past two hundred years of history, their lack of say or even mention in the events that seemingly shaped the world.

Though her mother and Susie had helped build the company and had always been strong women, Lena had never heard them talk about the barriers facing most women. Sunny and Susie had comfortable lives. So many women thought they had comfortable lives and now here was Lena Bergen with the audacity to say they had been duped.

"Ms. Bergen, tell us what you say to those women who don't support the Equal Rights Amendment."

Lena laughed with a bit of discomfort. "I talk to those women all the time." She smiled into the camera.

In the MacAlpine kitchen, her mother grinned with pride.

A NEW DIRECTION

After Lena returned home, Ellie told her, "You did so well. I just loved watching you."

Lena sat down next to her sister. "I'm glad you thought that, El. It felt kind of awful."

"But you know so much. And you're on television and you have a book. How can that be awful?"

"The thing is, it's all what I think and what I research and what I want others to know. But it isn't me exactly. It's my mind. So here I am with this mind, Ellie. You have two children and a husband. For whatever he's worth," she had to add.

They both laughed. "I'm pretty sure that's over, Lena."

"But you know what I'm saying. You have a life or you had a life that you're trying to sort. It's real, Ellie. It isn't just a thought. I mean, I don't know now how to go from this PhD poet person to having someone who loves me and a home and—I don't know—maybe children. It gives me nightmares."

Ellie shook her head. "But what about Jimmy Nelson or Bobby Kovacs? You've known those guys forever, and they're both interested in you. You know that."

Lena rolled her eyes. "Jimmy's only interested in his new car and the next fancy restaurant and Bobby just wants to talk me into bed."

"That doesn't sound so bad." Ellie grinned at her sister.

"I'd like something more in a man."

"Welcome to real life, Lena." Ellie meant it. She thought her sister's expectations were too high to be achieved. But then that was Lena. She always wanted to be at the top of every game. "Mom and Dad had a great marriage, but everything wasn't perfect. You know that. He wouldn't stop smoking for her and hardly had much to say with us kids. Look at Lars. If Dad had disciplined him once in a while, maybe he wouldn't be such a chauvinist pig today. And we don't know if Mom could really talk to Dad, if he was there for her, you know." Ellie lit a cigarette. "I say make a choice and just go for it."

"I know. That's what I'm thinking. I think it's time to be with someone."

"So who's in the lead?"

"If I choose Jimmy, I'll probably have a comfortable and kind of fun life."

"As long as you don't have to talk to him very often. Am I right?"

Lena didn't laugh. Of course, Ellie Mae was right. "Okay, but Bobby might burn out like a birthday candle. He's so intense. And he's never had much and here I am with this trust fund money we roll around in, this Bergen-MacAlpine wealth we're so used to. How is that going to go?"

"So you want Bobby to be rich or you want Jimmy to be smart."

"Yes, and the Mercedes in red. Thank you. Problems solved. Should we have a glass of champagne?"

They wandered to the kitchen, opened the wine and a box of crackers, and sat at the table. "Talking about love, I'd like to know a different kind of love," Ellie Mae said. "Not needing anything in return love. Total love. All-encompassing love, permanent and unwavering."

"So you're not talking about a man."

They locked eyes. "No. Something else. Truly something else. Large love. All I need to know is that I'll be loved forever. I've already been abandoned. I don't want that again."

"So God maybe. Is that where you're going?"

"What do you think?"

"I haven't had time to think about God, I guess. What do Lutherans know about God?"

And they both laughed again.

"I keep seeing myself in a quiet place, someplace where the sun rises and sunsets are like stained glass."

"Maybe you need some time away. From everything."

"I do. I do, Lena. I've been thinking about leaving, maybe be a hermit someplace. There are people who do that, aren't there?"

"There are monastics, El. Not Lutheran, though, that I know of. But I think a Catholic convent would take you in to think about God. You can donate or something." She poured more champagne. "What do you think of that?"

"Tell me about convents."

"When I was researching my book, I looked at women in convents, looked at their letters and their diaries, and what I would say is that these are places that are very accepting and thoughtful and even cheerful, Ellie. These are not depressed women escaping from the troubles of life, but women who have this calling and are into God like what you were saying and are friends to one another, even another whole kind of family." She looked over at her blonde, beautiful, tired older sister. "It would be very different."

"How would you do without me?"

"Maybe it's my time to move in a new direction too. Maybe we help each other get someplace new."

The two young women sat in silence then and drank some more in a slow kind of way until Lena said, "I think I should give Bobby a chance, don't you?"

WHAT SUSIE HAS TO SAY

Andrew did not make it home for Thanksgiving.

His mother called him the next day, just as he was returning from work, her voice so unbalanced that she forgot to say hello. "Andrew, this was the most bizarre Thanksgiving I've ever lived through. I just wished you were in town. You are the only sane person in all these MacAlpine and Bergen kids."

This made Andrew laugh. He would tend to agree with her but chose not to say.

"First of all, this group eats all day. We start with egg bake, they're all making a mess in the kitchen while I'm trying to get that turkey ready and then some come and some don't. Ellie Mae doesn't want to be here at the same time as your brother, so she came early with Lena and then Cameron had to come later with the kids. And the nanny, which don't get me started on her. So that's the logistics."

"Mom, that's the way it always is."

"No, Andrew. It's more. Your father was at the office again, like he is on every holiday and didn't come back until after the egg bake and then disappeared into the den to watch football. And honestly I'm not used to doing a meal like this with Sunny and you know how much I love her, but she isn't organized like I am and I felt like we were bumping into each other and doing the same things over, like how many times do we need to toss the green beans?"

"Mom, I thought you were going to tell me some news. You want to hear my news?"

Susie did, but she didn't want to stop telling her story. "No, let me keep going for a minute, Andrew. I just need to talk. You know Ellie Mae is leaving Cameron Junior. I could have seen it coming, but with the boys and all, I just didn't want to believe it. And here's the thing. She's leaving completely. She's going into a convent, Andrew. A convent! What

Lutheran ever goes into a Catholic convent? Which your father continues to call a nunnery. So here my grandkids are going to be half orphaned because their mother wants to "find herself" in a Catholic nunnery. I'm just sick. But do you think your brother even has tried to talk her out of it? No. No. It's almost like he's so numbed out on himself that he doesn't see how those children need their mother. Do you think I would ever have waltzed out the door and left you and Cameron Junior with just anyone? Or no one? Or whatever? I'm telling you, Andrew, I'm just sick. That nanny talks with such a thick Swedish accent, lord knows what those boys will sound like by the time they go to school."

"When is Ellie going to go? Is she well enough, Mom?"

"What's well enough? She's made these plans and her sister, if you can believe this, her sensible sister is helping her. She found some little place in North Dakota where these ladies keep a garden and pray all the day long. They showed us the brochure." Susie's voice continued to rise. "There they all are in those awful black uniforms like something out of the dark ages and smiling like everything's going so well. Carmelites, they're called, and I asked Barbie at the beauty shop what she knows about them, because she was raised Catholic you know, like half the rebels in the world were, and she says that these are the nuns that are so like hermits they go years, even decades, without seeing their families. You can imagine how poor Sunny took that. Losing Harold and now Ellie off to some cave—it might as well be a cave, Andrew. That's what we're thinking.

"And there's more. Honest to God, there's been talk and we've heard the talk, that Lars has been sleeping with women on his highfalutin book tours. When Sunny heard that, she cried for two days. And then he showed up for Thanksgiving like he's the new voice of the universe, swaggering around and putting down Ellie Mae, which even though we don't agree with her, she's not in the frame of mind to be pestered by him. And she has no love for him either, whatever went on over there. Sunny and Harold, bless their hearts, never set any boundaries on that boy and so no wonder. He doesn't eat meat now, so the Thanksgiving bird was beneath him, of course, and he prefers oatmeal to eggs in the morning and tea, not coffee, and then he drank all afternoon until I don't think your father has one bottle of whiskey left in the cabinet. And that's the truth, Andrew. I know you like how smart Lars is, but I could do without him in my house. I just get a feeling that I don't like. And it's my own house."

"I'm sorry, Mom. I know he can be a pain. Not too respectful. But he's got his own place in town, so at least you don't have to put him up for the night ever."

"Well, now let me tell you the good news. Lena is getting married."

"Lena? To whom?"

"Your friend Bobby Kovacs. From Hibbing. The hockey player who got all banged up in Vietnam, poor man, and now is limping and dragging that one leg, but he's still good looking, you know. Nice smile. And he's crazy about Lena, so thank the lord for that anyway. But still, Andrew, it was a lot to take on one holiday. And it was gray and kind of rainy." She had wound down to near tears.

Andrew felt near to tears himself. The woman he loved now seemed lost to him. "I'm sorry. A lot is going on, hard to believe." He tried to keep his voice level.

"What was your news, dear? I'm sorry I'm not as good a listener as you are."

"It's fine, Mom. I just got a promotion here. People seem to be noticing me. But I'm not sure when I'll get back to Minneapolis."

"Well, that's exciting, Andrew. Your dad will be proud." His news had cheered her, this younger son of hers who always did so well. "I'm glad you're happy."

"Thanks, Mom," he said, wishing it were true.

When Andrew told his mother that people in the CIA noticed his work, he was being modest. Over his years out of the Navy he had become one of the most respected investigative and strategic minds on staff. His promotion now was putting him at the center of a key sting operation intended to deceive the KGB into recruiting a US Naval commander who would then reveal secret information to the Soviets. Many behind closed doors at Langley thought MacAlpine the perfect operative to manage this sting, ensuring that the secrets leaked to the Soviets would only confuse and not inform them.

It was the most important opportunity of his career, and it would consume his time and energy until his team succeeded in arresting the KGB agents. He wasn't in a career that made relationships easy, he knew. But letting go of Lena Bergen might be more difficult than this challenging spy operation. He knew that as well.

WOUNDED WARRIOR

In 1970, Robert Sanford "Bobby" Kovacs had completed basic naval training and additional training on Swift Boats at the Naval Station in Coronado, California. Bobby's superior hand-eye coordination made it easy for him to master the operation of the .50 caliber M2 Browning machine guns mounted on the fifty-foot-long shallow-draft Swift Boats. Powered by two 480-horsepower marine diesel motors, Swift Boats could approach speeds of thirty miles per hour. After he learned that he had been assigned to a Swift Boat mission going up the Saigon River, Bobby boasted in a letter to his sister, "I'm going to water-ski right up to Saigon City."

The trip upriver dropped off a Navy SEAL Team successfully, uneventfully; however, they were ambushed coming back downriver. Bobby was the first causality of the firefight when an AK-47 round bit into the fleshy part of his left thigh and another round chewed up the bicep of his left arm. He held on to his guns while one of his buddies wound bandages tightly around his arm and leg. The bleeding appeared to stop but the firefight continued. The pilot zigzagged up and down the river to maintain contact with the attackers, and Bobby fired burst after burst from the big Browning into the underbrush where the Viet Cong remained hidden. Suddenly an enemy bullet hit his right hand, severing fingers and showering blood and bone onto his face. Bobby's first combat action was his last.

The commendation honored Bobby. "He stayed at his post until the Viet Cong guns went silent." In addition to his commendation, he received a Bronze Star and a Purple Heart. Bobby would later say, "I had just about the shortest military service you can have and still make it home alive."

Before he went into the military, Bobby Kovacs made his way on his highly skilled physicality, his grace and genius in athletics. He had never been much of a student, nor had he cared. All his needs had been met with sports. But on his return, he did not have that physicality to give meaning to his life. He was a wounded warrior who could no longer skate fast and shoot pucks, who needed to find a role for himself in the world. He took as his model the doctors and nurses who put him back together after his injuries. Within a week of being home, Bobby reapplied for school to complete his degree in sociology and did volunteer work at the VA. By the time he graduated in June 1974, he was well known in his field and easily obtained a job as a veteran service officer at the VA in Minneapolis. He'd been living on his own for years when Lena Bergen's father died.

The one thing that had not changed for Bobby was how he felt about Lena Bergen. He'd first met her when he'd moved into the house by the university where Lena and her sister would come to hang out with their brother and his friends. It seemed that he had fallen in love with her immediately even though she had no more interest in athletics than he had in feminine literature. Or poetry! But then she was back from college in England and he found himself calling her almost every day. "I had another thought of you," he wanted to say. "I'd like to take you for a ride. How about it? Do you have some time?"

She seemed to like him. He believed she did and after months of his asking and expressing his feelings, she agreed to marry him. Or maybe she suggested it to him at last and he, of course, agreed. They set the date for June 26, 1976, allowing one year from when her father had died.

By the time that day rolled around many things had happened. Sunny Bergen had reached out to Bobby's parents on the Iron Range to introduce herself and welcome them to her family. Cameron Junior and Ellie Mae had filed for a no-fault divorce which had become final before she made her first visit to the Carmelite convent in North Dakota. Though her mother was terribly distressed by this, she supported her older daughter as she always had, believing that her children were wonderful and whatever they did in life obviously had meaning and purpose.

Bobby had never been so happy in his life. On his wedding day he wrote a note to Lena saying, "This will be a wild ride. I'm so glad you're by my side." He was proud of his rhyme and thankful for his fate. Lena and Bobby wrote their own vows and Cameron Senior walked Lena down the aisle.

Andrew did not make the wedding. Ellie Mae could not leave her convent. And Lena's brother, Lars, arrived just as the newlyweds were coming back down the aisle.

THE WRITERS' WORKSHOP

Time just got away from Lars the morning of his sister's wedding. He was distracted by a lovely lady who lived down the block from his duplex on Lake of the Isles. She'd been walking her dog and he'd been strolling for inspiration; they'd chatted, and one thing had just led to another. It wasn't that he'd forgotten the wedding. And at least he'd made it in time to throw some rice and mingle with the old gang.

Overall Lars had lost interest in the friends of his youth. They did not live in the large sphere where he felt he now belonged. They seemed interested in settling down, as they called it, and watching television and joining men's leagues for one sport or another. Then, too, he was absorbed in his own writing that he preferred not to talk about. So what was the point?

His book, *Scenes from the Jungle*, had mythologized the war in Vietnam and made Lars most popular in military areas with military people. Places like San Diego and Norfolk. He was invited to read and talk and the women, in particular, just loved him—this extremely handsome, blond, Nordic man with that look in his eye. Lars was always on the prowl. He didn't hide it, women responded and military men, thinking him an idealized representation of themselves, offered no criticism and no obstacle.

The only woman who had slipped away from him was Annette Freeman who'd burned his brain at the stem. He didn't want anyone to know about it, but he could not get enough of her and when she left him, he'd felt the sting. Her intelligence frightened him, he couldn't keep up with her and she seemed to only want to talk. Lars didn't want to talk that much. It made him feel exposed. The less people knew about his dark inner workings the better really. Still he had not wanted to let go of Annette Freeman.

Lars wrote every day, even before he showered, he wrote every morning without editing, just letting it flow and most of the time, Lars loved everything he wrote. Then three years after Lena and Bobby's wedding, Lena had a baby girl and named her Angela—because she was their little angel, a dream come true. And that's when Lena talked to Lars about working together to host a writers' workshop in the Twin Cities.

They were both well-known writers, both teachers—Lena in the English department at the University of Minnesota and Lars at William Martin College in Saint Paul—and the two of them could pull the older writers and professors into a premiere annual workshop to be held each summer in a building renovated by Alpine Builders for just that purpose. In this way, Lena thought, she could make additional money and do it close to home.

"We could make our mark together," Lena said trying to coax Lars into her vision. She knew he would have preferred for it to be his vision.

"I make my mark every time I publish something." That was his initial response.

"We can build a national reputation, Lars. Like the Iowa Workshop."

"I'll be the director."

"Okay, Lars. You be the director. I'll take care of every other little thing." She smiled kindly, not bothering to mention how she'd half written his first book that had brought him such fame.

His eyes roamed in an almost delirium. "We'll call it THE Writers' Workshop. That's what we'll call it. The best of the best."

In the summer of 1980, they launched their endeavor. The building that Cameron Junior renovated had massive wooden beams and a brick exterior at the north end of downtown a few blocks from the Mississippi River. It had been cleaned up, floors sanded, glass windows installed on both the inner and outer walls and the elevator upgraded. The company named it The Cube because it was almost a full square block and ten stories high. Lars and Lena took offices next to The Writers' Workshop and Alpine Management rented out the rest of the building to a wide assortment of organizations that included two ad agencies, a small law firm, several galleries, *Citizen of the World Magazine,* and a New Age fitness and yoga studio on the main floor.

The first workshop was held from August 3 through August 16 and drew participants from twenty-two states and three Canadian provinces. Lena brought in one of her colleagues from Saint Hilda's College, Oxford, and Lars drew on two National Book Award finalists to do small-group sessions. It was a wonderful success and Lars took the final bow on the final day, thanking everyone for fulfilling the vision of his lifetime.

TRYING IS LYING

Ellie Mae did not like the cloistered life. She had been a wealthy socialite in the center of her own world and then, suddenly, she was in an environment of sacrifice and silence and much too much service to others. As she thought about what had happened to her, she concluded that she had burned herself to a frazzle. She had stayed up long nights waiting for her husband to come home from whatever place he said he'd been. She'd drunk cup after cup of coffee and smoked cigarettes constantly and worried and worried, knowing he was doing cocaine with Jimmy and spending time with other women. He lost interest in her and suddenly, her children hadn't needed her, and she had run from all of that to the convent to study and pray and try. And she had tried. But after three years, the head nun spoke to her in all sincerity.

"The women here choose this life, they run toward it, feel it. It's a calling. We know you are still contemplating your faith and your direction, but I don't think this is the place to find what you need."

Hearing those words, Ellie had cried—not because she disagreed, but because she had nowhere else where she belonged either. A month after that conversation, Ellie Mae moved from North Dakota to Los Angeles to study transcendental meditation with Maharishi Mahesh Yogi. She did not swing back through Minnesota on her way, did not inform her estranged ex-husband or her siblings. She contacted the bank, reclaimed her trust money, and flew directly west. Once there she wrote a quiet note to Sunny. Dear Mommy, she wrote, I'm still on my path. I'm in California where the sun is so healing. Mommy, you would love it. You were right that I could never be a Catholic nun. But they were lovely people. And I tried. But now I'm here and I love you and I have another idea. I will write again soon.

Her mother read the note so many times, the paper tore at its creases. Then she read it to Susie. "What do you think?" she asked.

"I hope she finds some peace there. I hope it's a good move for her. Do you think she told Cameron Junior?"

Sunny shook her head. She didn't know but suspected that Cameron Junior had no idea as to his ex-wife's whereabouts and very little interest either. Her absence hadn't seemed to affect him. He no longer had to be concerned. The grandmothers and nanny took care of the children, he had no one to answer to, and so, from Sunny's perspective, he looked to be a happy man, whatever he was up to.

Susie had not been lenient with her children and didn't like the latitude everyone else gave to her grandchildren. Although little Jack seemed a ray of sunshine, his eight-year-old brother, Cameron III, had become a demanding, exasperating child in her opinion and would be better off if his mother were home to parent him. She never said that to Sunny, who seemed happy as pie with anything that any child ever did—just as she always was. But she did venture to say, "I wish they'd all work it out and be a family. They should try to give it another go. Don't you think?"

Sunny smiled because she did not know how to answer. "We'll see," was all she could think to say.

"Cameron Junior is doing well with the business though," Susie said, trying to find some redemption for her self-absorbed son. "At our next board meeting, you'll be pleased to see we have more properties at greater values and all the condominium conversions have gone extremely well. Lucille, thank God for Lucille, has created a schedule that shows all the borrowings—you know, the leverage—that we used to buy all those new properties, renovate, and sell them for a profit and now almost all the loans have been repaid. That's the kind of thing Cameron Junior is good at. Cameron is so grateful that Cameron Junior pushed him to borrow and expand. You know, it's not the way we all did it in the early days. But the times they are a-changin' as the song goes. Cameron Junior says inflation is our friend."

Sunny had tuned out by this time. "Well, I'm happy to hear that. We do have to look to the future," she added, still holding on to her daughter's note. "Everyone has to look to their future."

Cameron Junior's vision of the future had been a family of Alpine enterprises. After Harold died and there were just the three principal owners,

Cameron Junior worked to convince his father that they should have Alpine Management Company and a number of other special-purpose vehicles such as limited partnerships to buy specific properties. Then when the properties sold, the money would be distributed to the partners with no tax owed by the partnership. It was brilliant. It was an enormous tax savings for the company and the families. The success of this strategy gave Cameron Junior the idea that he now led the entire operation. As long as his father did as Cameron Junior advised, he was the unanointed leader, the financial engineer. Unlike Cameron and Harold, he could not even pound a nail straight into a beam, but he had learned financing in college and in the days of no-fail real estate investments, Cameron Junior believed himself a wizard at making money. And who would argue with him?

When his mother told him where Ellie Mae had landed and subtly hinted that he could try to find her and restore his family life, Cameron Junior said, "That's okay, Mom. I think we're all doing just fine."

ENLIGHTENMENT GUARANTEED

Ellie Mae had chosen the Maharishi Mahesh Yogi because she'd seen him interviewed on television back before she'd gone to the convent. He had taught transcendental meditation to The Beatles and other famous people like Merv Griffin and she had been attracted to his wise demeanor, his flowing robes, and measured speech. Arriving at the Santa Ynez Inn where she would study with him, Ellie Mae told the receptionist that she was a seeker of ultimate truth, hoping to heal herself by finding ultimate answers to timeless questions. The receptionist pointed to a hallway and said, "Go all the way down. It's the last door on the left." She mouthed a smile and returned to the IBM Selectric on her desk.

Ellie Mae did as she was told, walking into a small room where a bearded man was seated, cross-legged. "Hello," Ellie Mae said, surprised that he wasn't the Maharishi. It was like going to the North Pole only to meet with one of Santa's elves.

The man motioned for her to sit, filled a small cup with hot tea, and handed it to her. "What brought you to us?"

"I've been in a convent for nearly three years, living there with the nuns and trying to find meaning," Ellie Mae said. "But I realized that I didn't belong there." She held the teacup in both hands, mimicking the way he held his, and took a small sip. "Hmm, this is good," she said.

"Yes?" His eyes held hers, gently, encouraging Ellie Mae to say more.

"I knew it wasn't working during chapel one morning. I saw five old nuns, eyes closed, deep in contemplation. I could tell that they had surrendered completely to the Holy Spirit. There I was examining the chapel walls and wondering if they needed repairing. A clue, don't you think?"

His face was one big smile. "Yes." He took a sip. "Then?"

Ellie Mae put down her teacup, put her hands in her lap, and took a deep breath. "I first learned about Maharishi Mahesh Yogi when he became spiritual advisor to The Beatles. I mean, that's when I became aware of him. 1967, if I remember correctly. I'm here to learn Transcendental

Meditation. That's why I came." She took another deep breath, adjusted her posture.

He smiled and asked, "Family?"

"Dad died five years ago so it's just Mom and my younger sister," Ellie Mae said, raising her eyes to his forehead so he couldn't observe her lie.

"Yes?" he said. "Do you have the means to pay your own way?" He took two deep breaths, as though the effort of speaking so many words all at once tired him.

"I do," Ellie Mae answered, adjusting her posture and rising to her full height.

His smile broadened and radiated outward until it filled their small room. "Let me ask, are you interested in a weeklong course—or would you like to study with us for a full year and receive a certificate of meditative proficiency." He continued to smile. "That would allow you to open your own studio, if you so wished."

"I'd like to do the full year, even if I don't open my own studio. I want to study for as long as I can."

The man with the beard took a piece of paper out of the pocket of his robe, handed it to Ellie Mae, and said, "Come tomorrow at two p.m. Bring your checkbook to pay your tuition. And so you will begin." He shook her hand, said "Welcome," then stood quietly and bowed from the waist.

She couldn't stop smiling as she walked to her apartment, pleased that the interview was over and pleased she had gotten her way. She felt better than she had felt in years. Happy to be in the warming California sunshine, happy she had gotten into the meditation classes, and especially happy that things were going her way after so many years of disappointment. So many years of not having her prayers answered. She entered her apartment and phoned her mother with the good news.

MORNING IN AMERICA

From Reagan's inaugural onward, America experienced massive changes in the social contract. The Moral Majority, big supporters of Reagan's policies, argued successfully for a new direction in the country, by busting unions, reducing their membership, and freeing businesses to control the destiny of America.

Ronald Reagan's Morning in America campaign made regular folks in the heartland feel good about themselves. "I'm okay, you're okay, it's the government that's the problem." His reelection against Walter Mondale and Geraldine Ferraro was an electoral college landslide. Some of the political messages of the 1984 campaign, such as "Government is the problem" could have come right out of George Orwell's book *Nineteen Eighty-Four.*

Lena and Bobby had been married for eight years by then and were raising their children in Reagan's America, continually angry with the president's notions on women, mental health, and social services which seemed to be leaving so many people in the dust. In response to his campaign, they gathered some of the old gang for a *Nineteen Eighty-Four* party and decorated their family room with quotes from the book like:

> "The Party told you to reject all evidence of your eyes and ears. It was their final, most essential command."
>
> "The best books ... are those that tell you what you know already."
>
> "War is Peace; Freedom is Slavery; and Ignorance is Strength."

The party was a smash. Everyone loved it. Partygoers conversed glibly about who might be a narc for the thought police, where they would put all the bugs needed for constant surveillance, why the schools, the press or the churches had not stopped the wholesale dismantling of national truths, and how the country could get them back, if ever. Several with advanced degrees blamed the pervasive lack of solid funding for educational necessities.

During a lull in the music, Lena pinned a new poster on the wall and read it aloud.

"No man in the whole world can change the truth. One can only look for the truth, find it and serve it. The truth is in all places." Dietrich Bonhoeffer.

Her husband, Bobby, watched her from the chair where he had been drinking for most of the party. "Truth, eh honey? Do you want to know the truth, Lena?" He pulled her toward him.

"Sure. Tell me the truth."

"My feet are too numb to dance. But it's a nice party, babe." He loved her so deeply he never could quite tell her how much pain he felt every minute of every day. And in this moment of her party, he also did not want to tell her he was out of his pain medications. Some truths were better left unsaid. And anyway, there were always more where those came from. He had two doctors willing to give him as much as he wanted for as long as he wanted.

Lena and Bobby had invited Cameron Junior, but he decided not to go. He didn't quite remember the book. The wrong people were in charge, maybe the animals were in charge and ate the people? Was it that? Anyway, he had a date with Bunny Divine which he did not want to break.

Overall, Cameron Junior liked Ronald Reagan. He hadn't voted for him the first time out, but this last election he did. Reagan's policies put money in his pocket. Cameron saw himself as one of the "captains of industry" that Reagan referred to and he very much liked that Reagan had reduced the regulatory burdens government had put on industry—Lyndon Johnson's clean water and clean air and whatnot. He especially appreciated that Reagan had slashed corporate and individual tax rates.

Cameron Junior was living the life he wanted. His home in Kenwood was perfect, in his opinion, his children went to the nearby private school, he owned three cars, two motorcycles, and a boat he had christened

The Bottom Line. In the years since his divorce from Ellie Mae, he had enjoyed being a single man of wealth and influence. Why would he ever want to mock Ronald Reagan?

EVERYTHING IS SWAT

Andrew continued working for the State Department in Washington, DC. Unlike everyone else in the Alpine Management family, he had no interest in owning a home, but lived in an apartment, which allowed him to lock the door when he left town and not worry about upkeep or maintenance or what the neighbors were thinking about his absences. He did not drive a car either. He didn't need one. Andrew spent much of his time traveling, most often to Europe and the Soviet Union where he used his facile language skills to fit in and spot trends that he reported on when he returned. He loved it all.

Though he visited home infrequently, he called as often as he could, usually reaching Susie, who was happy to fill him in on everyone in the family. Susie trusted her younger son. She told him anything, much more than she ever shared with her husband or Cameron Junior. So he learned about Bobby's continued ill health and the workshops Lena and Lars had begun so successfully, and their books as well. Susie told him how his father and brother were strategically leveraging and expanding the business, though they both worked too hard in her opinion. At least they worked too hard to spend very much time at home.

His mother never mentioned Ellie Mae unless he asked, and then she would say, "That girl will be the death of us all." If he asked her to explain, Susie would go on with something like "she's out there in LA with those meditation types," or "she should be here raising her boys." More often than not, though, she'd answer, "don't get me started," and leave it at that.

He tried to call on Sundays, hoping to occasionally reach his father at home, but it seemed Cameron Senior worked most weekend afternoons. So Andrew enjoyed his conversations with his mother, who would inevitably ask at some point, "What do you think, Andrew?" This was his cue to ramble on about what he actually was thinking or what she might do in a certain situation or the meanings behind the news as he saw it, pleased that his smart and insightful mother remained interested in his opinions.

From her reports, he understood that his nephew Cameron the Third was much like his father, even though he looked like Connie Demopoulos. He misbehaved and showed the same disinterest in school that his father always had. Jack, on the other hand, took after Andrew, curious and interested, toting thick books home from the library and devouring them without any parental probing. From Jack's earliest days, he had been so excited to see Andrew whenever he visited that he'd run into his arms as though they were long lost allies. Andrew always greeted him in Italian or French or Russian, prompting the little boy to ask what was the language, what was he speaking, and repeat it then for the rest of Andrew's visit. Andrew loved sending his little nephew books in the mail and had bought Jack a wall-sized world map for his bedroom.

The things Andrew never spoke to his mother about were the growing polarizations in society, the international observations he made in his work, and the arc of history that formed the basis of what the State Department asked him to do. Although it seemed democracy was alive and well throughout the world, Andrew had read enough and thought enough to know that authoritarians would always find their way back, would convince some part of the masses that they alone had the solution and would take control. In Russia, he saw Gorbachev rising to power with unusual ideas about transforming the Soviet Union, restructuring it and creating new openness so that democracy might have some possibilities. In the United States, however, he was sensing an opposite trend.

He was noticing the calcifying of the country. Mid-twentieth century had seen wonderfully daring experiments like the Tennessee Valley Authority and the National Endowment for the Arts, but after the protests of the 1960s and 1970s, a fear of change had emerged. Andrew saw society wanting to draw a line in the sand as if to say that this is where we are and no more changes or alterations were necessary. People had rejected Jimmy Carter's angst and desire to make things better and had welcomed Ronald Reagan's image of the city on the hill, the exceptional and perfect place to live. As a result, it was harder to understand how the United States could be number one in incarcerations and have workers' wages that were not keeping pace with inflation. Living standards were lowering. All this troubled Andrew.

Even worse, the inner cities that had burned in the 1960s remained destroyed with no money going into any kind of restoration and the people in those neighborhoods living without homes or opportunities unless they jumped into the growing drug trade that surrounded them. And the police working those neighborhoods—who did not live there and did not look like the people who lived there—relied more and more on military-style Special Weapons and Tactics (SWAT) and defense tools as they emulated elite military units. This was happening without any national outcry. That's what Andrew saw. He saw support in the country for fighting fire with fire, bigger guns and more guns.

Although these domestic concerns were not part of his scope at the State Department, he could not help but think about it and discuss it. In a rare conversation with his brother, Cameron Junior went off about the importance of guns on the street for the cops, the citizens, anyone. Andrew found himself saying, "I think that's a misreading of the Second Amendment, Cam. I mean it was meant to allow arms to defend the country before we had a military, not to arm citizens against one another. Or have cops with military rifles walking these poor neighborhoods."

"You ever even touched a gun, Andrew?"

"I was in the military, Cam." He wanted to add, unlike you, but refrained. Cameron Junior had been his buddy when they were kids and now it seemed they couldn't agree on anything.

"Well nobody's taking away my guns, even if I never use them again in my life."

"Right, Cam. A SWAT team of one."

THE AGE OF AQUARIUS

The mid-eighties knew crystals and energy, colors, meditation, mind expansion, and hallucination. Ellie Mae came into this world in Los Angeles with all her life experiences. She had melted, fallen apart emotionally and melted, then had put herself together and lived with the sisters in the convent where all the scruff and baloney of her previous life had been scrubbed away. Ellie Mae came to Los Angeles more pure and soulful than she had ever been. For three years, she had read and cultivated ideas, living there with women who were committed and smart and who enlivened her intellect. She already knew how to meditate, for what had those hours of prayer been if not meditation?

In her year-long program at the Los Angeles Center for Meditative Studies, Ellie Mae was noticed early for her ease in meditation and her overall wisdom and glow. By this time in her mid-thirties Ellie knew much and met the troubles of her colleagues in the program with a natural empathy because she had been wherever they had been. She understood crisis and trauma and the wants that could derail the meditative process, the part in a new movie or house in Laurel Canyon. Ellie Mae began to take on the role of an elder, one who could listen and understand and redirect. Her spirituality was visible to others. And, though she'd always thought of herself as pretty but not very smart, her absolute brilliant mind shone clearly. Everyone around her knew it.

So it wasn't surprising when Ryan Vatic, veteran actor and sometime jazz singer, suggested that Ellie start her own practice to guide people like himself and his poor brother who circled and circled and never seemed to find himself. He offered to put up the money for this venture, which she appreciated. But after a long walk along the beach, she informed Ryan that she would be starting her own practice and funding it herself. In a city where appearing was as important as being, Ellie would help performers to merge the two. That became her mission. She found a small house above Hollywood and Vine in the hills. She painted the walls herself and hired a professional to sand her floors and another professional to plant birds of paradise and English ivy near and around the door. She called her business Quiet Inspiration and had a small neon sign made in the softest color of pink.

She had clients before the year-long program at the institute finished. Ryan and his brother Geoff were the first, of course, and based on Geoff's ability to focus, it appeared they may be lifetime members. Her favorite client was an actress she'd admired since childhood, whose movies had won awards and whose voice was as familiar to Ellie Mae as her own. But she worked with her privately and never revealed her name.

When British actor Daniel Dana Brooke came to see her, it was not of his own volition but at the specific request of his director. Daniel, after years of successful movies and two plays, was stuck trying to develop his latest character. He felt wooden and unnatural and all the techniques he'd learned studying Method acting were not accessible to him. He parked his Bentley in front of Quiet Inspiration, glanced dismissively at the small vine-covered building, and went inside to face Ellie Mae whose beatific presence stunned him immediately. They sat in chairs and chatted for a while until she said, quite simply, "It's really crowded in there, isn't it?"

"In me?"

"You are very full of characters, Daniel, and," she said, smiling so naturally, "very full of you."

That was Ellie's way with her clients and it earned her loyalty, referrals, and significant fees. She settled into this life as a meditation queen in the hills of Los Angeles, the princess of positivity. She continued to call her mother at least once a month and hear the state of the Bergen and MacAlpine families. Sunny knew everything and loved "catching Ellie up" as she called it. So Ellie learned that when Jack was halfway through third grade at his private school, he had been moved ahead to fourth grade, while Cameron the Third was a wonderful wrestler, barrel-chested, strong, and energetic. She enjoyed the stories her mother told her about her children, whom she had not seen in years. At the time of her divorce, she'd been fragile and was hoping to live in the convent for the rest of her life. So she'd given full custody to Cameron Junior, knowing that his mother and her own would make sure her children had the best of everything.

She'd once asked Sunny if she should fight for joint custody now that she was a stable and functioning person again and her mother had applauded that notion until the two of them tried to figure out how it would work. The idea of the two boys shuttling back and forth between two households—even if Ellie Mae returned to Minnesota—did not seem right or kind to either of them. And then there would be the battle with Cameron Junior. And then Cameron Senior would get involved. And maybe it would affect Sunny's friendship with Susie. And the boys would feel the tension and carry it with them forever.

Weekly Ellie did send picture postcards of beautiful scenery, ocean vistas, azaleas, and Pacific sunsets along with positive notes to her sons. She would tell them how pleased she was with their accomplishments and ask them to send her a drawing or poem or note sometime. But they were very busy children and rarely sent anything her way. As Jack grew older, he began a regular correspondence with his mother and the two became great friends. But that was later.

Ellie Mae also talked regularly to her sister, who showed excitement and respect for Ellie Mae's work and only rarely mentioned motherhood. Every once in a while, the two sisters would have a laugh at their brother's expense. "Is Lars still lining his bookshelves with only his own books?" Ellie asked in one call.

"Of course, otherwise why keep writing?"

"Seriously, Lena, how do you stand working with him?"

"I don't exactly have to work with him. We put our names on the program roster and do our own thing."

"But still," Ellie returned, thinking how much she'd love to get her older brother into a meditative session and turn him around a bit.

"He's too busy to bother me," Lena said.

"And he still has one woman after another?"

"Oh sure. Or many women interspersed with many others. It's too obnoxious to think about."

"Well, I'm glad not to see him. It took me years to clean Lars out of my system."

"But maybe sometime you'd like to be a guest speaker at our writing workshop."

"I would love that, Lena. Really."

And though they both craved an opportunity to work together and both loved their talks on the phone, Ellie Mae did not come to The Writers' Workshop for many years.

WHEN THE WALL CAME DOWN

Bobby Kovacs had become an outstanding veteran service officer. He knew that servicemen and servicewomen healed better, and their healing lasted longer, if they shifted their consciousness away from the pain-filled present and into a future orientation. He knew these truths intellectually, from his college coursework. More importantly, he knew these truths from his own experience. He was reminded of them every working day by listening to the many soldiers and sailors and marines who only saw themselves as a diminishment of past perfection. He helped them craft a workable future.

Many veterans came to the VA rehabilitation center trapped in unhelpful ways of thinking. Many desperately needed to create a future centered on new ways of loving life. Many needed to trust that their hearts and minds could grow stronger, strong enough to lead them to a productive place in a society which mostly had not shared their wartime experiences.

Bobby had been helped by others at the VA when he himself was going through physical therapy, and at the university, as he finished his degree. He'd been helped to find his deeper self, had been helped to become a steady influence at the VA hospital, and to be the truly outstanding veteran service officer he had become. He knew he had been blessed to come home alive, to be in the bonus round, as wounded warriors often said.

Bobby was most grateful to be married to Lena, to have her as a loving wife, and to be blessed with two beautiful children who adored their daddy.

But Bobby's life was far from perfect. He had built a brilliant career in high school hockey without the ignominy of serious injury. His career-ending knee injury at the university was his first real pain. The multiple gunshots he'd suffered in Vietnam caused permanent, unrepairable nerve damage and excruciating pain. That was Bobby's Achilles heel. The pain that wouldn't leave his badly damaged body. He survived and was able to thrive only with large quantities of pain medications, the drugs he needed to make it through his days and nights.

Lena knew about his constant pain as only a loving wife and partner could know. She knew he took his meds with breakfast, lunch, and dinner, and before bedtime, and sometimes in the middle of the night. She was present, attentive, and fully aware. But in a way she didn't really know about Bobby's drugs. Not how many he took, nor what was a safe dose. She was awake and yet she was asleep, believing Bobby was in control.

Bobby and Lena were watching Peter Jennings on ABC's *World News Tonight* that Friday, November 10, 1989. They watched Germans celebrating the fall of the Berlin Wall. Angie and her younger sister, Sarah, had already kissed them goodnight and gone to their bedroom. Lena was glad the Berlin Wall had been smashed down and to be snuggling with her man on the couch, to have no place they had to be early in the morning. Bobby was glad to be home with Lena for the weekend, a bottle of good wine on the table in front of them.

"Andrew told us the wall would come down," Lena said.

"And he was right. We won the Cold War, just like he said we would," Bobby answered. "Do you think he's over there right now, in that crowd, watching history happen?"

Lena took a sip of wine, poured some in Bobby's glass, and said, "Susie would've told Mom and she would've told us, don't you think?"

"Maybe. But Andrew's under cover half the time, isn't he? Or in some stealth capacity?"

Bobby's body seethed in pain as he turned to hold Lena closer. When he groaned, she mistook it for contentment. When he took a gulp of wine, she did not see the handful of pills he popped into his mouth at the same time. He kissed his beautiful wife long and hard.

"I'm really sleepy, honey," he said as he slowly put his glass on the table. His body relaxed against her side, and when his eyes closed, it was not to sleep but to slip away from her forever.

RETURNS

It took Lena more than a year to feel normal in her house without Bobby. She saw him everywhere, even in the beautiful faces of her daughters. And she couldn't get over her lost opportunity, that she might have saved him, that she could have helped him more, or even that she would have been able to say goodbye. When he'd fallen asleep that night, she'd only propped him against a pillow on the sofa and gone to check on her girls. He'd lain there for more than a half hour before she realized that he wasn't breathing and by then, it was too late.

The only men Lena had ever loved were Andrew and Bobby. Andrew had never responded to her letter declaring her love and now Bobby had left her a widow with two children to raise on her own. At night she found herself rolling toward the center of the bed, to the place where her body would have met Bobby's, and found the emptiness there so difficult, she took to stacking pillows where he used to sleep.

She called her sister often, finding Ellie Mae, with her compassion and patience, more reassuring than anyone else in Lena's life, even her mother, who fretted and baked too many pies and continued to tell her she'd find someone new. Ellie Mae allowed her to ramble on about every anger and sorrow related to losing Bobby without ever judging or burdening her with platitudes. Lena had been shocked at how many people in her life—old sorority friends, work friends, and even her brother—continued to tell her how she needed to move on, move on, get over it, buck up. In so many words that's what they were saying. Quit moping and get a grip. But Ellie never said anything like that. What Lena learned in that year after Bobby died was how deeply experienced Ellie Mae was with loss. Ellie's love was Lena's lifesaver.

"You don't move on, Lena. Bobby is a part of you forever. But you move forward. Do your work. Love your kids. Talk to me. But don't fight your grief. Just let it roll right on to you and through you and honestly, it will eventually move past you."

And so she did. She took her daughters to Disney World in the spring, she rented a little cabin up north for two weeks in the summer, she bought herself a new deep blue Volvo and began to write a new collection of poems which she tentatively entitled "Returns."

And then in the fall, Andrew MacAlpine came to the university to teach a graduate seminar on "Living in the New World Order." The university was so pleased to get him. Not only had he received his bachelor's degree there, but he had gone on to earn a master's in international affairs from Georgetown University, a PhD from Princeton University, and had done post-graduate work at Johns Hopkins University. And Andrew was pleased to be there again. He took temporary residence in the guest house above the MacAlpine garage, a new addition they'd built for absolutely no reason other than to build it.

"Do you have any interest yet in joining the family business?" his father asked him. "You could really help out your brother when I retire next year," he added. "My two boys, running the business."

But Andrew respectfully declined.

And at the end of his first week in town, he called Lena.

He had not seen her since Bobby's funeral and at that time, she'd been so surrounded by people that he had not presumed to intrude. This time he arrived at her south Minneapolis home with presents. He had bought each of her daughters a book about Washington, DC, and a box of saltwater taffy and carried an enormous bouquet of fall flowers for Lena.

"Andrew, my goodness, you can visit without bringing presents."

"But it's fun to bring presents."

Lena introduced him to Angie who was eleven and Sarah who was nine. Both had dark hair in braids and big smiles. Andrew thought them two of the most beautiful children he'd ever seen. Of course Lena was beautiful and Bobby had been as well.

"Andrew is Grandma Susie's son. You met him before, but you were young then. He works for the government, right, Andrew?"

"What do you do?" Angie asked.

"I broker in secrets, Angie. Do you like secrets?"

"I guess I do. Except you can never tell anyone ever."

"That's exactly right. So I'm a guy who knows how to keep my mouth shut—if you ever want to tell me something nobody should know."

Lena's daughters laughed and after hearing a story or two from their mother and Andrew about "the good old days," they left to watch a movie video.

"How have you been, Lena?"

"It's hard."

"Of course. Bobby was such a good guy, such a patriot. I can't say how much I admired him."

"Ellie Mae's been a big help to me," Lena offered. "You know she's gone through so much herself and she knows how to listen and just be there."

Andrew nodded as though he would have expected that from Ellie Mae. "You two have always been so close," he said. "It's good to have someone like that."

"Are you and Cameron close?" Lena knew the answer, but she wanted to hear what Andrew would say.

"Not really. My brother loves making money and I don't think about that much. He let Ellie Mae slip away from him and he lets our mothers raise his kids. It's nothing I would do, I guess. But we talk once a month. The usual. Weather, sports, our parents. He loves to tell me about his latest car and I get kind of a kick out of that."

"Do you even have a car?"

"Of course not. In DC? I'd actually love to see my brother maneuver the DC streets in that monstrous Range Rover of his. Can you picture it?"

They both laughed. It felt so good to Lena to laugh like that.

"Thanks for coming today, Andrew."

"I'm always here for you, Lena, you must know that."

She was thinking about the letter she'd written during the war. They'd never talked about it. Andrew had moved to Washington and Lena had gone off to Oxford and they'd never really been alone in all the nineteen years since.

"I wrote you a letter when you were in the service. Why didn't you answer it, Andrew?"

"I always answered your letters." Andrew seemed confused.

"It was just before Ellie Mae's wedding. I told you I loved you. I wanted you to give me a chance, to maybe be together."

Halfway through her sentence, Andrew began to shake his head and continued shaking it. "No, Lena. I never got a letter from you like that. My God, if I'd had a letter like that, I would have returned to you in a heartbeat. You must know that. I loved you for years. My God." He'd lost his composure.

"Why didn't you get it? I don't understand."

"I was at Pearl at the time. But it was war, I guess. Things happened. You know our mail tended to travel on military vessels. Wow, this is something to learn though."

"Well," Lena started, but she couldn't finish.

"Do you want to try again? I mean, with me? Is it too soon? What do you think, Lena?"

"We live so far apart, Andrew. You have so much your own life."

"I have more degrees than I know what to do with, Lena. I'm three months from my government pension. I can do about anything I want just now. That trust fund is still sitting there." He listed all these as he would list arguments to an opponent. "I mean, I'm yours."

"Let's try, Andrew. But let's take it slow, okay?"

"We'll see what happens then."

"We'll see what happens. The girls like you," she added for encouragement. "And you know my mom's favors you."

"Right. Did I beat out Lars and Cameron Junior then?"

Again they laughed and it felt better than ever.

THREE:
The Slide

THE CRASH

Andrew had such a wonderful visit with Lena. The graduate seminar was good, but the time with Lena was perfect. They hadn't connected in years and there they were together, the same as when they were speaking French, going to anti-war marches, and talking for hours about the state of the world. They didn't have to fill up the space with words, their conversations were like music. And she was still so beautiful. Andrew had all the same feelings that he'd had before and Lena, too, was willing to see what might happen.

He had to tear himself away to get back to work in Washington, DC, and left during the morning rush hour. On the drive from Lena's house to the airport all he could think about was what it might be like to be with Lena and her girls in Minneapolis. He could teach at the University of Minnesota, be near his family and old friends, start a different life. Andrew was in the middle lane, cars to the right, left, and ahead of him, when he saw a semi-truck coming from behind.

He saw it clearly in all three mirrors of his little rental car and could tell it wasn't slowing down. The truck was getting larger and closer by the instant as Andrew instinctively calculated its speed and mass as it barreled toward him.

It wasn't slowing. Why couldn't the driver see him?

Andrew was stuck in that little car with nowhere to escape. He realized he was about to be crushed to death, that this car obviously couldn't withstand the massive force of a full-sized semi coming toward it at highway speed. The cars in front of him had slowed, then come to a stop over the bridge so there was nowhere he could go. Not left or right or forward. Andrew felt a rush of adrenaline as he realized that his life was ending. The damned car would be demolished and everything in it would be destroyed.

Einstein was right, time slows down.

Andrew said a final prayer as he braced for impact. Then the thin metal frame of the little car exploded into pieces as the truck cut through the rear end. The force of the collision ejected Andrew. He was weightless for an instant and then—nothing.

* * * *

The rehabilitation nurses at the hospital told Andrew that he should accept each new day as a blessing, a special gift, a fresh chance to reduce his suffering. They urged him to greet each new day as an opportunity to be present, mindful, and live happily in the here and now.

They also said all humans are fighting a continuous war, battling an ancient monkey brain that threatens to doom us all to life in a persistent reactive state. They told him he should sit quietly and breathe. That the only tool within his control was his breath. That he must breathe in, breathe out, and focus only on that breathing.

Every morning Andrew practiced breathing deeply, in and out. Time passed. Some mornings he imagined he had split his mind into two halves. This bit of device, this self-trickery—this intellectualized construct, this conceit—urged him to imagine that a real self existed, that he controlled that self, and could will that half of his mind to become ascendant.

Beautiful images and sensations flooded into Andrew's mind, filling whole moments with an intense awareness of possibility. He experienced an overwhelming calmness and knew, as philosophers and priests, artists and lovers do, that his core was spiritual—not merely material. He was a creative spirit.

Onward is the only vector time knows by heart, he thought. Perhaps he'd read that somewhere, but surely he knew it was true.

One morning he was moved out of the ICU and into a regular ward. That was the first time Andrew saw Lena after the accident. Before that, his mother had visited with photo albums that included pictures of their family at the beach and he and Cameron throwing a baseball in the front yard, one photo of the two of them in cowboy outfits, photos of family Easters, Andrew in his Naval Officer uniform, all to stimulate the recovery of his memory. There was not one of Lena Bergen. But the minute he saw her, he knew her and reached out his hand.

"I wasn't sure you'd remember me, Andrew." She started to cry.

"You look just like an angel."

She came over to hug Andrew gently around his shoulders and he noticed that she winced when she bent toward him. Then she pulled over a chair and they talked.

"I was so worried about you. When Susie called me—and then I saw the picture of your car on the television news. I couldn't understand how you even survived." She cried a bit again.

"How are the girls?"

"Pre-teenagers?" She rolled her eyes in drama. "You can't imagine."

They were quiet. Then Andrew said, "I want to marry you."

She cried some more, nodding her head and holding his hand.

"I think I have a month more of this recovery. I'll have to go back to my job to wrap things up, then maybe by January I can return here and we can be married by Easter. What do you think?"

"That simple?"

"That simple." It was the best he'd felt since he'd driven away from her house. He'd been in a coma for seventeen days and in recovery for his bones and blood and mind for another three weeks. But it had been a century. To him it had been a century. "I think this is the best day of my life, Lena. I love you."

She stood up and hugged him carefully and kissed him, a lovely perfect kiss, but there was that wince of pain again.

"What was that? Did you hurt yourself?"

"I don't know. This just started recently."

"What is it?"

"It's in my stomach. Kind of a sharp pain when I move a certain way."

"I think you better see someone to check that out. I mean, you might have pulled a muscle or who knows. You'll do that?"

She nodded and looked concerned. She told Andrew she would make an appointment immediately but said nothing about the many other symptoms she had been experiencing for weeks.

He didn't remember how that day ended.

It was the best day and then there was a shadow.

That's what he remembered later.

THE WORLD GETS SMALLER

Lena sat alone on the deck where she took her morning coffee. A beautiful, thoroughly modern woman—well-educated, well-traveled, well-read—but lately worried about her health.

She seemed to be having a jumble of thoughts about her life and had been jotting some of them into her private journal. She looked down and saw a recent entry. "I've dedicated my life to my daughters," she'd written. "What will happen to them when I'm gone?"

She had married Andrew in the spring of 1991, and they had finalized his adoption of Angela and Sarah a few months later. After healing from his accident, he had retired from the State Department and secured a job at the Humphrey School of Public Affairs at the University of Minnesota, where he worked with graduate students on public policy and international relations. He loved his life just then—his wife and daughters—and had never been happier. Except for the imminent threat of Lena's health.

When he'd encouraged her to find out about her stomach pain before they were married, her diagnosis had seemed horrific and numbing to them. She had stage four ovarian cancer which was immediately treated with surgery and chemotherapy. Even so, they'd moved ahead with their plans to be together and treasured every bit of time they had. She decided not to continue working with Lars on The Writers' Workshop project, which though only an annual event, still consumed her energy from spring through late summer. Instead she stayed home to be with her daughters and Andrew as much as she could and to do her own writing. Poetry particularly was helping her to cope with the trauma of being sick.

And the world was changing, something that fascinated both Lena and Andrew who loved being able to talk again about the events occurring everywhere. They were both so happy when Nadine Gordimer won the Nobel Prize in Literature in October of that year for her work questioning the privileges of white people in South Africa. They were both very unhappy at the confirmation of Clarence Thomas to the Supreme Court seat of the retired Thurgood Marshall that same month. Thomas drew all the ire they had felt years ago for Nixon, maybe more. "He's disgusting," Lena said again and again. Andrew, of course, agreed.

In that same month, a relatively unknown governor from one of the smallest states in the union joined the challenge against President George H. W. Bush for the presidency, saying that the middle class was forgotten and he was a centrist Democrat with a plan. "It's the economy, stupid," William Jefferson Clinton reiterated throughout his candidacy.

The family spent hours together following the campaign, which got even more interesting when a Texas billionaire named Ross Perot decided to run as an independent. The CEO of an electronic data company, he shouted to the American public that their jobs were being sucked up by overseas companies. "You hear that sucking sound?" he'd say and Lena, Angela, and Sarah would roar with laughter.

The CNN twenty-four-hour news cycle that had emerged over the previous decade and become respected during the Gulf War, brought the world right into the Bergen-MacAlpine home, providing hours of engagement for all of them as Lena's health declined that summer of 1992.

She slept more and more as her family sat near and, whenever they could, curled around her as she slept. Angela and Sarah had lived through their father's death and now found themselves battling anger and despair at their mother's stealthy, deadly disease. They fought their feelings for Lena's sake, but Andrew heard them fighting with one another, wailing in their bedrooms, and whispering sweetly in their mother's ear. He watched them leave their childhoods behind them at the tender ages of thirteen and eleven.

On election night, Lena huddled under one of her mother's crocheted coverlets, sedated with morphine. She managed to open her eyes to watch Bill Clinton's acceptance speech and to smile at her family sitting flopped all over near her. It seemed to Andrew that was the last time she smiled at him. It's what he remembered—and he thought that was another one of the reasons he always liked President William Jefferson Clinton.

GOODBYE MY LOVE

At Lena's grave site, Pastor Jensen said "Amen" at the end of his prayers for her, and her daughters cried uncontrollably yet quietly, holding hands with one another. They bent forward and threw white roses onto their mother's polished casket, followed by Andrew, Ellie Mae, and Lena's mother who held on to Susie MacAlpine for support. Many others in the small gathering added their white roses to the cascade of flowers which had been Lena's favorite.

Susie MacAlpine turned to her grieving son and said, "It's all about the girls now that they've lost both their father and mother, Andrew. Your life is no longer about you. You must be there for them. But you already knew that, my dear."

Andrew felt the sting of tears in his eyes. "Yes, Mom. Lena and I promised the girls that. I'll never leave them."

Sunny Bergen moved toward Andrew for a long hug. "I'm thinking about a line that Lena loved: The best way to find out if you can trust somebody is to trust them. Do you know that line, Andrew?"

"Ernest Hemingway," he answered. He knew it well.

Susie and Sunny walked away from the grave site together. "I wish Lars were here, Susie. What is he going to think when he comes home to find Lena gone?"

Susie wondered. Personally, she found Lars so self-absorbed, he hardly seemed to care for anyone. "You couldn't reach him?"

Sunny shook her head. "He's all over Europe. We have no idea."

"Well, it's something to lose a sister like Lena. I'm sure it will break his heart."

Angela and Sarah came to Andrew, and he drew them close, one on each side. "Your mother and I had some times over the last several months when we allowed fear to come into our life. But we never let it take control, did we?"

Angela spoke first, "No, we never did."

Sarah nodded agreement. "Keep on living. That's what Mom told us." Her young voice sounded mature.

Angela agreed. "That's what Mom said. Can we come visit her here every Sunday?"

Andrew choked back his feelings. "Yes. That's what we'll do every Sunday."

Then he let everyone drift back to their cars and whispered, "Goodbye, my love." It was a gray November day, but at that very moment when Andrew let go of Lena, a cloud shifted and the smallest shaft of sun came through.

THE PEACE DIVIDEND

Andrew pushed the doorbell buzzer on the front door of his parents' home and stamped the snow off his boots. "I'm so hungry I could eat a horse."

Sarah sighed. "Oh, Dad, that's an old joke. It's not even a joke!"

The three laughed together at Andrew's expense. The weeks since Lena's funeral had been sorrowful and they were looking forward to a nice dinner with family at the MacAlpine home.

Cameron Senior opened the door and waved them in.

"Well, look who's here! Mighty brisk out there tonight. The women are in the kitchen preparing some appetizers."

"How are you, Dad?" Andrew asked. Even though he had lived in his hometown for the last couple of years, he didn't see his dad much.

"Keeping busy," Cameron Senior said. "Your brother thinks he runs the joint, but . . ." He rolled his eyes. "He's off skiing with the boys. You probably know that. Hey, how's my favorite granddaughters?" He gave Angela and Sarah hugs, though somewhat gingerly. He was still getting used to having two granddaughters in his brood. Little Sarah reminded him of Harold. Maybe her eyes.

The girls went out to see their grandmothers and auntie. By the time Cameron and Andrew had followed them into the kitchen, Ellie Mae, who had stayed in town after the funeral, was deep into discussion with the girls while Susie and Sunny worked together at the stove. The scene calmed Andrew, who found himself more anxious than relaxed since Lena's death, as though waiting for the next bad thing to happen or for the universe to reveal exactly how he was supposed to move forward now.

It was a wonderful meal and the talk mostly light and comfortable. Susie and Sunny were taking a poetry class at Normandale Community College just for fun and chatted on about that. Cameron tried to get the group to care about the Vikings with him and Angela and Sarah answered questions about school and friends. Nobody went very deep and nobody wanted to.

Andrew said to Ellie Mae, "How are you liking twenty below zero, El? Are you adjusting?"

"I was born and raised here. I haven't forgotten frost on my nose."

Susie jumped in, "Frost is good. I could never live anywhere that didn't have four different seasons."

Ellie Mae asked, "What are you teaching this semester, Andrew?"

"We'll be discussing a paper titled 'The End of History' written by Francis Fukuyama."

His father looked up and said, "Fukuyama? I think me and Harold and the 101st Airborne parachuted into Fukuyama during WWII."

Everyone laughed except Sarah. "What's so funny?" she asked.

Andrew continued. "The paper was written a couple of years ago and everyone at the State Department is making new plans based on its predictions."

Susie said, "So for those of us who don't read Fukuyama, what did he predict?"

"Peace and prosperity. Democratic governments around the world and an end to conflict. Things like that."

"Sounds too good to be true, if you ask me." Susie stood up to move some plates off the table.

"No conflict with Communist Russia and China would be a good thing, Susie," Sunny called to her.

Ellie Mae interjected, "I've heard it called the peace dividend, Mom. Maybe people will begin to have an attitude of abundance and gratitude rather than a mindset of scarcity and fear."

Everyone turned her way. Ellie Mae's family was not used to this side of her, the mind she'd been cultivating all her years away. "It could happen. Don't you think, Andrew?"

"Well, these are the exact questions the graduate students are tackling. They'll work to figure out their own answers, then assess the prospects for everlasting peace, prosperity, and goodwill amongst all citizens of the world."

Cameron Senior excused himself in favor of the television and his granddaughters trailed after him asking questions about World War II. Sunny and Susie had cleared the dishes and were singing some song out in the kitchen, leaving Andrew and Ellie Mae at the table.

"How are you doing?"

"One day at a time."

"Yes, one day is all we ever experience, really." Her voice stayed soft. "Lena went so quickly, Andrew. I should've moved back sooner."

They were quiet for a minute before Andrew asked, "Are you back for good?"

"Yes. Mom isn't getting any younger. And she just lost her baby. And I can spend more time with my boys—my young men—before it's too late."

Andrew took a breath. "Susie mentioned to the girls that you might come back. Angela and Sarah love being with you, El. They're delighted you're coming home."

"Good. I love them too. So, Professor MacAlpine, what say you on Fukuyama? Be you yea or nay? Are we humans irrevocably flawed and incapable of permanent peace?"

"I'll say this. I did predict that we would win the Cold War against the Soviets. However, I don't subscribe to intellectual triumphalism. I don't believe for a minute that Western-style liberal democracy, free markets, rock-and-roll, and blue jeans will rule forever. Greed and petty prejudice will soon arise, if I'm any kind of historian."

She nodded thoughtfully and stood up. "Let's go see what tall tales Grandpa is feeding those girls."

LARS IN NORWAY

Lars Bergen had overseen another successful Writers' Workshop in August, after complaining all spring and summer that with Lena home ill, he'd had to do all of the organizing himself. But he was careful not to voice this complaint to anyone who knew that Maarika Heikkila had ably assisted him, perhaps doing the lion's share of the work before and during the workshop.

Maarika—everyone called her Rika—had been one of the brightest English literature students in her graduating class, but had decided to live in the real world for a while before pursuing a graduate degree. So Rika had needed a job just when Lars needed an assistant. Lars knew she was a gifted writer and poet and believed she'd be perfect as his assistant, though it was said she did not suffer fools gladly. That was fine. Lars was confident he could handle her rough and unpolished side, which came into view when anyone fiddled with projects she considered completed.

When that 1992 Writers' Workshop was over, Lars left town for a long-awaited sabbatical. He flew to Oslo, Norway, packed his tent and supplies into the trunk of a rented Admiral Blue Saab 900, and drove five hours on the E16 highway to the northwestern shore of Lake Vangsvatnet where he wanted to camp for a while. When he needed supplies, he visited the village of Vossevangen, but mostly he reread Ayn Rand and wrote in his journal.

Lars had long believed that the individual should be supreme, that collective action through any form of government should be reduced or eliminated, and that enlightened selfishness and capitalism offered the purest forms of individual freedom. Individual freedom had always been uppermost in his hierarchy of beliefs. Lars titled his journal "*Bootstraps and the Survival of the Fittest,*" and imagined his notes could become the architecture of a book. He believed a person's journey through life would inevitably produce the realization that human interconnectedness is a misguided myth and a dangerous illusion. Lars had come to understand that all men and women should organize their lives with the sole purpose of maximizing their pleasure through the acquisition of material goods. He exhibited extreme adherence to the scarcity mindset.

There in Norway, Lars also contemplated his ancestry.

> *My people come from the land of the midnight sun, a land of deep snowfall and bitter cold wind, a land where many souls lose hope before the sunlight returns. Perhaps it is because of this genetic history that I have become strong, independent, and successful. All I have accomplished has been me, me alone, all through these years. I—the way I think, what I believe—I am the reason for my success.*

That was another thing he wrote.

By the Autumnal Equinox the days had grown short and the nights too cool for comfort in his tent, so Lars drove almost nine hours to Trondheim. The vast expanses of the beautiful country, the great forests and fjords, the minutes without seeing another car or person symbolized to Lars that one's journey through life is intended to be solitary, even secret and, ultimately, filled with foreboding.

He did not believe that a god or God offered any signs to show humans the way to live rightly. He'd never believed there were eternal paths to spiritual enlightenment and correct living. Instead, for Lars, the only truth was whatever his intellect found persuasive. And so, blinded to much of the wisdom centuries of thinkers had produced, he was seeking the innermost meaning in the Ayn Rand books he'd carried with him, confident in her ability to give him his own ultimate liberty.

In Trondheim Lars went directly to the luxurious Scandic Solsiden Hotel. The rental car was safely parked by an attendant as Lars checked in for an indefinite stay. A porter took his bag to his room while Lars went to the bar for a much-needed drink. The bartender poured out a snifter of the best cognac and Lars began to relax. His neck and back muscles were stiff from the long drive, but the cognac was beginning to work its magic on him when another patron in the bar approached him.

"I heard you order and recognize that accent. You're an American, aren't you?"

"Yes, that's right. Why'd you ask?"

The man pointed to the stool next to Lars and asked, "Mind if I sit?"

"Suit yourself."

The stranger nodded to the bartender, pointed at his empty glass, and looked intently at Lars. "You Americans have the power to destroy us all and none of the good common sense to avoid it. When you get back home, please tell everyone to do something about that. Okay, friend?" He reached for the freshened drink, slid off the barstool, and returned to his own table where he began speaking softly to two women and another man.

Lars ignored them. People like that had no ability to rouse him. An hour and two cognacs later, Lars signed his bar tab and headed out to the lobby, the elevator, and his own room upstairs. But as Lars walked past the other tables, the same annoying stranger called out to him, "I thought someone should tell you—you're not the only people here on Earth. It's the only Earth we've got, you know."

Everyone else in the bar heard him which stung Lars. His face flushed and his ears burned, but he did not answer. He strode past the stranger and his laughing friends with his eyes on the lobby ahead.

The stranger's remarks stayed in his mind long after he'd gone to his room. He found himself, uncharacteristically, fuming as he pictured the sneer on the stranger's face when he'd said "the only Earth we've got."

What exactly did that mean? The nerve. Interrupting a guest who was minding his own business. "You're not the only people here on Earth." I know that, Lars thought. Did the stranger mean we're supposed to be our brother's keeper? Interfere with someone else's enjoyment of material things? Or was he referring to that Desert Storm initiative? What was that man implying? That we should all become vegetarians and ride bicycles, throw away our automobiles and forget about protecting the oil industry. The oil which lubricated the wheels of commerce and made the world go around?

Lars didn't see the stranger again, that nosy native who had so rudely interrupted his cognac and reverie, but the encounter gave him the idea he should perhaps write his more ambitious philosophies using a pen name. Perhaps "Thor." He liked that, writing as the Storm God.

On Monday, he took the train down to Oslo to do some sightseeing—fjords, waterfalls, and beautiful blonde women—which was, to Lars, the most pleasant part of his Norwegian odyssey.

He had not lost his winsome ability with women, but he held back a bit. He didn't need any more difficulty just then.

From Oslo he flew to Rome, where he planned to spend months in museums and on beaches, eating and drinking well and enjoying the sight of beautiful Italian women wherever he went. The flight to Rome was so bumpy, however, that it crossed his mind he may not ever make it safely back to that planet Earth that he was supposed to be saving. The Fasten Seat Belt sign was lit throughout and the captain frequently reminded passengers to stay buckled up. For a brief few minutes, Lars wished he'd had children to carry forth his brilliance if he were to die so young. The small airplane bucked and dropped and bounced its way south and when it finally bounced and screeched onto the runway in Rome, all the passengers applauded.

Lars stayed for many weeks in Italy before moving on to Morocco, Bulgaria, and Greece. He had no contact with family or friends during the winter and spring of 1993, remaining wherever the sun was shining and preparing to return to Minneapolis only as the flowers began blooming.

He was gone for so long and had been so out of touch, that he did not know that Lena had died and that Ellie Mae had returned to Minneapolis and was renting space in The Cube for her Quiet Inspiration meditation classes and readings. Nor could he know that his young assistant, Rika, a fan of Ellie Mae Bergen, had invited her to be a keynote speaker at that summer's Writers' Workshop.

Left alone to organize that year's workshop, Rika had decided that it should be women-centered, feature a retrospective review of Lena's *Letters to American Women,* and include the growing movement called the human potential dimension. She grew so excited about her ideas that she began making plans, and so it was natural that she reached out to Ellie Mae regarding meditation training for writers. It wasn't that Rika wanted to save the Earth, necessarily, but she certainly did want to bring people together in authentic ways. Lars wasn't there to give his input.

And so it was decided.

THE FIRST TUESDAY IN JUNE 1944

Cameron MacAlpine liked to tell the story about when he and Harold Bergen jumped out of their low-flying plane into the night skies of Normandy way back in June of 1944. They were Screaming Eagles, members of the feared 101st Airborne Division, and their company's mission that night was to parachute behind enemy lines and secure route N13 and the village of Sainte-Mère-Église.

The Screaming Eagles had to be there, Cameron would say, because Allied Headquarters expected route N13 to become flooded with Nazi forces roaring through the old village toward the beaches of Normandy once it was obvious that the D-Day invasion was underway.

Cameron and Harold landed just outside Sainte-Mère-Église and fought their way slowly to the church at the center of the village. When telling the story, Cameron described the sound of gunfire, single rifle shots and bursts of machine gun rounds from the hostile forces in the village, but he never mentioned the names of his comrades who fell that day. He did say that the 101st Airborne Division overcame the enemy, occupied the town, and freed the residents, making the little village one of the first towns to be liberated in the Battle of Normandy.

Cameron always lowered his voice when he said the longest hours of his life began when his boots touched French soil and ended when the enemy had been killed or forced out of the village, even before some 25,000 American troops began landing at nearby Utah Beach.

Sometimes he would go to his old Army footlocker and pull out war souvenirs: a Luger, a Nazi Iron Cross, an enemy bayonet. He rarely showed anyone his Purple Heart, two Bronze Stars, and other medals which remained secure in their gold-colored boxes deep inside that footlocker.

He regularly received the Screaming Eagles newsletter and made travel plans as soon as he read that a reunion ceremony was planned on site in France. He was looking forward to being with the survivors of that day and that campaign. Paratroopers from the US 82nd and US 101st Airborne divisions had collaborated, joined forces, fought, and died to gain a foothold in France. Then his band of brothers had soldiered on to liberate Paris. Such a celebration, Cameron would say, although he never said exactly how he and Harold celebrated. Cameron Junior once asked his dad if that old footlocker had souvenirs from the liberation, something uniquely Parisian, feminine. Cameron laughed, rumpled his son's hair, and changed the subject. If Cameron had such mementos, he never produced them.

The Screaming Eagles marched north into Bastogne in late 1944, during the coldest December in memory. Cameron and Harold were both wounded during The Battle of the Bulge. Both were bandaged to stop the bleeding, given back their rifles, and continued fighting. Cameron especially liked telling the story of the senior United States Army officer who earned fame as the acting commander of the US 101st Airborne Division troops defending Bastogne, Belgium. The German commander asked General McAuliffe to surrender his outnumbered and besieged troops and McAuliffe is reported to have said "Nuts." Cameron's favorite souvenir was a large cylinder made by the townspeople of Bastogne by melting down the brass casings from the large shells which bombarded the Screaming Eagles. It was dedicated to the battling bastards of Bastogne with a drawing of McAuliffe in the center. He was giving his "Nuts" answer to a German officer.

That had been fifty years earlier.

Harold had accompanied Cameron to their twenty-five-year reunion which had been in San Diego back in 1969 when Sunny and Susie had gone along as well. It had been a small gathering just for their company. They had missed the thirty-year get-together and then Harold had died in 1975. Now Cameron was off to Normandy for the 101st division's fiftieth reunion on his own, flying from Minneapolis to Paris before boarding a train for Sainte-Mère-Église.

He'd spent the morning with Lucy, lying with her for two hours in her comfortable king-sized bed. He had loved Lucy for years, just as he'd loved Susie throughout their marriage. Both seemed to understand that, though Susie never mentioned it in any obvious way. But he was certain she knew.

"Call me when you get there, Cam. You know how I worry when you're flying."

"I will, Lucy, the minute I get to my room."

"Okay, mister. I'll be waiting by the phone."

They both chuckled. "I love you, my dear," he said to her.

"Your secret is safe with me."

"Try to keep Junior out of trouble until I return, okay?"

She looked directly into his eyes, "You think I can lock him in a room without a phone?"

Cameron laughed. "There's an idea. You certainly have my permission."

"Are you all ready to go?"

"Packed last night. Susie said we should leave for the airport no later than four p.m. She and Sunny will chauffer me there in plenty of time for my eight o'clock flight."

"Do you have to leave this very minute?" Lucy slid her hips closer toward him.

Cameron felt that familiar excitement growing. "How about I stay for lunch?"

Four hours later he was buckled up in Susie's car on his way to the airport as she ran through the pre-flight checklist. "Passport? Wallet? Traveler's checks?"

Cameron answered in the affirmative—like a good soldier.

From the back seat, Sunny chimed in too. "Got your Dopp kit? Prescriptions? Sunglasses?"

"Yes, yes, and yes. Thank you both, dear ladies."

Susie chuckled. "I love that old story about the first time you and Harold flew commercial."

They all laughed. "There you are, flying to Chicago for some home-builders' convention and Harold looks at you and sees you sweating like nobody's business. White knuckles and all."

Cameron picked up the story. "Right. Harold asks me, 'Why so nervous, Buddy? You've been in lots of planes before.'"

Sunny finished the story. "So you said, 'Yeah, but I've never landed in one before.'"

They all laughed. "That's my favorite story," Cameron said. "It's a real paratrooper tale. God, I miss Harold."

At age seventy-two, Cameron was not the oldest World War II veteran at the Screaming Eagles reunion. And he was not the oldest paratrooper to go up in a C-130 and jump out at 3,000 feet with a carefully packed parasail strapped on his back.

The parasails were brilliant splotches of color against a cloudy sky that day and a large gathering of townspeople, French veterans, American veterans, friends, and family cheered as the old-timers floated down to the village green then gathered to tell stories of the war, their wounds, and what they had done in their "bonus round." The celebration was still going on after the last light of day had disappeared. Cameron told his comrades, "I'm going to head over to Utah Beach. I want to see what everyone saw when they came cruising in that morning."

Neither Jimmy Dow, Tracy Newlands, nor any of his old unit wanted to go anywhere, or get up from their barstools, for that matter. They couldn't dissuade Cameron, so he left the bar alone.

He wandered around the village until he found the taxi stand where an old battered Citroen was parked. Cameron woke up the driver, pointed toward where he assumed Utah Beach would be, and put a handful of bills in the driver's hand. The big Citroen surged forward and they were on their way. If Cameron thought the driver was going too fast or noticed that they'd missed a turn in the deep of the dark woods, no one would ever know. In the beat of a second, the taxi crashed into a tree, rolled over, and exploded into a huge fireball.

THE RAGS-TO-RICHES STORY

In 1968, when Alpine Homes was in its peak growth, a local reporter had asked the Bergens and MacAlpines the secret of their success. The two men looked at each other and shrugged before Cameron answered, "Just lucky, I guess."

Then Harold had ventured, "If you mean luck is being in the right place at the right time with the right houses."

Their wives had opinions on this as well. Sunny said, "Pure stubbornness. We worked ten to twelve hours a day for six or seven days a week to make sure we didn't fail."

Susie had smiled graciously at the reporter. "Just say we're not quitters. We've all got grit."

The day after Cameron's fatal accident in France, WCCO radio broke the news that the long-time local business leader was dead. The newspaper followed the next day with a page-one story about Cameron's rag-to-riches-success. His obituary was two columns long and featured two photographs. One was young Cameron in his Army uniform, the Screaming Eagles patch visible on his arm and his many medals and ribbons festooning his chest. His Army hat was tilted at a rakish angle and so was his smile. The other photograph had been taken for the fortieth anniversary celebration of Alpine Homes with Cameron dressed in a dark suit and serious tie.

The funeral was Saturday afternoon, June 11, 1994, with bright sun and temperatures rising toward seventy-five degrees. Though there had not been a drop of rain all month, lawns had been watered so that the grass would not burn up in the endless sunshine. The church was filled to overflowing, and for those who didn't know Cameron's whole story, the memorial brochure informed them that he had been born in Big Piney, Wyoming, on February 22, 1922, to Malcolm & Agnetha MacAlpine. His mother died in childbirth, home alone in the winter, in the wilderness. His dad died by electrocution as a lineman when Cameron was three. He was raised by his maternal grandparents. His grandma died when he was ten, he dropped out of high school after eleventh grade, and he joined the CCCs, making roads, planting trees, and fighting fires.

Pastor Lindquist said a few words, offering comfort to the family assembled in the front row. He looked directly at Susie as he spoke of the mystery beyond understanding which is death. Susie had Cameron Junior on her left and Sunny on her right. Then came Andrew, Sarah, and Angela, Cameron III, and Jack. Behind them sat Ellie Mae, Lucy Shea, and Lucy's niece Ramona Riley Krauss, who was next to Lars Bergen, and Cameron's two old Army buddies, Jimmy Dow and Tracy Newlands.

When the pastor nodded to Cameron Junior to come forward and speak for the family, the young man's eyes were red and his voice trembling. He began, "Welcome," then fumbled with his notes, coughed, and looked down and around and finally looked up at Andrew, beckoning him. Andrew came to the podium, his brother handed him his crumpled notes, and Andrew looked out over the family, friends, and fellow mourners.

"Let me begin with a thank you from the entire MacAlpine family and the extended family at Alpine Homes. Your sympathy and condolences have lifted our spirits." Andrew slowly scanned the group. "For those I haven't yet met, I'm Andrew, Cameron's second son. Some of you might know Cameron and his best friend, Harold Bergen, volunteered for the war the morning after Pearl Harbor."

Andrew saw nods of recognition and approval as he spoke.

"Dad and Harold were appalled at what happened at Pearl Harbor, a sneak attack on our Navy just as Japanese ambassadors in Washington, DC, pretended to be negotiating in good faith. So each volunteered the very next day," Andrew repeated. He was a practiced public speaker and needed no notes to share stories about his dad with all those in the church that afternoon.

"The recruiter told them they could be submariners or paratroopers. They'd never been on a submarine and never been in an airplane either, but the idea of being cooped up in a small space didn't appeal to them. So they told the recruiter jumping out of airplanes sounded just fine."

"That's how Dad and Harold became Screaming Eagles. They decided to jump out of planes and get shot at while floating to the ground rather than be underwater for long periods of time. You got to love that. That was Dad and Harold. They were warriors, you know. Both got shot up in Bastogne at The Battle of the Bulge."

"The Battling Bastards of Bastogne!" Jimmy Dow exclaimed. His unexpected outburst caused some laughter to erupt. "Forgive my language," he concluded. The crowd laughed and Andrew continued.

"Dad and Harold knew all about the London Blitz. They had seen it in the newsreels, read about it in magazines and newspapers, and heard about it on the radio. The German Luftwaffe began bombing runs in September 1940, continued almost every single day for nearly two months, day and night, hoping to bomb Britain into submission. Almost 50,000 innocent lives were lost that autumn—but they did not surrender. They did not give in or give up.

"That's how we should remember Cameron—and Harold. They never gave up."

There was not a dry eye in the church.

Andrew walked back to the front pew, hugged his mother, and stood next to his daughters.

"Thanks for stepping in," Cameron Junior said to his younger brother. "I kind of lost my place there for a minute."

"I was glad to help. You know that, Cam."

"Well then, help me get some more stock in the business," Cameron chuckled, nervous yet determined to plow ahead with his agenda. "You know mom and Sunny will listen to you."

"Not now, Cam." Andrew clapped his brother on the back and left him to mingle with the guests.

As most of the congregation took the stairs down to the fellowship hall for lunch, Ellie Mae moved easily from one old friend of the family to another, offering and receiving condolences and heartfelt expressions of sympathy. When Lucy Shea passed her, Ellie Mae graciously shook her hand before noticing Lucy's niece close behind her. "I think I remember you. Don't I? Weren't you working in the hospital when Cameron Junior was knocked out on some drug? Oh my gosh, years ago."

"This is my niece, Ramona Krauss, Ellie Mae. She's my pride and joy."

"Well, of course, Lucy. She looks just like a MacAlpine, doesn't she? What a coincidence." All three women smiled. Only later did Ellie Mae understand. Cameron Senior had known Lucy Shea for many years. Things happened. She shook her head in amazement, wondering if Susie had any idea. Families and secrets seemed to travel well together.

Andrew's remarks had lifted the spirits of the mourners, a rare gift at a time of such sudden loss. Andrew had spent a lifetime knowing that his father had little interest in him or his accomplishments. Cameron Junior was the first born and the most like his father, interested in the business and content to stay close to home. For some reason, this had never bothered Andrew. As former military, he'd always respected his dad and admired his relationship with Harold. He might even be the son who would mourn him the most.

For Sunny, Andrew's remarks brought Harold back to her for a few minutes, just as though he himself were at the pulpit telling those stories. He'd been gone for almost twenty years and she still missed him every day. Poor Susie. She was about to know what it felt like to wake up every morning without her life companion at her side.

But Susie wasn't thinking that just yet. Sad as she was, she found herself surveying the people at Cameron's funeral and drawing some conclusions. Lucy Shea's grief, for example, did not go unnoticed. Nor did the sight of Lucy's niece, who might have been Cameron Junior's twin, they were so alike in coloring and features. Now that her husband was gone, she wished he'd told her what she always knew. Lucy had always known about Susie, of course, which gave her more insight into Cameron. She'd had the upper hand in his life, Susie thought. She couldn't help but think that.

And as she observed the full church basement of people eating and talking, she also couldn't help think that the groups had sorted themselves in a certain order—Cameron's business friends at one table, the civic leaders near them at another table, his few Army friends clustered at their table, and all the company's workers at theirs. The carpenters did not sit next to the attorneys. The bricklayers did not mingle with management. When Harold had died, she remembered how different it was, with everyone mixing freely, all of them friends who worked for the same company and who drank, ate, and bowled together at least once a week, taking no note of position or pocketbook.

Somehow, that distinction made her all the sadder.

THE NEXT GENERATION

Cameron Senior's death brought many childhood memories back to Ellie Mae, almost as though an era had ended for her. Her sister had died, she remained estranged from her brother, and her widowed mother focused much of her energy on her relationship with her best friend, Susie MacAlpine, who now needed her more than ever.

Weeks after Cameron was buried, Ellie Mae showed up at Andrew's house with take-out food and two bottles of champagne. "Surprise," she said, sliding out of her shoes and walking barefoot into his kitchen.

Andrew followed her, delighted. "A celebration?"

"Not so much. Let's call it a planning session."

"And what will we be planning, El?"

"Well, maybe it's a review session."

"Okay. So what are we reviewing?"

She unpacked the food, found glasses for the champagne and poured for the two of them. "Where are the girls?"

"Off in their very busy lives. It's summer after all."

"Good." She tapped his glass with her own. "You've become a perfect and perfectly wonderful dad. That's why I want your opinion. I have not been the best mother, leaving Cameron III and Jack with Cam. Tell me what you think of my sons."

"What do you want me to tell you?"

"How are they doing in life, in your opinion? How have they fared with such an absentee mother?"

"You're hard on yourself, Ellie. At least you kept in touch. I mean, I always thought they knew you were available if they needed you."

Ellie Mae shrugged. She wasn't so sure. "Cameron III seems like something of a wild child," she offered. "Is that what you think?"

Andrew nodded. "It's what I see. Wrecking cars, staying out late, running with a bad crowd. My mother worries about him all the time. But my brother isn't exactly a straitlaced type either, so she should be used to it."

"Do you think it's because Cameron III doesn't look like anyone else in the family?"

Andrew was the only one who had always understood Cameron III was not his brother's biological child, that Ellie Mae had spent some hours at least with their Greek friend Connie Demopoulos just before she married Cameron Junior. Everyone saw the physical differences, Cameron's stockier stature and swarthy skin, but only Andrew seemed to have put the pieces together.

"Maybe," he replied. "He's good looking though. That might be all that matters at his age. And he has a place in the family business."

"Unlike you," Ellie Mae joked.

"Or Jack," Andrew added. "First-born sons are heir to the land, isn't that how it goes?" He poured them both more champagne.

"Sunny told me that before your dad died, she, your mom, and your dad hired a business lawyer—great name of Franklin Delano Johansson—to reconstitute and recapitalize the business. They did that when your dad turned seventy. Anyway, as part of the legal maneuvering, the new company adopted a modern business succession plan giving Cameron Junior ownership interest if any of the other partners died. And now that your dad has died, Cameron Junior is a full partner. Did you know that?"

Andrew nodded. "My mom hinted at it. She knows I'm not interested. But still, I think she feels guilty about it sometimes. You know Susie. She's like a general—what's fair for one is fair for all."

Ellie laughed. "Well, it certainly allows Cam to bring in my son to whatever degree he chooses."

"Keeps him close to home."

"Unlike Jack," Ellie said with a bit of a sigh. "He's like you, isn't he?"

"Wanting to roam the world? Work undercover? Be gone for years at a time?"

"That sort of thing. Is that Jack?"

"I think it is. He's doing so well at Georgetown. He seems to be leaning toward the Navy, joining the Office of Naval Intelligence. He's such a great guy for that kind of work—smart and creative, easy to know and easy to like."

"Do you miss it, Andrew?"

"That life? No. I loved it then and I don't miss it now. Isn't that perfect?"

"But Lena's daughters, your daughters, will be on their own soon. What then?"

He grinned at her. "You returned. How do you like it?"

She had to laugh. "We're here then, aren't we?"

"Drinking champagne together."

"Here's to you, Andrew."

"And to you."

"And to the next generation."

THE QUACK SHACK

Connie Demopoulos's family had sent him to the United States in 1967 when the Greek colonels staged their coup d'état. It was a disruptive period of time, and the very wealthy Demopoulos family feared retribution. After Papadopoulos's senior officers rebelled and negotiated a change, free elections were held and Connie's father believed it was safe for his son to come home, which he did. That was 1974. Although the family's business took Connie to the East and West Coasts regularly, he had not seen his college pals in years, but Jimmy Nelson called him now and then to talk about the state of international business—and to see if he might want to buy any additional insurance as well.

Now his friends had asked him to join them in November of 1998, for five days at a duck hunting shack near a place they called Lac qui Parle, which translated to the "lake that speaks." He'd know why when he heard those ducks honking, Cameron Junior had said, and the hunting did not get any better. For Connie it was too good to refuse. He arranged his schedule so that he could fly from Athens, Greece, on a Monday morning, get to New York City late that night, meet with three longtime import-export clients there for several days, then fly on to Minneapolis to see his old friends early Friday morning. His wife of twenty-two years kissed him goodbye in the same whole-hearted, passionate way she did everything. "Be careful with those boyfriends you have," she teased as she waved him off.

It was a good week for Connie. He booked new orders, ate his favorite foods in Little Italy, and popped in at stores that sold the high-end trinkets of his industry. But on the morning he was to leave for Minnesota, he ran into trouble. There was a storm over the city, incoming planes were delayed, and outgoing planes canceled. Passengers like himself stormed from one airline to another trying to get a flight out only to be told they could not. He called Cameron Junior to tell him of the delay but got no answer. When he called Jimmy Nelson's phone, he heard, "Gone out to the Quack Shack to shoot some ducks. Be back sometime next Wednesday. Ask for Helen if you need anything."

But Connie didn't have a number for Helen, and after many hours waiting around the airport, he gave up and returned to his hotel. He called his wife, who only laughed. She thought her husband's Minnesota friends were not to be taken seriously anyway. Perhaps he would be better off staying in New York an extra day or two and coming home to his family. "You don't even like duck," she said.

In Minnesota, Jimmy picked up Cameron Junior in his newest toy, a 1999 Ford F250 Crew Cab. "What a beauty," he thought every time he drove it, pleased with the glossy black exterior and plush leather interior. He had ordered the four-wheel drive option, paid extra for a matching camper top, and had had a car phone factory-installed.

Jimmy took delivery on election day, November 3rd, hours after he'd voted for Jesse "The Body" Ventura for governor. He'd been as shocked as the former pro wrestler when Ventura won, becoming the first Reform Party candidate to achieve statewide success. He'd won 37 percent of the vote, outdistancing Norm Coleman and Hubert "Skip" Humphrey III. Jimmy smiled, excited that a guy like Jesse was really going to move into the stately governor's mansion on Summit Avenue and be in charge for four years.

The truck had less than 100 miles on the odometer and still had a new car smell. Jimmy's 12-gauge shotgun and extra boxes of shells were in the back, under the camper top, locked in a chest. Two large Styrofoam coolers were filled with food and liquor. Rubber waders and a fishing rod were nestled near a duffel filled with enough clothes for the five-day vacation.

This trip was extra special since it was to be their friend Connie's first time at the Quack Shack, first time duck hunting, and first time fishing for the wise and wily walleye. He was coming all the way from Greece to savor this unique experience. Jimmy picked up his car phone and dialed Cam's number.

"Hey, Cam. You guys ready?"

"Connie's plane never came and I don't have his mobile phone number. Do you?"

Jimmy did not. "Jesus, now what do we do?"

"The airlines said planes are delayed, bad weather, I dunno. I wasn't home this morning if he called."

"Yeah. Don't even tell me where you were. Shit. You want to wait around and see what happens?"

The truth was that, as much as the guys loved their friend from Greece, they loved this annual hunting trip more. On his truck phone, Jimmy made a few calls only to learn what Cameron Junior had already told him. Fights were not leaving any time soon. Jimmy didn't think to check his home phone for a message and when he called Helen in the office, she had not heard from their friend. And so, near noon, he and Cameron headed north without Connie, smoking as they drove to dull the disappointment.

At some point along Highway 7, the two of them let go of what could have been and started thinking about the "flyway" zone ahead, where maybe eighty million ducks came through each season, about ten or twelve million of them mallards.

Jimmy joked that he could "just point my gun at them and pull the trigger. Bang! We'll cook some for dinner tomorrow in a nice marmalade."

"Yum!" said Cam. "I can hardly wait."

The pickup ate up the miles and the men talked easily about current events and political affairs.

"Got to feel sorry for Clinton," Jimmy suggested. "Seems like a perjury trap to ask a married man if he's been sexual with someone other than his wife."

"Poor bastard," said Cam. "Too bad she kept that damn dress."

More than three hours later, Jimmy eased his big black beauty off the main road and carefully navigated a long private driveway through woods and fields until, around a long bend an old farmhouse came into view.

"Here we are, Cam," Jimmy said. "Let's go pay our respects to the old man."

Cam laughed. "I love this guy, what a character."

Karl Nelson owned the farm and leased land to Jimmy's family. He appeared at the door now and yelled, "Come on in and stretch your legs. Warm yourself in front of the fire before you unpack your gear."

After some friendly chat, the old man said, "How come your lawyer friend didn't come?"

"Lewis Wright? Too busy at the office this time."

"Hmmph," Karl said. "Too bad. I had a lawyer joke all ready for him."

"Come on," Jimmy chided, "tell it anyway."

"Okay, here she goes. What do you say about a lawyer up to his neck in sand?" He paused for effect. "Not enough sand."

All three men laughed and downed a shot of whiskey like they did every year.

Saturday morning the weather was perfect. Jimmy and Cameron Junior ate a leisurely breakfast, drank a couple of cups of coffee each laced with enough brandy to drown out the taste of the coffee, and walked down to a stream. They paddled their aluminum canoe a short distance into a large lake where they could see hundreds of ducks. They shot three before the flock took off in a thunderous flapping of wings.

"They'll be here again tomorrow morning," Jimmy said and took out his flask of whiskey. The men took the ducks back to the shack, wrapped them, and set them in the refrigerator before sitting in fat chairs by the fire to spin yarns and continue drinking.

They shot more ducks on Sunday morning, then spent the afternoon and evening telling more tall tales as they put away a fifth of bourbon, another of brandy, and too many beers to count.

When they were wakened Monday morning by wind gusts shaking the windows and rattling the walls, Jimmy went out to check the weather. "Looks like we got some wind, for sure, but that'll keep the ducks sheltered right around the corner. I say we go get some before the wind gets any worse."

They downed their breakfast coffee and brandy, put on their gear, and headed out. A light but steady snow was falling as they paddled their canoe down the winding stream and out into the big lake, right into the flock. The ducks had huddled together, seeking shelter, and were startled when the canoe came into view. One by one, then ten by ten, then in hundreds, the ducks flapped their wings and headed straight for the men.

"Jesus," Jimmy called above the racket, "what the hell is this?" But Cameron couldn't hear him, nor could he stop Jimmy when his friend stood up in the canoe to take a shot at the ducks. Just as Jimmy pulled the trigger, the foot of his rubber wader slipped on the frosty floor of the aluminum canoe. Struggling to get his balance, Jimmy reached out for Cameron who was pulled toward his friend in a grip so clumsy, Cameron knocked his head on the rim of the canoe.

Jimmy toppled into the lake, calling out for Cameron to help him as the freezing water closed around him and his waders pulled him down. Instinctively Cameron dove in to get his friend, but was shocked by the frigid water and the blinding snow that came harder and harder, shrieking louder than the men and pushing them farther away from their overturned canoe and the safety of the shore.

In the roar of wind and snow, Jimmy's last thought was that he was being run over by a locomotive—and where was Cameron? He'd always thought Cameron Junior would save him, that's what he'd always thought.

Monday passed into night. By Tuesday morning, Jimmy's beautiful black pickup was covered with thirteen inches of snow, and the telephone lines out of the Quack Shack had been snapped by sixty-mile-an-hour winds and the heavy wet snow. Karl Nelson drove his snowmobile over that afternoon expecting to find the two men passed out cold from drinking their way through the all-day storm. He chuckled at the fancy truck buried in snow. “Those boys will have a hell of a time getting out of here.” They were all city slickers to him.

But when he finally shoveled his way to the door and entered the shack, the old man found only breakfast dishes left haphazardly on the table.

Eight hundred miles away, Connie Demopoulos conferred with one of his favorite customers on the displays that were top sellers for the season. He had not been able to connect with his college friends but thought of them as he continued his business trip, knowing that even without him, those two characters would be having the time of their lives.

THE BIG CHILL

The news shocked Jimmy and Cameron Junior's friends who had known them from their school days. It didn't shock them that the men would do something dangerous and lose the battle, but that they were gone. Those who knew them well found it hard to imagine a world without their larger-than-life personalities.

Jimmy's brother Richie got word to Connie who changed his plans and flew straight to Minneapolis, blaming himself for not making the Quack Shack trip. He didn't tend to drink as much as those two. He would have been a cautionary influence and perhaps they would't have gone out in bad weather if he'd been there. He couldn't shake that nagging regret. In fact, he never did. The deaths of Jimmy and Cameron Junior followed Connie for the rest of his days, a story he told now and then when men sat drinking their glasses of ouzo and telling their tales.

He attended both funerals, saying little to the men and women he'd known at the University of Minnesota where he'd lived with his friends in that run-down mansion near campus. But at the large gathering afterward, he sought out Andrew MacAlpine.

"I should have been there," he confessed.

"Connie, my brother and Jimmy did things their way. You couldn't have saved them."

"I think I could have. You know the weather was bad in New York and I couldn't get my flight. I cut it too close. If I'd come in one day earlier, I would have made it here to go with them."

"And supervise?" Andrew smiled, a kind man always. "Nothing is predictable, Connie."

"Your poor mother. Such a nice lady. And your daughters—I saw them looking out for her in the church. Like angels." Andrew agreed, they were angels.

"What about Cameron's kids? How're they doing?"

"We'll see. The younger one, Jack, is my godson. He's been kind of following in my footsteps, so I've felt responsible for him anyway. You have lots of kids, Connie. You know how that goes."

"The other boy, the older boy. You see he looks like me?"

"Yep." Andrew waited to see where Connie would go with this idea.

"He's a good kid?"

"A bit spoiled. Probably not his fault. Ellie Mae left when they were young and Cameron Junior liked to work." Andrew shrugged as if to say, what do you expect.

"Ellie Mae's around now though, right?"

"She's been back in town for almost seven years and I think that helps."

Without elaborating, Connie said, "Maybe the boy is good at business like me."

"He certainly has your good looks!"

"I'll reach out. Maybe he comes to visit us in Greece sometime soon." He stared across the room to where Cameron III was drinking his way through a long story with one of his friends. "I take care of my own," he concluded and thumped Andrew on the back.

Overall Andrew had lost his brother long ago. For him, this gathering of people revealed feelings and memories of the past that had almost nothing to do with Cameron Junior.

He stood watching the old crowd drink and reconnect. Ruth Ann Kovacs was the first to come his way and express her grief. Her restaurant—The Iron Miner's Daughter—had opened a second location across the river. Life was good for her, she said. "But Bobby and Lena, now Jimmy and Cam," she reflected to Andrew. "We have lost our brothers, Andrew. We have both lost our brothers." Her tears started again, but Andrew said nothing. He just listened as she reminisced. Andrew had always been such a good listener.

He was happy to see Linda Horton too. Good old Linda Horton, he thought to himself. Still brilliant and all-knowing, still working the floor as she always did, her lifelong partner, Annette, radiant at her side. He saw Ellie Mae in deep conversation with the two of them, speaking of life on other planes, he supposed. She caught him watching her and broke away to come toward him.

"Lars just told me I shouldn't be sad about Cameron because we were divorced anyway."

"Lars is always so sensitive to the situation, El. We know that by now."

"My poor mother. She lost Dad and Lena, I took off for years, and her only son is Lars Bergen."

Andrew had to laugh. He'd thought the same thing many times. Poor Sunny. "Our mothers have each other though. I mean, since my dad died, they have become so close."

"You know, Andrew, I think they always were close. Especially after Harold died and my mom moved in with your parents. They're best friends like sisters and business partners all these years too."

It was true. At that very hour, the two women were driving home together discussing the business situation. Sunny very diplomatically asked Susie if she thought her grandson was ready to take over Alpine Homes. The agreements they'd drawn up now gave him leadership. "Do you really think he's ready?"

"He's got Lucy Shea and Jake Bachman. They can get him up to speed." Susie did not want to think about any more trouble.

"Yes, of course," Sunny pressed, "they can advise him. But is he ready to make the executive decisions?" She was thinking of the years her husband and Cameron had worked hard to build the business and the comfortable lives they'd all been able to live because the business had done so well. "The big decisions will be up to him now, you know, and he's only twenty-six."

Hands on the wheel and eyes straight ahead, Susie answered, "We'll find out soon enough."

At the gathering they'd just left, Cameron III had no trepidation as to his ability to lead Alpine Homes into the new century, nor as to the gold mine he had in his grasp. His father's college friend Lewis Wright was already circling him, hoping to be the new outside general counsel to the company. Lewis was a brand. Having escaped military service in 1969, he'd gone on to become an attorney, expert at advising on the buying and selling of real estate. He was powerful and persuasive, with L.A.W. embossed on his bespoke starched cuffs.

"Sorry about Cam, kid. I always loved those trips up to the Quack Shack. Your dad was a hell of a good time." He moved in close to the young man. "If there's anything I can do . . . You know your dad and Cameron Senior tended to like that old attorney Franklin Johansson, but a young guy like you, you're going to find Franklin to be a bit conservative. Not a financial engineer, you know what I mean? No, Franklin is not the guy to help you explode this business, Cam. Real estate is my specialty. My first born, as it were. Your dad always consulted with me on the side, but he wasn't up for the commotion of taking the business to the moon." He handed Cameron III his business card. "Give me a call next week. We'll see what we can do for you."

He left the young man holding his high-gloss card. The grieving crowd around him straggled out of the assembly hall into the chilly November evening.

IN LOVE IN PARIS

Jack MacAlpine watched his brother working the crowd at their father's funeral. The heir apparent was now head of Alpine Homes and ready to make himself so rich nobody could ever touch him.

But Jack didn't care. The deaths of his father and grandfather had left him with enormous wealth in his own right. The patriarchs had not only invested in Alpine Homes but also in land, stocks, bonds, and annuities, and then during the boom years, those had compounded over and again and were protected through a variety of trust funds. So money never had been a concern for Jack and never would be.

Moreover his brother had always been something of a stranger to him, a guy so focused on himself and so unwilling to behave with discretion, the complete opposite of Jack. Even their father seemed a bit foreign to Jack, who put reason and intellect above reaction and raw emotion. Jack was more his mother's child, he thought. Or his grandmothers' child, as it turned out, since he had spent more time with them than any other adult in his childhood. But now that Ellie Mae was back in town, he found her company reassuring. She was quietly smart, modest, and deep, and very devoted to the people she loved. He saw her devotion to him and that was reassuring as well.

Ellie Mae now had a close friendship with Andrew, who had been a role model to Jack since he could remember. Jack loved his time with Andrew talking about political and economic events, and their diplomatic repercussions. They had spent hours together studying ancient and modern maps, learning how old and new religious and ethnic conflicts shaped worldviews, and practicing the correct pronunciation of country names and capital cities. No one was surprised that Jack followed in Andrew's footsteps and attended The School of Foreign Service at Georgetown University. It was perfect for Jack. He graduated near the top of his class and stayed for a master's degree.

In graduate school, his already mature view of the modern world grew and became more nuanced. He conversed fluently with professors and peers, expressed and defended viewpoints with skill and panache, and maintained cordial relationships with hawks, doves, and those who fluttered between. Jack was on the short list for highly sought-after jobs at the State Department, in both civil and foreign service positions. He had also been approached by various agencies in the intelligence community for national and foreign service.

Jack reached back to Andrew in Minneapolis for advice, knowing his uncle had been employed by the State Department and freelanced for the intelligence community. "What do you think would be best for me?"

"If you want a wife and family, choose the State Department, but if you're not interested in settling down, choose the intelligence community."

"You did both."

"I felt a passion for the service, Jack. And when the CIA needed me, I accommodated them too. Now I'm happy to be a middle-aged professor in middle America raising two daughters. So are you in love with someone?"

"Yep. Her name is Laura Pollard. I met her at Georgetown. She's like me, Andrew, but a lot more beautiful." This made them both laugh.

After Jack's conversation with Andrew, he called Laura and asked her to dinner. And when they were seated in a corner booth at Old Ebbitt Grill, he proposed that the two of them join the foreign service together. "Maybe Paris," he teased. "We really do speak such impeccable French."

"Bonjour, Paris."

They toasted to that. Then for the next six months, they both did everything they could to make it happen, and in October of 1999, they took their positions as attachés in Paris, helping Americans in France or those in France who wished to become American. They lived together in a third-story flat in a decrepit building near the American Embassy. They loved their work and they loved Paris. They also truly loved each other.

Not everyone they worked with their first year in Paris loved them. The French had given up Morocco and wondered when America would do the same with Puerto Rico and let it become a state. People challenged Jack and Laura about the equality in America's empire. It may not have been personal, but Parisians were worldly and freely lectured the two young attachés on American inequities. Vietnam. The Gulf War. The Philippines. Despite their training, neither Jack nor Laura was prepared for the worldviews and broad scope of the average French citizen, nor the anger toward America that they experienced.

The American Century was nearing an end. Some talk in some circles was that in the twenty-first century, the world would shift to the East. What if Asia would be unified and organized and would approach the United States in GDP and ultimately surpass it? America was constraining its population, spending its national treasure on military, and becoming more and more a debtor nation. Meanwhile the country was not spending money to rebuild roads that had not been updated since Eisenhower was president and not spending money on education and not preparing the power grid for the twenty-first century. It was almost as if the country had forgotten the benefits accrued from the GI Bill of Rights where millions of veterans went on to colleges and trade schools, forgotten the fact that everyone does better when everyone does better. That belief had been exchanged for ideas like greed is good, for financial engineering, and the offshoring of jobs to lower the cost of goods produced. The United States was experiencing an epidemic of amnesia.

The middle class of the post-war era had eroded to gated communities and MacAlpine-Bergen wealth. This is what the French seemed to know. But it was something that had rarely occurred to Jack before.

Laura and Jack talked as they walked to their apartment after a long day at the embassy. Jack was mad. "The French are always right about everything. And they want everyone to know it."

"Anton again?"

"Arrogant prick. That guy doesn't let a day go by without reminding me what an imperialistic dumb shit I am. Which I'm not."

"Of course not," Laura said, poking him in the ribs. "You're never a dumb shit, Jack."

"He thinks I don't know that we have an American empire. He's always bringing up Guam and American Samoa like I'm the one occupying them." He was walking faster as he spoke, feeling fury at being chastised every day for something he couldn't change. "It's not that we don't agree, for Chrissake."

"You think he's just trying to be one up?"

"He thinks I should be out demonstrating in the streets to free Guam."

"Well, they like to march in the streets in Paris, you know that."

"It's not my style," Jack answered, but he didn't really like how his answer sounded. "If I have to defend America every time I turn around, then maybe I shouldn't be a diplomat at all."

Laura was not surprised to hear him say this. She'd been thinking the same thing herself. Paris was such a wonderful city and she never grew tired of it. But work as an attaché seemed to her to be excessively polite and rigidly bureaucratic. Not her dream. "Maybe we shouldn't be diplomats."

"You either?"

It was the beginning of their conversations about a next move, and the beginning of reaching out to the intelligence community. By August of 2001, Jack and Laura were in deep cover and undergoing intensive training at a secret CIA facility.

SHOW OF FORCE

Everyone seemed very optimistic, even joyous, at the start of the new century. Though some aspects of the financial market were floundering, real estate was still doing well and so Alpine Homes continued to thrive no matter what Cameron III did. In the summer of 2001, the national intelligence services were picking up signs of terrorist activity around the globe—a suicide bomb here and a train attack there, a garage blown up, a buzz that should have sounded some alarm but did not. America was not paying attention. When the horror of September 11 was upon it, the country was not only shocked but indignant.

Lars Bergen was actually enraged. "We'll get whoever did this, goddammit," he hollered to the walls in his East Isles home. "Just like Pearl Harbor, we'll never forget where we were when this war began." He had been drinking imported coffee, the television news muted as he scribbled notes for a new poem. If he had not glanced up to pour some cream into his cup, he would not have seen the second plane crash into the south tower, burning jet fuel that sent black smoke high into the air above Manhattan.

In the days that followed, President Bush ordered an immediate halt to all civilian air traffic. The New York Stock Exchange closed, not to reopen for a week. And although Al-Qaeda and Osama bin Laden denied responsibility, Lars knew in his heart that they were responsible, and he also knew what the US should do. America needed to show them who was boss.

"I hope this second Bush has more guts than his old man," he muttered to himself. "This is why we have a military. We should bomb them back into the ninth century, for chrissake!"

On a military base 1,600 miles away, Lars had a son he did not know. Richard L.B. Scott carried only his biological father's initials in the center of his name. The only father he had ever heard about was a guy he'd never seen who he believed had died in Vietnam before he was born. He had not heard the story of how she had spent a night with an up-and-coming writer on his first book tour. In September of 2001, he knew none of it. So, of course, he could not know that a man named Lars Bergen had similar views to his own.

Richard had enlisted in the US Army as an eighteen-year-old. Growing up without money, with few prospects or role models, it had seemed to him that his most logical course would be military. Within a year, Richard was recognized for his intelligence and motivation. He moved into special operations, learned to be a skilled marksman, and became a believer in the American empire. In 2001, Richard had been in the service for almost a decade. The news of the attacks upset him and all his buddies on the base. As soon as the president declared war, they knew where they were heading. "That's the way it goes," one of Richard's friends complained. "Let's just hope we come back in one piece." It wasn't that they weren't brave, and they certainly were loyal patriots. There was no doubt about that. But the longer Richard and his fellow soldiers stayed in the military, the more they understood their reality. None of them were rich, educated men. They were of many colors and from many poor neighborhoods and they rose through the ranks because of how they performed, not who they were or whom they knew. The longer Richard and his fellow soldiers stayed in the military, the more they understood the class system in their beloved country.

Even so, Richard agreed with the father he did not know. "We've got to show them who's boss," he said after the attacks. None of his friends disagreed with him.

Jack and Laura were only a few years younger than Richard, but they were in that other class, that class of the educated and comfortable. They, too, wanted the United States to fight back and win. But they saw it through idealistic eyes. If anything, the attacks on the United States only solidified their commitment to be instruments of the government. Soon they would be done with their training. They planned to marry quickly in a civil ceremony that would not involve all the relatives making a fuss and would allow them to operate as a team, a rarity in the intelligence world, they had been told. They could hardly wait to begin. They might overthrow regimes, collect intelligence, pretend to be different people all over the world. In the sadness of the tragedy and the indignation of what had happened, Jack and Laura were ready to defend the greatest power on earth.

Susie and Sunny did not know what to think about anything anymore. They had felt so thrilled to cross over into the twenty-first century, as though living out a science fiction story, some kind of futuristic dream. But this? Men flying planes of innocent people into buildings? Random and unthinkable murder? "It's a good thing Cameron and Harold aren't alive to see this," Susie said over and over to Sunny. "It would have broken their hearts."

THE 9/11 COMMISSION REPORT

Richard returned home to North Carolina for his thirty days of furlough after eleven months in Kandahar. His wife, April Louise, did not let him have even one full glass of beer before telling him she wanted a divorce. April worked as a receptionist for an auto body shop and had fallen hopelessly in love with the lead mechanic. His name was Brad and, "Guess what," she told Richard, "he looks just like Brad Pitt." She apologized, but nonetheless asked him to take his things, which she had kindly packed for him, and please leave before Brad came by to take her out to dinner. "You never took me to dinner much, Richard," she added, with something like sadness in her voice. "But you're a good person. You'll find someone else." That was it.

He lugged his two boxes of personal items, which included his high school yearbook from Beattyville, Kentucky, over to the Motel 6 until he could get a room in one of the open barracks at Fort Bragg. For that first weekend, he didn't want to be around his fellow soldiers anyway. He had no heroic tales to tell and no wife to compare to the other wives and he was extremely tired.

He sat on a stool at the first 3-2 joint he could find, ordered a hamburger and a couple of beers for starters. The guy next to him had his eyes on the television above the bar. "Now they want us to believe the 9/11 attacks were our fault. The goddamn Arabs were flying those planes, we all know that, but now after three years of some bunch of lawyers poking around, they got this report, you gotta listen to these guys, you won't believe it, they think it all happened because we didn't catch 'em in the first place. The Arabs didn't want to learn to land a plane, how's that for a big fuckin' clue. Honest to god. My old man is rolling over in his grave what this country is coming to." He glanced at Richard. "Have you been listening to this crap?"

"Just got back from Afghanistan," Richard answered. "Feeling lucky to be alive."

"Shit. You don't want to listen to these guys then. Let me buy you another draft. Thing is we all love America, right? You go over to that hell hole of a desert and risk your life, so I know you love America. But all these commissions and committees and reports and baloney just take my tax money and yours and get us nowhere. Now they say we need another head spy to be on top of the CIA and FBI and then they'll hire more spies to spy on those spies to make sure that they all know that me and you are sitting here drinking beer two miles from Fort Bragg. Like we don't have enough people looking at us already. Goddamn television there is probably some kind of two-way bullshit watching us right this minute."

Richard had to laugh. This guy was actually cheering him up. Only in America could a military lifer sit next to a paranoid drunk and get the real take on what was happening. "Here's to ya," Richard said and knocked his glass into his neighbor's. "You're America, pal. That's what you are."

"Damn right. And so are you."

They watched television for a minute before Richard had to ask, "Do I look like anyone you ever saw in the movies?"

The guy took a long look. "Yeah maybe. Remember Tab Hunter? Could be you look like him."

Richard accepted that though he had no idea who Tab Hunter was. "Thanks," he said. "Good to know."

In fact, he looked just like Lars Bergen. But it would be several more years before he knew that.

Lars had reactions to the 9/11 report too. He was furious that it had taken so long and angry that the blame was on the United States for its "failure of imagination and failure of communications and failure of management." He didn't agree with any of it any more than Richard's companion in the 3-2 bar did. And the result of all that wasted time and energy was to enlist another level of management on the spying community. He'd made the mistake of showing up at his mother's seventy-sixth birthday party and having to listen to Andrew MacAlpine and his nephew Jack use all their government terminology to justify this new level of spy activity in America. It was enough to make him choke.

And though he started to argue his limited government views, he realized he was upsetting his mother, so he let it go. He'd wait until he got home, write an article under his pseudonym, Thor Larsson, and submit it to his favorite neoconservative publication.

Cleaning up after that party, Susie had asked, "What do you think Lars meant when he said that the attacks were a wake-up call? Did you understand what he meant?"

Sunny shook her head. "I don't think I understand Lars anymore at all, to tell you the truth. Every time he talks, I wonder did I really raise him. He's certainly not the Lars who worked so hard at his little lawn service. Remember that lawn service, Susie? If Harold were alive, I swear he might die all over again to hear his only son say America needs to know what it feels like to be attacked."

"Well, he's a professor, Sunny. He leads that Writers' Workshop and they all seem to love him, so maybe he just rambles when he's around all of us."

"I think he wants Andrew to argue with him. I really do."

"Why?"

Sunny put the last dish back into the cupboard. "Andrew's such a natural with everyone, you know. People just take to him, he's such a gentleman and a good listener. Look how Lena's girls have thrived with him and how kind he is to all of us. I mean, really Susie, he is nicer to me than Lars is. You know that. He stops by to visit us. He brings little things like those Scandinavian sweets or bouquets for no reason. He just makes my day, Andrew does." She sat down at the table. "And I think my son knows that. I think Lars knows that Andrew is the favorite and so without meaning to he just wants to strike Andrew down in some crazy argument about the United States being meddlers all over the world. Of all things. Payback. Did you hear him say that?"

Susie thought about the night's discussions. "Andrew didn't say much about it though. I mean, he just let Lars talk, didn't he?"

"That's what I mean. I think Lars wants Andrew to roll around in the dirt with him. Darn it."

"Don't worry about it," Susie said, but she was thinking how sad she felt for her friend to have lost one of her daughters and to have a son who didn't seem to care very much about anyone.

"Well, he's not too old to get married. Look how happy Jack and his new wife are. I love it when boys get married," she added, dreaming for a minute that her son would transform to someone tender and generous like her husband, Harold, had been.

"We were so blessed, weren't we, Sunny, to have husbands who were not only good businessmen and left us all so comfortable but also patriots who fought for our country? I'm proud every time I think about it."

"Me too. And I think we'll always have a great country. I mean, this new young man who spoke at the Democratic Convention, what was his name?"

"I can't remember his name," Susie answered, "but I remember he said he was a skinny kid with a funny name and that America had a place for him too."

They both smiled, recalling. "It was a good speech. I like thinking about hope, don't you?"

"The audacity of hope. That's what he said."

"Better than the audacity of gloom," Sunny said. And she meant it.

GEOGRAPHY AS DESTINY

Andrew MacAlpine was well aware of the underlying tensions between Lars Bergen and himself. Over the years, Lars had become a pre-WWII Lindbergh-America-First isolationist, whereas Andrew saw events globally. He believed in the largeness of the world's problems and the need for cooperation. But for the most part, Andrew chose not to think about Lars, who taught creative writing at his private college across the river, while Andrew held his distinguished fellow position at the University of Minnesota.

That fall semester of 2004, just weeks after the release of the 9/11 Commission's report, Andrew was thinking very much about what was causing the combustion in the world. When a student in his graduate seminar asked him what he thought happened to cause the 9/11 attack, Andrew stepped to the large world map on the wall to explain. "I would say 9/11 is a pressing example of the role geography plays in history. In destiny.

"Let's talk about Afghanistan," he said, "which has been feared for thousands of years because of her desolate deserts, rushing rivers, treacherous terrain, brave nomads, and fierce warriors. Centuries of invaders and traders have traversed the Silk Road through Afghanistan, and yet Afghanistan remains Afghanistan, not China, not Great Britain, not Russia, not the USSR. Or the USA, for that matter.

"You can see on this map how Kandahar Province sits between the southern tip of the Hindu Kush Mountains in central Afghanistan and the Registan Desert, with the desert forming the southern border of Afghanistan. That geography created tribes, and these tribes were separated from other tribes by mountains, valleys, rivers, and deserts. These separate tribes developed, over time, into political entities and states and nations. So the history of southern Afghanistan was shaped by the rivalries among tribes. These tribal warriors are some of the fiercest fighters in the world. Which is why Afghanistan is a perfect case to illustrate how geography becomes destiny."

Andrew took a moment and looked around the classroom, connecting with his students. "Please remember this, those who choose to go to war in Afghanistan do not go to war against only the Taliban, or the warrior tribes—they also go to war against the deserts and cave-filled mountains and rushing rivers.

"As we discuss the conflict in Afghanistan, please consider all the nations which blunted their swords, consumed their precious treasure, and forfeited their moral leadership when they attacked Afghanistan. History can be an excellent teacher if we listen to her lessons."

A SMALLER NUMBER OF PROPERTIES

Unfortunately Cameron III did not inherit his biological father's instinct for business, nor his inherent loyalty. Instead he seemed to have absorbed all the reckless tendencies of Cameron Junior and hated anything that was difficult. Being CEO of Alpine Homes was much more difficult than he'd ever imagined. Situations were dropped on his desk every day and he was expected to make snap judgments—and be right all the time. He was constantly being asked about things like whether zoning variances should be requested for Alpine Homes' new construction projects, how much to spend for remodeling aging buildings, what wages and benefits should be paid to non-union crews, and whom they should hire and train to replace Lucy Shaw, Jake Bachman, and other long-term team members who had left the company.

Cameron was certain the stress and strain of his job had caused his first marriage to fail. Annie had said as much during the divorce, and Bianca had been saying the same things lately, that he wasn't home enough and was distracted when he was home, a drink always in his hand. He didn't want to suffer through a second divorce. The idea of being a two-time loser at the marriage game was too painful to ponder. How would he ever get hooked up if he had to tell the truth about two failed relationships.

Now, in the summer of 2005, Cameron hoped the answer to his prayers might come from a complex real estate transaction Lewis Wright was pitching. Lewis claimed it would provide real estate diversification and a public-vehicle exit strategy. Lewis had assured him that he would structure the transactions in the most tax-efficient manner using an innovation called an Umbrella Partnership Real Estate Investment Trust known as an UPREIT.

Cameron got a bit dizzy listening to Lewis glibly rattle off tax code sections—a lot of fancy language, Cameron thought. But in essence, Alpine Homes would go to a Wall Street investment bank and exchange some of its main street properties for interests in a real estate vehicle. Meaning Cameron would have less work to do and more investments. The strategy involved several steps, including a Delaware Statutory Trust, but Lewis promised it could withstand IRS scrutiny if they dotted all the

I's and crossed all the T's. Cameron would be required to hold the real estate vehicle for a number of years before it would become fully liquid, a lock-up period, Lewis called it. However, if it worked, if nothing bad happened in the next three years, the countless questions and the endless pressure would be greatly reduced. Cameron could simply sit back in the chair his grandfather and father had sat in and rake in the dividends from the real estate vehicle.

Cameron smiled. Bianca would like that, he thought.

Lewis's proposal was very enticing but having the approval of Susie and Sunny was also important. He didn't want to downsize the business they and Cameron Senior and Harold Bergen had built without giving them his reasons. It wasn't as though he needed their permission, not legally anyway. Still, he invited himself to lunch at the home of his two grandmothers to share his plan. He would be positive about the UPREIT proposal and hope they agreed it was the right thing to do.

It was hard to be a star executive in a firm that his grandfather cofounded, that his dad ran day-to-day as president, and in which his younger brother had no interest. He knew how much his grandmothers prayed for his success now that the two previous Cameron MacAlpines had died.

Being close to the helm of their family business all his life had made Cameron III imagine he was ready to take control of the ship, be master of the everyday details, continue the good fortune of the family enterprises.

"You have the right ingredients," Grandma Sunny constantly told him. "A business degree, a good head on your shoulders. You can be the leader of a very successful firm."

But Grandma Sunny's encouraging words only glossed over an otherwise tired narrative. Cameron was third generation. He did not have what his grandfathers had. Cameron MacAlpine Senior and Harold Bergen had had grit and persistence, a desire to be in charge of their own fates, and a willingness to work the long hours needed to move their dreams to reality. Cameron III had never had to work long hours at anything. Everything had been handed to him. No amount of cheery bluster from a doting grandmother could mask Cameron III's obvious deficits in the critical areas of grit and perseverance.

The truth was, he was spoiled. He believed he was entitled to be on top, to be successful because of who he was. He had no concept of what it took to produce real estate properties for the community that were attractive and worth a second look. But he did like making money.

And so he invited himself to lunch with his grandmothers and told them the tale. Gold at the end of the rainbow. A tax-deferred exchange of some of their real estate holdings for stock in a real estate company which would be listed on the public securities markets.

They listened carefully, nodded encouragingly from time to time, and drank their tea. At the end of Cameron's dissertation, Sunny spoke. "If you think it's the right thing to do, then you should go and do it."

Cameron looked at Susie. She looked back and said, "What is the problem that this transaction is intended to solve?"

After some thought, Cameron shook his head.

Susie continued, "Does it take too many hours? Is that it? Because how you spend your days is, of course, up to you. Only you can choose how you spend your life."

Cameron nodded and finally said, "I'd be more comfortable with a smaller number of properties."

And so Cameron III accepted the proposal pitched to him by Lewis Wright. He was as happy as a kid in a candy store as he signed the necessary documents and smoked the celebratory cigar Lewis Wright handed him imagining how he would spend the dividends he would receive.

He and Bianca splurged and flew to Paris for a romantic getaway at the Four Seasons Hotel George V. The heavy burden of responsibility which had weighed him down was now removed and Cameron was light on his feet as he squired Bianca down the Champs-Élysées toward the Eiffel

Tower. Their days were filled with shopping and sightseeing and their evenings began with sumptuous dinners and ended with passionate love-making. They were sad, but sated, as their weeklong vacation ended and they returned to Minneapolis.

The Wall Street firm which had done the real estate exchange referred Cameron to a concierge wealth advisor. The advisor recommended Cameron take out a line of credit against his real estate holdings until they could be sold in the public securities market.

Cameron and Bianca spent lavishly throughout the autumn and winter of 2005-2006 and continued their sprees in the spring and summer of 2006. The properties still owned by Alpine Homes continued generating steady rental income throughout that year, even though 2006 saw steep increases in national foreclosure rates. Bianca remodeled their house in time for an elaborate celebration that Christmas of 2006. Everyone who was anyone in the Twin Cities was there.

In 2007, Cameron and Bianca relied on their line of credit to make ends meet. Grandma Susie wrote in her diary that she feared her grandson was living a champagne life and wondered how it would end.

The credit crisis of August 2008 took most people by surprise. Subprime loans and collateralized debt obligations crashed in value and so did the not-yet-liquid real estate interests Cameron held. He was told to repay the balance on his line of credit immediately and had to liquidate his investment portfolio to do it.

All that was left were the few properties Alpine Homes hadn't sent to Wall Street.

And, learning this, Bianca filed for divorce.

FOUR:
The Fall

COAL COUNTRY

Rose Mary Scott was born in Coal Country, in Eastern Kentucky, far away from the American Dream, that part of America where hillbillies mined coal. Where the white underclass lives and dies. Rose Mary grew up in Appalachia in a pocket of aching poverty surrounded by a land of wealth and opportunity. She was ten years old in 1964 when, in response to a national poverty rate approaching 20 percent, President Lyndon Johnson came to a small town in Eastern Kentucky and made it the face of his War on Poverty. The television coverage of Johnson's visit to Appalachia was all Congress needed before passing the Economic Opportunity Act in March. The nation had seen for themselves, in black-and-white or full color, the ground zero of poverty—its broken porches, rusted cars, and barefoot children.

Like her ma and pa, Rose Mary always dreamed of escaping. Growing up, she imagined the life she would have with marriage, children, a home of her own, and self-reliance. Then just like her ma she got pregnant. She'd taken the bus to Louisville, her first trip to a big city to see if she might like it there someday, might aspire to Louisville or some city like Louisville for the grand life she'd always imagined. She was so pretty back then, so rounded out and unsuspecting.

She'd wandered into a bookstore because she'd never seen one before and there was a writer reading from his book about the Vietnam War. He looked like a god to her, powerful and larger than life. His voice boomed out into all the store and he caught her eye and she stayed to see what would happen. She remembered riding home from that trip on a gauzy wave. Three months later she knew she was pregnant.

When little Richard L.B. Scott was born, Rose Mary deposited him with her parents, who already had so many children, it seemed one more would not tip the scales any more in their disfavor. She took a mail-order bookkeeping class. Correspondence school, she called it. She graduated with a certificate of completion and was grateful to eventually find a part-time job at the Star Motel on the county road outside of Beattyville. At least she wasn't waiting tables, she told herself. She dressed in a skirt and blouse every day and fixed her hair kind of tame—like a bookkeeper.

The Star Motel was a place where newlyweds driving through the mountains would stop for the night, and traveling salesmen as well, and retired couples out to see the world. The rooms were clean, the televisions and telephones worked, and the little soaps in the bathroom smelled like the pine trees out back. Rose Mary was proud to say she worked there. But then the new expressway came through and the Star Motel struggled. Cars just zipped past Beattyville, possibly not even aware it existed.

When her job at the motel disappeared, she was fortunate to be hired as a teller trainee at Home Federal, the local branch of a regional bank, right in the center of town and across from the Presbyterian Church. Rose Mary was happy to have full-time work as a teller before she had even turned thirty. She made a little more money, helped her parents out with their bills, and spent time teaching Richard math and card games. Every Saturday night she went out for dinner and dancing with a guy she'd met when she worked at the motel. He sold cleaning supplies in the region, moving from town to town all week until he could zip by Rose Mary's on his night off to take her out on the town. They always went to the same roadside restaurant and ordered the barbeque. Then they went to another roadside joint to dance the two-step. Robby John Wills was his name, and he was a very good dancer.

She was surprised the first time she got a severe headache. She'd never known such pain before in her life and had no idea where it came from or why it fell on her. Nobody in her family had ever had such things though her ma coached her to spread Vicks VapoRub on her forehead and lie still in the dark. But it didn't work. After she'd missed a few too many days at the bank and had staggered in too many more days barely able to function, her best friend Wilma came to her rescue.

Wilma, who was the lead teller and someone to trust, offered Rose Mary something she called her pep pills which she said had changed her life. "I never get sick," she told Rose Mary. "Honestly, you won't believe how good you feel. The headaches will go away, you'll feel twice as happy and twice as productive and you'll lose weight in the bargain. Not that you need to," she added, "but it's amazing how you never feel hungry on these pills. They're a true miracle."

Wilma was right. The pills were like a miracle and Rose Mary made sure she had prescriptions to take her from one day to another. It was the 1980s then, a decade that turned out to be good for her. She saw her son grow tall and strong, good at sports and destined to be an all-star athlete. She didn't mind that her mother needed more financial help after her father died, although that made it harder for her to set aside a dime for any rainy days to come. She did, however, always manage to have money for the little white pills that got her out of bed in the morning.

When Bill Clinton won the presidency in 1992, she thought life would get even better in Appalachia since he had been governor of Arkansas. He had that hillbilly feel for life, she thought, and he'd raise them up some. She was also secretly in love with him but so were half the women in the South. One thing they knew about Bill Clinton—he liked women.

By this time she was dating a coal miner named Billy Ray who always seemed to need money for his car or for gambling. Rose Mary often loaned him money, which was never repaid. She tried to reform him but he couldn't seem to stay away from Big Bob's tavern and the illegal poker table in the back room. Late Saturday night, December 19, Rose Mary sat on a barstool and watched the television news. The House of Representatives had voted to impeach Clinton for perjury and obstruction of justice. A wave of fury overcame her as she strode into the back room and dragged Billy Ray away from his losing streak and out of Big Bob's place. She noticed a twinge of pain in her back as she drove her drunken boyfriend to his trailer. Rose Mary broke up with Billy Ray that weekend. In the weeks that followed, her back pain got so bad she could hardly get out of bed. She asked Wilma to help her with the constant pain and Wilma handed her a container of OxyContin pills. "When did I ever steer you wrong?" Wilma asked as she watched her friend take the pills that, in Wilma's mind, were gold in a bottle. Rose Mary felt immediate relief.

But in the world, things were sliding downhill. Bill Clinton made way for George Bush and the dream of an Appalachian revival simply died. The 2000s were just plain bad. The price of coal continued its decades-long decline. Employment in Kentucky dried up as mining companies moved their operations to the cheaper fields in Wyoming. Senator McConnell claimed to be protecting his state from the people who were against coal, but Rose Mary knew there were fewer and fewer paychecks being deposited in bank accounts at her branch and more and more residents receiving public assistance. Rose Mary's paycheck was barely enough for groceries, rent, and her pain pills.

The real estate collapse and financial crisis on Wall Street hit the banking industry hard. Rose Mary drove to work through an early season snowstorm on the day her branch was closed and she was laid off. She was fifty-four years old. Fifty-four and out the door. By the end of 2008, Rose Mary—like much of Appalachia—was struggling with joblessness, hopelessness, and opioid addiction. Her parents had both died, her son was a soldier in Afghanistan, and her life seemed something like leftover twigs on the outlier's path.

SEEDING THE FUTURE

There were those who didn't suffer. Unlike Rose Mary, Sunny Bergen and Susie MacAlpine were in that 1 percent sufficiently protected, a financial cushion wrapped around them like down coats in winter. In their many talks over coffee in their Kenwood kitchen, they considered what they might do to help others not as fortunate as they were. The Bergen-MacAlpine Family Foundation was the ultimate result of their considerations. And Susie decided to use the occasion of her eightieth birthday in June of 2009 to announce this endeavor—and to urge everyone to contribute as well.

In honor of how much Cameron and Harold loved to fish, Susie threw a down-to-earth fish fry on Saturday, June 20, out in the backyard with river birch and mountain ash draping all around them. The kids all came, and many of their lifelong friends. Even Lars chose to grace their presence for a plate of fresh fried walleye.

Andrew picked up Ellie Mae and drove over to their mothers' house in Kenwood where she had lived with Cameron Junior, briefly, after their marriage. The two had already biked that neighborhood earlier as they did many Saturdays. For almost twenty years, since they both returned to Minneapolis and Lena died, they were the best of friends, true siblings of the heart, and turned to one another for understanding and companionship.

Ellie Mae went in to let Susie and Sunny know they had arrived as Andrew stationed himself halfway between the greenhouse and the party tent, perfectly positioned to see everyone as they came up the walk.

Jack and his wife, Laura, were the first guests and Andrew was right there to greet them. "Good to see you. It's been forever since you were here."

Jack and Laura answered together, "Good to see you." Laura laughed. "Married seven years and we still talk at the same time!"

Jack chuckled. "That's a good sign, isn't it, Uncle Andrew?"

"It is indeed."

Ellie Mae squealed when she saw Jack and Laura. "The spies! Oh my goodness, the spies have arrived." She hugged her younger son and his wife and for at least a minute would not let go. When she did, she whispered dramatically, "The grandmas have their cameras ready to go, so be prepared to have your pictures taken."

Just then Richie Nelson and Lewis Wright walked into the yard together. They saw Lars standing just to the side of the drinks table, a flute of champagne in hand. Lars waved a careless greeting to them, spilling some bubbly on his sleeve. "Drinks over here, guys." He handed a glass to each man as they approached.

Lewis took a sip and said, "How's the teaching business?"

Lars scowled. "Can't say a damn thing nowadays. Too politically correct, if you ask me."

"We're living in a new world, Lars. Better get with the program."

"I liked it better the way it used to be."

"It's a good time to be an attorney though, Lars. Everybody is suing everybody."

Richie piped up, "Your problems are nothing compared to living in the post Bernie Madoff era." Richie's financial services business had made it through the recession and was now inundated with regulations and paperwork beyond anything he had ever imagined. "If Jimmy were alive and working with me now, he would die all over again."

The three men laughed. Thinking of Jimmy cheered them up. "Wonder what your brother would have thought of our new president," Lars said, rolling his eyes.

"I'll bet you think he's a Muslim," Lewis poked at Lars.

Lars scowled but did not answer. He saw Annette Freeman and Linda Horton coming his way and hurried across the yard in the other direction to avoid having to talk to them. The thought of Annette Freeman in a lesbian relationship with Linda Horton was more than he could face. As he left his friends, he called over his shoulder, "I don't know what news you guys watch, but I'd like to see Obama's birth certificate."
Lars always made an exit.

Andrew saw Tommy Buffalo and Nelson Coleman coming toward him, one tall and one short. Close friends since rooming together at the university, they were outwardly different, one Native American and one African American, but both inwardly driven to serve their own communities in need. Andrew waved and called out a pleasant greeting. "Gentlemen. Welcome."

"It's good to see you, brother Andrew," Nelson said, in his deep and pastoral voice. "Mrs. Coleman had some family business, but she gave me a card for Susie. She's quite a person, your mother is, Andrew. You are lucky to have been raised up by a woman of such substance."

Ellie Mae saw her old tennis friends arrive together. She was happy to receive messy lipstick kisses from Carol, Diane, and Merrilee. All four had married early and all four were divorced. They still played tennis together and the other three were regulars at Ellie Mae's yoga classes, hoping Quiet Inspiration would descend upon them. Ellie Mae was chatting comfortably with them as her older son made his entrance.

Cameron MacAlpine III, holding the hand of a very young and slender woman, walked to Susie's table and introduced Chloe to his grandmothers. When they wandered off to find a place to sit, Sunny turned to her friend and asked, "Do we call her his girlfriend or his significant other?"

"Maybe we just call her Chloe."

After the plates were cleared, Andrew rose, tapped his water glass with his knife, and called out, "Where are my tenors?" After the laughter died down, he led the gathering in a heartfelt rendition of Happy Birthday.

"And many more, mom. Do you want to say a few words?"

"Yes, Andrew. Thank you. Thank you one and all for coming to celebrate my birthday. I'll be an octogenarian on Monday. Can you believe it?" Susie smiled. "My granddaughter Sarah gave me a lovely birthday card with a bunch of calculations on it. She wrote that I've been on this planet for more than 29,000 days."

"Two and one-half billion seconds, Grandma, don't forget that!"

"Thank you, Sarah. I grew up over by Seven Corners and have lived in Minneapolis my entire life. I was the youngest child so I was raised mostly by my sisters after my mother died. I met Sunny my first day of school and we've been best friends since. We've been together during warm summers and cold winters, nourished by our school and church communities as often and as much as by our family and friends.

"A birthday is a great time to celebrate one's blessings. Here we are today in the community which has permitted Alpine Homes to succeed beyond my wildest dreams. I know how fortunate we've been. Sunny and I are blessed to have accumulated wealth beyond our earthly needs. Now is the time to give back some of that wealth.

"We have created the Bergen-MacAlpine Family Foundation. Lewis Wright helped us with the legal paperwork that was required. He kept his mouth shut, as he promised to do, so I get to tell you our secret tonight. The Bergen-MacAlpine Family Foundation has been granted tax-exempt status by the IRS and will soon distribute money to those who have so little and need so much.

"We looked past this high hill where we make our home and saw the sad harshness of life just north of here, and southeast of here. With this family foundation we make a public pledge to do good for our youngest neighbors. The focus of our effort is on children in poverty and we ask you to join with us.

"Our first grants go to two pre-kindergarten programs. They are the Minneapolis programs organized by Reverend Nelson Coleman on the North Side and by Tribal Elder Tommy Buffalo in the Phillips neighborhood.

"In making these initial grants, we chose action instead of despair. We know the deep joy which comes from giving and we're confident of the good work Nelson and Tommy will do with these added resources. Sunny and I invite you to help us build a more just and equitable future. Please give what you can. Thank you."

Everyone was still clapping as Ellie Mae rose to her feet, "You can count on me!"

Andrew, standing next to Tommy Buffalo, congratulated him on his work. Tommy's childlike quality and artistic sensibility had always made him a natural with young people. "I admire what you're doing, Tommy."

Tommy grinned. "My grandpa the Medicine Man would be surprised to see me off the reservation, working with these young pups and making art out of old Detroit auto parts."

"You know, I could use some car art, Tommy. It's what these Kenwood yards need, don't you think?"

"Well, I've got mobiles too, Andrew. Think of that. Some old carburetor hanging from your ceiling?" The two men laughed amidst the happy energy around them.

Susie's announcement had put a wonderful signature on a special birthday gathering. Pledges of support were enthusiastically made by almost everyone. Except Lars Bergen and Cameron MacAlpine III.

Lars didn't believe anything Susie had said. Some people's kids just needed to pull themselves up by their bootstraps, he thought. He slipped away from the enthusiastic crowd and walked home. On his way, he began composing a Thor Larsson op-ed about the dangers of socialism.

Cameron tried to hide his disappointment behind a forced smile. He and the shrunken Alpine Homes portfolio had barely survived the Great Recession. He had secretly hoped his grandmothers would give him some money so he could buy more properties.

A VISIT WITH LUCY

Since The Cube warehouse enterprise was established in 1980, it had continued to thrive. Occupants like The Writers' Workshop, *Citizen of the World* magazine, and the Neurological Rehabilitation Clinic had maintained offices since the building was refurbished and opened for lease by Alpine Homes. Cameron III had inherited this successful venture and had managed to hang on to it throughout his leveraging maneuvers and the recession. But it was starting to get a little shabby and he'd been hoping his grandmothers would give him additional funds to upgrade The Cube to a Class A property with WIFI throughout and LEED-certification so that he could raise the rents and attract new and larger businesses to the building. He was dreaming big for a reason. Under his leadership, Alpine Homes had shrunk in value with fewer assets under management and a much-reduced stream of monthly income. They were no longer a major player in the city and that's what Cameron III wanted. He wanted to be a major player.

He didn't blame Lewis Wright for his leveraging advice. Nobody in the family blamed Lewis Wright. Who knew that the stock market would crash and they'd have to pay back the debt so soon? Nobody could have known that would happen.

But the result left Cameron III with this small-potatoes company and not much obvious path back to what it used to be. His father and grandfather had the benefit of the administrative expertise and discipline of Lucy Shaw who was now seventy-nine years old and had been retired for nine years, though she still lived in the Alpine building where the company had its offices. Cameron III had never been very interested in the old woman, but now he was feeling desperate. His grandmothers' plan to be do-gooders all over town with the family money scared him. Was he really on his own?

On a cloudy, gloomy Wednesday in January of 2010, he walked down the hall from his office to Lucy Shaw's apartment and knocked on the door. She answered, dressed as always in a crisp blouse and tidy skirt. She was clearly surprised to see him, but she kept her voice neutral. "Is something wrong?"

"I was hoping you'd give me some business advice, Mrs. Shaw." Cameron had always been afraid of her formality and didn't dare call her Lucy. He glanced nervously into her apartment.

"Come in, Cameron. I'm having a cup of coffee; may I pour one for you?" She pointed him to a neat table in her tidy kitchen, and he sat where she indicated.

"I take mine black. Will that be okay, Cameron?"

"Yes, please."

She handed him a cup of steaming black coffee and sat across from him.

"Now, how can I help you?"

"Well, I know you helped my dad and grandfather with this business and I was wondering if you could do the same for me too. I mean, maybe give me some advice."

"What do you want to accomplish, Cameron?"

"I'd like to grow the business, Mrs. Shaw."

"Yes, it's a much smaller company now than it was." She took a sip of her coffee and waited for him to continue.

"I'm thinking I'd like to upgrade The Cube downtown, you know, make it a real landmark. And then maybe do the same with a few other buildings down there close to the river. It's a hot area, don't you think?" The woman made him so nervous.

"It is a very hot area. Your grandfather always said it would be. He had good instincts about real estate." She smiled to remember her former employer and the love of her life. "He would have liked making The Cube a landmark." She nodded to herself. "But you will need cash, won't you?"

"Well, that's what I'm thinking. You know the family money is going into that foundation now so..."

"Yes, that's a good thing Susie and Sunny are doing. You can always try for a loan, Cameron. Do you have a good relationship with your bank?" She saw in his face that he did not. "Or you could do some work with the city and perhaps get financing that way. I seem to recall Cameron and Harold discussing that possibility years and years ago. What do you think of that?"

"Yeah, I suppose. I don't know anybody." He gulped his coffee. "What do you think if I asked some others in the family for financing. I mean, it's a family business, right? And you think my idea is a good idea so maybe they will think so, too, right?"

Lucy Shaw nodded. Clearly Cameron III preferred money that was handed to him rather than money he went out and negotiated. He was not interested in taking on risk, possibly because he knew he would somehow manage to trip himself up one way or the other and lose. She did not know what else she could say to him.

"I wish you luck, Cameron," she concluded, but she did not invite him to come and chat with her again in the future. Cameron III had negative attitudes toward women, deep feelings that they couldn't be trusted. Like his father, he knew in his bones that women ultimately deceive and disappoint their men, and soon after leaving Lucy's apartment, he understood she'd dropped him flat.

The next day he went to visit his Uncle Lars about putting some money into The Cube, knowing Lars had offices in the building and loved it. They met for lunch at the café on the main floor. Cameron III jumped right into his pitch, "Uncle Lars, I need money to renovate this building, make it a Class A property. I could boost the rents and turn it into a real gold mine. What do you think?"

Lars was skeptical, "Rents are already pretty steep, Cameron. What needs doing?" He leaned back, drank his wine, and listened to Cameron share his vision for The Cube.

"Have you talked to your banker? Any luck there?"

"No loans from them until I get more private capital."

"Typical." Lars chuckled. "It's a rare day when a banker says yes."

They finished their lunch in silence, and Lars picked up the check. "I might be willing to talk to my bank, cosign on a renovation loan, if you and I agreed to some side terms. Got any interest, Cameron?"

The younger man nodded without hesitation. Money on the line was worth any side term his uncle could come up with, of that he was certain. And he flinched only slightly when Lars detailed his interest in Cameron's beautiful ex-girlfriend Chloe and her equally beautiful young friends. "Just an introduction, Cam," Lars concluded. "Just an introduction."

RIKA'S REVOLUTION

By age sixty-five, Lars Bergen had evolved into his alter ego, Thor Larsson. Thor was just as brilliant and good looking as Lars, but he seethed publicly, his rage against women who wanted power or minorities who wanted equality the topic for any editorial, article, or book he thought it important to write. Now, in the presidential campaign of 2012, Thor climbed on his stallion to lash out against the incumbent Barack Obama. It was the campaign of Makers Versus Takers, with white and wealthy Mitt Romney against the bleeding-heart Democrats who were always willing to give handouts to any ne'er-do-well who couldn't find a job. All the deficits for hundreds of years through every president that came before were laid to rest at the feet of Barack Obama.

While Lars Bergen cavorted at night with several of Chloe's willing friends, Thor Larsson wrote by day of the darkness that was encompassing America. *You Will Not Replace Us* spun out tales of a country in decline and in fear of a revolution—debt, decadence, and the wrong people thinking the wrong things. His publisher loved it, knowing there was a ready audience just waiting to revel in the exciting vitriol on every page. Survivalists and supremacists were hungry for just this kind of rhetoric and the publisher hurried to release the book early in 2013, just as Barack Obama began his second term as president.

Lars as Thor did not accept any speaking engagements, of course, because he chose to keep his college creative writing position, though it was often difficult to listen to the impassioned liberalism of his students. Moreover Lars did not want to jeopardize the national reputation and cachet of The Writers' Workshop. Rika Heikkila, who had worked for Lars for over twenty years, had sensed his true nature for a very long time. He was happy to have her run the workshop, but he had no interest in her as a person. Sometimes Lars would work in The Writers' Workshop offices for whole days without ever even seeing her there. He ignored her completely and dismissed her totally, and whenever she mentioned anyone who was a humanitarian hero in her opinion, she saw Lars freeze and his jaw tighten. She did not know he was Thor Larsson but, in her intuitive and poetic way, she knew there was evil within him. She stayed simply because she loved the workshop each year and she loved all the people she met doing the annual event. The job paid her bills and kept her in a circle of talented and successful writers. Her longevity had nothing to do with Lars.

In 2014, on the last day of The Writers' Workshop, Donovan Miller of the British Columbia Federation of Writers, offered Rika the executive director position for his organization beginning immediately. "You are a gem in this business, Rika," he told her. "I've admired you for years." It didn't seem that Donovan quite realized Lars Bergen existed.

But Lars did exist and he was furious. "After all I've done for you. You came here a nothing little poet with not a credit to your name and now you go behind my back with my mailing list of contacts and solicit a job offer. You ungrateful bitch."

She chose not to argue. She turned and left him still spewing expletives at her back as she put her laptop into her book bag and closed the door behind her. Lars could not begin to know everything she had done each year to prepare for the workshop, mailing list or not. Driving away she laughed at the thought of Lars Bergen trying to organize the event that she had nurtured for twenty-three years and that his sister Lena had nurtured for a decade before that.

Lars stayed angry for weeks. Once a day he stormed into Rika's office and rummaged through the files in a hopeless rampage looking for some magic clue to what she had done, but he had no idea where to find anything nor where to turn for assistance. In truth, Lena had trained Rika. Lars had never run The Writers' Workshop and he knew it. Worse, he knew Rika knew he knew it. He returned to *You Will Not Replace Us* and reread his chapters on the misguided power of the American woman. Fuck them all.

RICHARD'S UNREST

Richard Scott was awake half the night in his bed at Camp Swift near Austin, Texas. For the past two months, he'd been involved in a realistic military training exercise code named Jade Helm 15 and would be there one more month until September 2015. Everything about this assignment weighed on him. He could hardly wait to get back to Fort Bragg and his normal duties as an instructor for US Army Advanced Special Operations Training.

Jade Helm, a routine US military exercise, was causing mass hysteria in the American Southwest and bringing out the worst in his soldiers. As their chief warrant officer, Richard was always separate and alone. He hadn't had a woman in his life since his divorce, he was too old to pal around with the soldiers in his charge and was noticing more and more the divisions around him. The military reflected the nation it served. This combustion in the ranks could only be a sign of larger trouble in the country. That's what was keeping Richard awake.

The afternoon before, he had broken up a fight during an Infowars broadcast. Host Alex Jones had said that the federal government was preparing to invade Texas. "They're going to practice breaking into things. This is going to be hellish," Jones said. "Now this is just a cover for deploying the military on the streets . . . This is an invasion . . . preparation for the financial collapse and maybe even Obama not leaving office." That was what the soldiers heard.

A Green Beret took offense at Jones's remarks. A Navy Seal expressed a contrary opinion, and the fisticuffs began. Richard stepped between the men and took a few blows before the combatants obeyed his order to stand down. Getting cooperation from competing military units during realistic military exercises was always a challenge. Nowadays the airwaves were so filled with alternative facts and conspiracy theories that keeping discipline was almost impossible. When had the United States lost its civility? He could not believe the trash bombarding his men daily.

Richard mentally prepared for another day of Jade Helm exercises. He was confident guns would not be confiscated, no attacks would be made against civilians, but he feared another right-wing evangelical insisting that Obama was a grave threat to God and country could spark violence amongst his soldiers.

Earlier that week he had been in a briefing with Army brass. A colonel told them that a survey showed one-third of Republicans believed the Jade Helm conspiracy theory, this wild-eyed story that "the government is trying to take over Texas," and another survey said 28 percent of GOP voters hadn't made up their minds yet about the matter. The right-wing frenzy over Jade Helm had even swept up the Republican governor of Texas and several other GOP leaders who wondered aloud and in public if the drill was part of Obama's plan to seize Texas, impose martial law, and throw conservatives into closed Walmart stores that had been converted into FEMA camps. It was all sad and impossible to Richard.

He remembered his hot and dusty drive from Fort Bragg down to Camp Swift. Radio stations provided some distraction as he drove, coming in clearly at first and later fading into a maddening buzz of static. Many stations covered Donald Trump's ride down the golden escalator at Trump Tower, as well as his remarks, "When Mexico sends its people, they're not sending their best . . . They're sending people that have lots of problems, and they're bringing those problems with [them]. They're bringing drugs. They're bringing crime. They're rapists. And some, I assume, are good people." Richard was not particularly partisan; however, he decided he could not vote for the star of *The Apprentice* reality television show. Richard was proud to have served with many honorable Latino soldiers and was disgusted at the un-American nature of Trump's remarks.

Richard had been raised to believe that God was on the side of America, that it was God who wanted white settlers to dominate the people and lands of North America. One nation under God with God on our side. He was no longer certain of this. More and more lately, he wasn't satisfied by the old narratives. He had doubts about America's wars and his role in them and his sleep suffered.

Richard was a soldier, had become a lifer in the blink of an eye, and had seen combat in hot spots for almost twenty-five years. Morning came and he pulled himself together as usual. He looked like the career soldier he had become, lean and mean and prepared to meet the day. At the same time, he realized he was dreaming about the day when he would drive away for good.

ELLIE MAE TALKS WITH SUSIE

Ellie Mae had always loved Susie MacAlpine. Susie was practical and solid and not nearly as accommodating as her own mother. She knew the business of Alpine Homes better than anyone in the family. These days Ellie found herself more and more troubled by her older son's business dealings and needed Susie's input. Ellie jumped right in when she heard Susie's strong voice answer, "Hello, Ellie. How nice to hear from you."

"Susie, I want to talk to you about the calls I keep getting from Cam. He just about breaks down telling me he hasn't made much progress getting The Cube rented up. He sounds so desperate and I don't know what to make of it. He inherited the family business!"

Susie could hear the concern in Ellie Mae's voice. "I'm sorry, I guess it was inevitable. Ever since Bianca walked out and hit him with a divorce claim that locked up his home equity, if he has any, he's been asking all of us for funds. He's already asked Sunny, and me, and Lucy, and Lars, so it's not surprising that he would come to you. We think his cash flow wasn't big enough to support his lifestyle with Bianca. Lifestyle, that's what they like to call it."

"Cam also said he needed a big check from me to pay off some back taxes. Is that true?"

"Not exactly. Your son got caught inflating valuations on his bank loan application at the same time he got caught trying to persuade a county appraiser to lower the real estate assessment on The Cube. Cameron settled that thing with the county attorney, but the bank got suspicious and called in his loans. Now he's trying to find a new lender at the same time he's still fighting the county about what would be a fair assessment. He's got more lawyers than Carter has liver pills."

Ellie Mae was silent for a moment, realizing the stories Cam had told her weren't truthful. "Did Cam do some deal with the price of gold?"

Susie made a noise. "Your son should steer clear of stockbrokers. He didn't learn his lesson when he leveraged up that fancy tax deal years ago. Now he's on the wrong side of gold bullion, I guess."

"Gold bullion?"

Susie paused for a moment. "Actually it was options on the price of gold futures, that's what it was. He's in over his head again. Confidentially, Ellie Mae, your son cannot swim with the sharks. They eat him up every time."

"At least he didn't buy a franchise in Trump University," Ellie interjected. "The fraud trials over that scam are in the newspapers every week."

Susie agreed. "I guess we can be thankful he didn't get hooked by that con man." She paused. "Are you thinking of helping him out?"

"I don't know. I'm not sure if that's the right thing to do."

"Your mother and I have decided not to give him any more money. When we told him that, he asked us for an advance on his inheritance, like we were steps away from the grave. It broke your mother's heart."

Ellie Mae was stunned. "I'm so sorry to hear that. It's hard to understand his desperation when he had so much to start with—the business, his trust. How can you blow that much money?"

"I agree, Ellie, but he thinks big and can't make it happen. Then he gets angry. He seems to be angry all the time."

"He should be doing meditation with me. That's what I'm going to talk to him about. I moved into The Cube years ago just to give him my rent. I guess it didn't make any difference."

Then Susie changed subjects. "Ellie, have you talked to your brother lately?"

"Not for a while."

"You know how Lars has always gone his own way. Last week the public radio station was doing its fundraiser so Sunny started moving the dial around to find something interesting and you won't believe what she heard. A man on another station was talking about a coming civil war. A civil war here in the United States. And Sunny was certain it was your brother. Stopped her cold in her tracks. Of course, we hope it wasn't him, but Sunny kept saying she could recognize her son's voice anywhere."

"I wonder why Lars would be talking about a civil war on the radio? What does that have to do with his Writers' Workshop?"

"He gave a different name. But Sunny said it was definitely his voice saying those crazy things. Sunny got so scared she turned it off."

Susie MacAlpine reflected on her conversation with Ellie Mae for days. The world was becoming a place she did not know in that comfortable way she had known the world when she, Cameron Senior, Harold, and Sunny had built their business on hard work, decency, and a love for their country and its citizens. Her oldest son had drowned drinking. Cameron III could not hold on to a marriage and had no children to carry on the business. Lars thought there would be a civil war in America. A man like Donald Trump thought he could be president. This was not where she ever imagined things would lead. Her husband would have been so sad to see it. The death of dreams. That's how it seemed.

RICHARD GOES HOME FOR CHRISTMAS

Richard Scott threw his duffel, packed with a few civilian clothes and toiletries, into the back seat of his car and began the 420-mile drive northwest toward the small town in Kentucky where he had been raised. Nearly three months had passed since the successful completion of the Jade Helm operation, but Richard had not been able to get that realistic training exercise out of his mind. He'd imagined a visit with his mother during the holiday season and a change of scenery might improve his mood.

Richard realized his fingers were numb from fiercely gripping the steering wheel as he stopped to refuel two hours away from home. Easing his large frame out of the car, he rubbed his hands together briskly as he walked toward the service station. He'd been driving for almost six hours, thinking about his mother and her life, thinking about his place in her life. He'd left her the day after graduating high school and had built a successful military life. Expert Infantryman Badge, Ranger Tab, Airborne Badge, Bronze Star, and other medals of honor had been bestowed on him by a grateful nation, but he'd failed at marriage and had not gone home to see his mother in years. He hadn't given her any grandchildren and he hadn't given her much thought.

Now he drove into town a stranger. Richard turned onto River Drive, glanced down at Crystal Creek, and remembered himself as a teenager, swimming and fishing in the cool waters which flowed into the Kentucky River, a tributary of the Ohio. Nearly a quarter of a century had passed by and the Scott family had left this small town or died, as had his grandpa and grandma. Richard turned onto the road which led to his mother's house and immediately slowed his car to a crawl, bumping along, trying to avoid the largest of the potholes on the old gravel road. Richard could barely make out the scrawled Scott on the mailbox, which was nearly rusted through, leaned precariously, and appeared to have a newspaper dangling on the lid.

Back in Beattyville again, Richard thought, as he parked where grass and weeds showed through the oiled gravel. The wooden house Rose Mary had inherited from her parents needed paint, shingles, and care, reinforcing the gloom of a late afternoon day without sunshine in one of the poorest congressional districts in the nation. He'd known during his growing-up years that the Scotts were dirt poor. No one needed to tell him that there wasn't enough of anything. That was one of the reasons Richard had chosen a military life, a cot and three square meals a day were promised to those who served.

He grabbed his duffel, arranged a smile on his face, and walked toward the door. He did not expect the woman who opened it. Rose Mary had lost at least thirty pounds. Hugging her, Richard could feel the sharp bones beneath her bulky sweater.

"Mama, are you sick?"

"Never mind me. You look very fine, Richard," she said, and started to cry. "Things here kind of falling apart."

Richard glanced around. The house was shabby, needing cleaning and color. "Do you want me to go out and chop you a Christmas tree? We could make some popcorn and decorate like we used to?"

He found himself stroking her hand almost feverishly, as though it were up to him to keep her blood flowing.

"Nothing's like it used to be. I got some kind of cancer here, Richard. Lost my appetite. I don't know. Old Doc White tells me to take it easy, not to worry."

It was clear to Richard that his mother was dying. He should have come sooner. He could have saved her. If he lost her, what would he have left in the world?

"Mama, I'll take care of you."

She leaned her head back on the worn sofa and sighed. "Maybe you will, Richard."

That afternoon, Richard called the Kentucky River Medical Center in Jackson, persuaded a doctor to come to the house, and heard Rose Mary admit she was in quite a bit of pain. He saw the doctor frown and tell Rose Mary that pain relief was the only thing that could be done for her. After the doctor administered a dose of morphine, arranged for daily hospice visits, and left, Rose Mary slumped onto her pillow. "That's better than any stuff I've ever had before."

Once his mother was resting, Richard went out behind the house, cut a small pine tree, and secured it in a bucket of wet sand. He put it in the corner of Rose Mary's room and draped several of her colorful scarves along its branches. When she opened her eyes a few hours later, the sight of the tree made her laugh, the deep and pained laugh of the dying.

"I'll be damned. Aren't you something."

Richard pulled a chair over to sit close to her. "I'm sorry I've been gone so long, Mama. I'm so sorry about that."

"You made me proud, son. I always had a story to tell around here and that's something in life."

Her smile was so weak. "You do have a father out there somewhere, you know."

She closed her eyes so that she wouldn't have to see her son's reaction. It was nothing she ever planned to say or expected to say. Her encounter with Lars Bergen was so far in the past that most of the time she had trouble believing it was true. But her son looked just like Lars Bergen. He was the living memory of that encounter.

Richard thought she was drifting out of reality. "Tell me," he said.

And quietly she did. She was young and on her first trip away from home. The writer in the bookstore looked like a god to her. She didn't remember much else about him. Perhaps he was arrogant or brilliant or both, but those were nothing to her. She just loved his confidence and his looks.

"His name is Lars Bergen. That's why the LB in your name." She tried to laugh. "You've always had him and you didn't know."

"Is he alive, Mama?"

But her eyes were already closed again. Except for brief, incoherent moments, Rose Mary's eyes remained closed. Christmas Eve and Christmas Day came and went. The hospice worker stopped by daily and Richard sat diligently at her side.

On January 3, 2016, Rose Mary took her last breath. Although Richard had continued to talk to her through those last days, his mother never seemed conscious. Certainly not conscious enough to tell him if his father was still alive.

RICHARD FINDS HIS FATHER

Richard drove back to Fort Bragg considering his future. His mother had left him her house, and although it was in shambles, the old homestead was his free and clear, including some valuable acreage adjoining a new development project on Crystal Creek. She had told him he had a father named Lars Bergen who was a writer and she had left him with the idea that she'd always had pride in his military accomplishments. He watched the strip of highway roll beneath him thinking about what he might do next.

He returned to his Special Forces unit and was summoned by his captain. "We're suiting up for another African engagement. They need more help," the captain said. Richard gathered his unit and handed down the order. A young soldier named Willson called out, "What about Super Bowl 50? My Denver Broncos are playing in two weeks' time."

An older sergeant laughed. "Fuck football. We've got work to do."

Richard had been to the Sahara before in a counterterrorism effort policing arms and drug trafficking across central Africa. He knew the primary mission of Army Special Forces was to train and lead unconventional warfare forces, or a clandestine guerrilla force in an occupied nation. The never-ending Global War on Terrorism. He prayed he'd live through another operation.

As he got his gear together, Richard's mind flitted back to Kentucky. His mother had lived her whole life in and around Beattyville, except for that one fateful trip to Louisville. The funeral at the Assembly of God Church was nearly filled with old friends and neighbors. Many at the service shook Richard's hand, reminisced briefly, offered sincere condolences for his loss, thanked him for his military service, and said they'd pray for his safety.

Now Richard finished packing his kit and led his soldiers out to their transport. His military training had taught him that a good plan set into action can create reality. One step at a time, he thought. "We're going to Africa," Richard said. "Get your mind straight." One step at a time, first things first. Richard could find Lars Bergen on the Internet after this operation ended, approach him face to face and show him he had a grown-up son.

A C-130 brought his unit to Chad where they deployed to counter Al-Qaeda forces operating there. On their first nighttime recon maneuver, Richard urged his men to stay alert, stay alive. Ten minutes out of camp, one of the soldiers was hit by a bullet. He fell to the ground without a sound as the unit took fire from an unseen enemy. Richard and his men returned fire but minutes later the enemy force slipped away and the night became quiet again. Minutes later the sergeant told Richard that Corporal Willson had died. No one spoke as they brought their dead comrade back to the camp.

Richard went from man to man, consoling each, making sure they were as okay as could be. His calm exterior comforted his troops but inside he was exasperated, furious, full of rage. He'd fought in the war on terror since it had been announced. But nearly five years had passed since Osama bin Laden's death and he was still acting as one of the world's policemen, risking his life everywhere on the globe.

That was it for Richard. If America wanted to do nation building and act as the cop on the world beat, let somebody else do it. The concern he'd had for the direction of the country, the craziness of Jade Helm, and now the loss of this young man who only wanted to be sitting home watching the Denver Broncos pushed him to the edge of his military career. He wanted out. Wanted to turn in his shoulder boards and dress uniform, the cap with the gold band which alerted enlisted men that he was to be saluted. Come June he'd have his twenty-five years and that was more than enough. The rest of his life called to him. He would put in his resignation, claim his military pension, and sell the Beattyville property. Then he'd have the money to fund his search for Lars Bergen.

Rose Mary had said he looked like his father, so Richard had a face in his mind, an older version of himself, equally hardened by life, equally alone. He imagined a writer of deep wisdoms, a traveler and warrior who never knew that women had loved him though always wishing they did. Such was the picture Richard sketched in his mind. It was this image of Lars Bergen that pulled him toward the man and fueled his sense of purpose in finding him. This man, this Lars Bergen, needed a son like Richard as much as Richard needed a father.

By mid-June Richard's plan was in high gear.

He got back safely from Chad, mustered out, and moved his belongings to his house in Beattyville. The developers of the Crystal Creek property persuaded Richard to sell them his land, but he insisted on keeping the small house as his home.

Using a computer at the Estill County Public Library in nearby Irvine, Richard was surprised to see fifteen million hits from his Internet search for Lars Bergen. Overwhelmed, he spied the reference librarian and went to her for help. "I'm wondering if you have any books by a guy named Lars Bergen," he said and watched as she searched her computer for any titles by that author in her library.

"We have one at the main library in Manchester. Yes. It's *Ancient Aliens and the Age of Giants* and was published in 2014. Is that what you're looking for?"

"Sure, sure. You got anything else?"

"He also wrote *Ancient Aliens and the Lost Island* and another one, *Renegade Genius; Starborne III.*" She looked up at him over her glasses. "Do you want me to request them from the Clay County Library in Manchester?"

Richard could feel his heart racing. "No, thanks a lot, Ma'am. I think I'll drive over there and see for myself."

It took only an hour for Richard to arrive in Manchester and check out two of the titles on his list. Reading the back cover, he found the question, Who Is Lars Bergen? And the answer that followed:

> Lars Bergen is a shadow on a moonless night. You will not see him. You will not hear him. Because he is always behind you. Moving silently through the backways in search of Earth's

> extraterrestrial history where the dust lies thick, hidden in the mists of time.

This left Richard stunned. If the man who was his father could not be seen or heard, then his chances of finding him seemed impossible. He again sought out a librarian. "I'm looking for a writer from the 1970s named Lars Bergen. I don't think it's this author here," he said, showing the fantasy titles. "But I think there must be another writer by this name. My mother knew him. She met him at a bookstore before I was born."

He watched as the woman logged on to a computer and searched a database, scrolling and scowling for at least five minutes. "I see a book that's out of print here entitled, *Scenes from the Jungle*. Written by Lars Bergen. And here's another one, *My Life as A Warrior*. Both out of print and both from the 1970s." She kept searching as Richard watched her intently. "Do you want any biographical information?"

"I do, I would love that."

"This author was born in 1947. Let me do another search for you. Here we go. I'll print this out for you." She met his eyes kindly. "Good luck," she said and he knew that she meant it.

He took the printout and walked outside reading it:

> Lars Bergen was born in Minneapolis, Minnesota, in 1947. His father was a partner in the development company Alpine Homes which was responsible for major suburban growth in the Minneapolis area after World War II. Bergen graduated from the University of Minnesota and was in his master's program when he enlisted in the Army and was sent to Vietnam in 1970. His experiences in the war were the impetus for his best-selling book, *Scenes from the Jungle,* which was published in 1973, propelling him onto the international stage as an important writer. The book was sold to Hollywood with Peter Bogdanovich to direct it and Clint Eastwood to play the lead, but Bergen's desire to control the script killed the effort. His biographical novel, *My Life as a Warrior,* was published in 1975.

> In 1980, Bergen and his sister, the poet Lena Bergen, created the renowned Writers' Workshop in downtown Minneapolis housed in the family's renovated warehouse. The Writers' Workshop attracts writers from all over the world who submit their work for inclusion and convene as a group during the first two weeks of August every year since its inception. After Lena Bergen's death in 1992, Lars has run the workshop on his own along with a seasonal literary staff.

The photo that accompanied this biography showed a man who looked almost identical to Richard. Like an older brother. Like a dad. His father had been a warrior just like Richard and this knowledge comforted him like nothing he'd encountered before. His mother had chosen a smart and heroic partner to father her son.

He could hardly wait to make a connection.

THE PHONE CALL

The summer of 2016 was turning out to be the worst of Lars Bergen's life. One of the students at the college had started whispering loudly that she was going to marry him, while several other women at the college were saying quite clearly that he was a sexual predator, not dissimilar to the candidate Donald Trump.

Sunday evening marked the end of the first week of The Writers' Workshop. One of the participants criticized Director Lars Bergen in an email to the other attendees, saying of him, "His lectures on 'good writing' are an army of pompous phrases launched from behind his safe podium, never to be questioned. His literary self-absorption is so thick it oozes into every classroom, and throughout his endless bloviations comes nary an original idea—the intellectual landscapes he creates are words in search of ideas. This past week has been a colossal waste of time and money. I'm sorry I ever applied."

The email struck some sympathetic nerves and the thread quickly garnered replies from three female participants. Lars Bergen was described as "a has-been writer in need of a good editor," "a terrible teacher," and "a would-be sexual predator with a voracious appetite." That last email said, "Bergen requires applicants to his workshop to send a recent photo of themselves. I see now that I was chosen mostly because of how I look. I'm so pissed off I could just kill him!" As the thread grew, all of those complaining decided that their tuition should be refunded.

The email thread was forwarded to Lars Bergen by Daniel Morton, one of his supporters. Bergen's first reaction was to phone his attorney. "You have to do something right now, goddammit! If these emails become public, they'll destroy me and the workshop."

Early the next morning, the attorney filed a lawsuit against the complaining attendees claiming libel, slander, and defamation of character, all damaging to Bergen's professional and personal reputation. The lawsuit requested that the court issue an immediate cease-and-desist order against the students, forbidding them from further dissemination of their views. The legal papers requested millions of dollars in monetary damages for loss of reputation, special punitive damages for the infliction of pain and suffering, and recovery of all attorney's fees, court costs, and expenses.

On Monday afternoon the second week of the workshop, Lars strode to the podium and said, "Some of you published slanderous lies in emails yesterday. A friendly soul forwarded these vicious attacks to me and I have turned them over to the lawyers. The matter is now in court and subject to a confidentiality order. Stay or go, I don't care. For those who stay, keep working on your assignments."

With that he spun around and headed out the door, his rage running rampant. He returned to his office to find the phone on his desk ringing, another intrusion. He grabbed the receiver and hollered, "Writers' Workshop, Lars Bergen."

"Mr. Bergen, my name is Richard L.B. Scott."

"Are you trying to sell something?" Lars had had it.

"I'm not trying to sell you anything, Mr. Bergen. My mother knew you. Her name was Rose Mary Scott and she met you at a bookstore in Louisville in 1973. And she was probably in love with you."

"I have no idea what you're talking about. I've got a workshop going on here, so good luck to you," Lars said, though he didn't mean it the way the librarian had, and he hung up abruptly.

Richard took a deep breath, counted to fifty, then called again.

Lars's phone showed the same number on his screen and though he thought to ignore it, he found himself accepting the call. "What do you want?"

"I want to meet you. My mother died a few months ago and told me I had a father named Lars Bergen and I did my research and I know it's you. I look just like you, Mr. Bergen. And I'm a warrior like you too."

Lars liked remembering that he was a warrior. He certainly had been in battle the last twenty-four hours. "A warrior you say?"

"Twenty-five years in Special Forces at Fort Bragg. Chief warrant officer."

"Congratulations. Good for you. Did you read my books?"

"They're out of print, sir."

"Well, they're good. Try Amazon. I think they still have copies."

"I'd still like to come and meet you. Talk to you."

"No need for that. I don't know you. I don't remember your mother and I don't have any interest in pursuing a relationship with a total stranger. What did you say your name was?"

"Richard L.B. Scott."

"Well, Richard, let me set you straight. I slept with many women in my day. I kept in touch with none of them. I married none of them. I have no intention of marrying any of them. I have no children that I've claimed or plan to claim. I'm sure your mother was a lovely person, and I'm sorry you lost her, but I have no interest in being a father to anyone. And now I'm going to hang up and I do not want you to call me ever again."

Lars pounded his desk with his fist. One more thing. Dammit. He turned off his overhead light, locked his office door, and pulled the blinds. Then he took out his latest article on immigration and scribbled for hours about keeping the caravans of savages out of the empire.

On the other end, Richard did not move a muscle for almost an hour. When he looked at the clock on his dashboard, it was after six p.m. and he realized he had not eaten the entire day he'd looked for the man who was his father. Over the next few days he puzzled over what had happened on the telephone and decided that he needed to be face to face and man to man with Lars Bergen. Nobody dismissed Richard Scott when he was on a mission and this man was his father whether he liked it or not. He stopped at a gas station for maps of every state between Kentucky and Minnesota, planning his moves to meet Lars Bergen in person. Given his history, Richard was certain that once Lars met him and shook his hand, he would not ignore him ever again.

DINNER AT THE RUSSIAN EMBASSY

Laura and Jack had been equal partners in careful spy careers for more than a decade. Since 2013, when Putin went after Crimea, the two had worked in Sofia, Bulgaria, running the All is Well International Map and Bookstore. They were professional listeners. They listened to Russian television and to various radio stations. They listened to the tourists who roamed their store and to the dealers from whom they purchased limited edition books and maps. They read every Russian magazine and newspaper printed and they fed what they learned back to their intelligence unit in McLean, Virginia.

They loved working out of Sofia, a city with an ancient history and landmarks dating back more than 2000 years. Their bookstore opened onto a winding stone street next door to a café where both locals and tourists gathered. Jack and Laura could stand in their doorway sipping strong coffee, watch the café patrons and passersby—and listen. And so they understood that Putin was fomenting division in Ukraine and bolstering the wealthy in Moscow and laughing as he promoted the American named Donald Trump. That's what they knew.

Now, late in 2015, they were back working in Washington, DC, using what they knew. They had returned with some regret.

Eastern Europe had settled on them over the years—their little bookstore and unsuspecting neighbors, the intrigue of being so close to the action. Dinner at the Russian Embassy was their first domestic assignment and, though it was only an evening, the work was delicate and crucial.

They found traffic more tangled than usual as Laura drove the two of them across town to Wisconsin Avenue Northwest and through the front gates of the monolithic Russian Embassy, where a valet took their Mustang to park. They sailed confidently through security and joined a short line in front of a table where their credentials were checked again. "The chandeliers are beautiful, don't you think?" Laura smiled at Jack. How they loved the grandeur of Russian culture. They continued to admire the decor quietly until their diplomatic passports were returned to them.

Relatively young and beautiful in the crowd of career diplomats, Jack and Laura knew that many eyes followed them around the room, and that was fine, that was what their cover was all about and had been for years. Being attractive and friendly, bright and energetic, made them pleasing to the good and the bad. It all just worked.

They did not search for their contact. He found them instantly. "Welcome," the tallish youth said in the distinctive English of those who speak it as a second language. "My name is Peter and I'll show you where you want to go, please." He escorted the two of them past the center patio, down a long hallway, and into an expansive private dining room. They could see four round tables on the main floor, each set for eight, a long table on a slightly raised dais where several old men were seated, and a sextet of musicians in the far corner.

"You're at table three," Peter directed, bowed, and shook Jack's hand vigorously with both of his. Then he did the same with Laura and watched as they moved to their places.

Jack and Laura had been given this embassy assignment just three days earlier, summoned by one of their bosses and told they would attend a reception on Friday evening using their US State Department attaché credentials from previous days. Jack would be given a memory chip containing top secret documents by an official inside the Russian government, which Jack and Laura would then deliver to their boss. The documents supposedly contained all the disinformation efforts, memes, and messages used by the Internet Research Agency known as Glavset, as they worked to interfere and agitate the US presidential election on behalf of Russian business and political interests. The CIA had reason to believe Putin ordered this disruption and that he favored Donald Trump.

The tall polite man who ushered them into the room had deposited the memory chip into Jack's hand during his welcoming handshake. Jack slid this into a pocket until the lights dimmed and the pre-dinner concert began. Though Jack had never been a fan of this Schoenberg piece before, he now decided it was one of his favorites for how it captured the attention of the audience. Jack could see that all interest was on the cellists and violinists in the front corner of the room.

Closing his eyes to absorb the music, Jack took out the memory chip, squeezed his legs together, then unscrewed the bezel of his watch. The crystal of his watch came off easily along with the very thin watch face, revealing a space large enough for the memory component. That tucked securely in the tiny area, he replaced the crystal and bezel, then screwed them both into place. He looked over to see Laura smiling at him, her head swaying to the music. He smiled in return. Nothing unusual. The music so lovely.

The rest of the event passed as such evenings do, with a few awkward jokes and several dull speeches about the future of the New Russia. The roast beef was dry. The air slightly fusty. When the waiter offered him an after-dinner glass of cognac, he decided to say yes. Laura was driving after all.

"Did you two enjoy the music?" Peter asked as they were leaving.

"It was the highlight, so absorbing," Jack responded.

Nodding, Laura added, "We could not take our eyes off the musicians, the proficiency of such playing."

"Yes, that is good," Peter said with a satisfied nod.

Jack and Laura held hands waiting for their car, but once inside the Mustang, they fell purposely silent. A superstition between them, they never talked when they were in possession of secret information. Not that someone would ever hear them or they would stumble. No. Silence, they both believed, honored their profession. It wasn't until they had made their delivery and were on their way home that they talked about Jack's trip to Minneapolis the next day.

"I still think I should go with you," Laura said, repeating what she'd told him every day for a week.

"Cam will only aggravate you. Nobody understands him the way I do. We grew up alone in a house with Ellie Mae gone and our dad out living his own life. He wants my advice, so I will go home and talk to him."

"He wants your money, Jack, you know that."

"Of course. And you think you can protect me from that?"

They both laughed. "Anyway, he's got this notion about putting a police station in one of the buildings and I'm kind of interested."

"You think he wants to help the city?" Laura was incredulous. "You two are nothing alike. You don't even look alike. All his dark hair. Where did that come from?"

"I'll leave that for you to decipher, my dear."

BRUNCH AT THE CUBE

When Claudio, the head waiter, showed Jack to a table with white café chairs, Jack chose one that allowed him to look across the 150-foot courtyard to the space where his mother conducted her Quiet Inspiration Yoga Circles. She had told him she liked being near to the high-end workout studio on the main floor. Plenty of air and light for her yoga students, she'd said. Eight floors above, Jack knew, was where his Uncle Lars had his office and classrooms for The Writers' Workshop. The Cube was not unfamiliar to him, but he had tended to avoid it if he could. Family enterprise and all.

But then Cameron had nagged his brother for months to come home and be part of this meeting today. And maybe he thought that having Jack's brilliant mind on his side would clinch the deal. At any rate, Jack liked the idea of The Cube having a police presence and was happy for the chance to visit his mother and grandmothers. As he sat near Cameron, he asked, "You feel ready to make your case?"

Cameron III shrugged. "It's got to happen. There's that whole space empty over there." He directed his brother to the area on the other side of the courtyard. "Sure rent, that's what I need. These retail places, they come and go, come and go. Honestly, Jack, I just want some government money to anchor me a bit here. Say, order whatever you want," he added magnanimously, glancing toward the door every few seconds. "Great food here. That's one thing for sure."

"I hope it works out the way you want," Jack said and meant it. His brother's instability seemed to him an unnecessary and debilitating condition. It made the women in the family worry too much.

"You know, Cameron, I think I'll have French toast. I haven't had it in years. Laura thinks it's not healthy." Jack laughed at his own comment, but his brother did not. Instead he jumped to his feet, jarring the table so that the ice water sloshed onto the cloth, and stretched out a hand to greet the tall woman approaching their table.

"Jack, this is Mayor Linda Kendall. This is my brother, Jack; just flew in from Washington, DC, this morning. I think I told you he does intelligence work, right, Jack?"

Jack stood and shook the woman's hand. "I've never met a Minneapolis mayor before," he said and smiled.

Linda sat directly across from him. "And I've never met anyone who worked in intelligence." She had a sincere manner. Jack understood how she had come to be mayor of Minneapolis.

When Claudio ushered a couple to their table minutes later, Cameron leaped up again, hugging them both. "Jack, Penny Carmichael-Rossiter and Giles Rossiter." He enunciated their names slowly, a signal to Jack that he had been drinking for possibly hours before the brunch began.

"Penny is chief of police in our fair city. Been with the department since she got out of the Army."

Penny grinned at him and added, "Twenty years this summer; almost two years as chief."

"And Giles came here from Thunder Bay to play some hockey," Cameron III said, forgetting that his brother had never cared much for sports. As they studied the menu, the mayor and chief of police chatted comfortably with one another. This was their town, Jack thought. They probably spent hours together on all sorts of projects and with people like Cameron who wanted something from the city.

As the waiter brought pitchers of coffee to the table and Cameron III began drinking another gin and tonic, he launched into telling them why the city needed a police station in the warehouse district, the level of crime, the density of businesses, and the reluctance of new businesses to come into the area with conditions as they were. His voice got louder and sweat covered his face. It seemed to Jack that Cameron was delivering a well-rehearsed speech to sound as coherent as he did. Something of a miracle, really. "Because the population in the warehouse district has tripled, it's time to provide more services. These people should be taken care of, don't you think?" His eyes scanned the group around the table. "Lots of voters here, Linda. They'll remember on election day, you know that."

Linda Kendall was silent for a minute. Then she shifted the topic somewhat. "Your family has owned this building for some time?" She looked to both Cameron and Jack who said yes that was true. "You have a fairly upscale clientele coming here to shop and exercise, take classes, eat at this lovely café. How do you see this type of customer responding to a police presence? There probably are not many cops attending Quiet Inspiration Yoga, am I right? It's not a natural fit as I see it. Though I tend to agree that this neighborhood overall could use some type of police presence, I am not convinced The Cube is the right place."

"But the parking here is real good," Giles threw in, eager to add his two cents on Cameron's behalf.

Jack was just about to support his brother by saying that there were many options for how the police could reside in The Cube when the glass ceiling of the building's atrium exploded above them, and a body crashed onto the floor of the courtyard.

A woman near them screamed and Chief Penny Rossiter jumped up and ran toward the scene while phoning for a squad to come. The mayor and others at the table scrambled just behind her and followed her to the center of the courtyard where an older man lay crumpled in a heap, his blond hair showing gray and his tweed jacket torn.

Cameron III gasped.

There was no mistaking that Lars Bergen was dead.

Others in The Cube that morning gathered around, taking photos with their cell phones which were posted real time to social media. Within minutes of the accident, the world knew the famed poet and founder of The Writers' Workshop had fallen eight stories to his death. And within seconds the chief had secured the scene so that no one in the crowd had access.

Jack looked for Ellie Mae, somehow wanting to protect her from seeing her brother in that state. But she didn't seem to be in the crowd and he had no authority to remain in the building. Instead he put his arm around his brother's shoulders and guided him outside where they joined a huddle of frightened and confused tenants and customers.

To calm his brother, Jack said, "I think the mayor might be willing to consider some proposal, Cam."

"This ruined it, Jack. My god, Lars falling through the glass like that." He searched Jack's face for a reason, some sense of rationality to what had just happened. "I mean, I know nobody liked the guy, but who would have thought this?"

"It could have been an accident," Jack said, though he somehow doubted this was true. "Lars was famous, you know. He drew attention to himself." Jack talked on thinking how this was going to kill his grandmother Sunny. Losing Lena was so terrible. Now her son too.

The brothers walked away from the commotion to Cameron III's silver Corvette. He gripped the handle, yanked open the door, slammed himself inside, and revved his engine. "Nothing ever goes my way," he said. And he drove off leaving his brother alone in the lot.

RICHARD SCOTT IN MINNEAPOLIS

Richard had arrived in Minneapolis late Friday, found lodging overlooking the Mississippi River, and rested after his marathon journey. Waking late in the morning he saw the mighty river moving fast on its way down South. He knew he had to get moving too. He was anxious to find The Cube and anxious to meet his father face to face. The thoughts in his mind bobbed up and down like the white-capped waves on the river outside his window, not really connected to one another, and yet all connected to whether Lars Bergen would accept him as the son he knew he was.

He showered quickly, dried himself, and dressed in a light blue short-sleeve shirt, khaki slacks, and a sport coat. He stepped out of the room, closed the door tightly, and walked to his car. Richard did not notice the humid air or overcast skies as he drove west on Washington Avenue, rumbled across Hennepin Avenue, then turned left into The Cube parking lot. The building loomed large, covering almost a whole city block, and stood more than 100 feet high, its old brick exterior and paned windows reminding Richard of the factories he'd seen in southern cities.

He walked through the double doors and took off his sunglasses to survey the building inside. The only activity he saw was at the International Café and he instinctively walked up to the man standing at the doorway. Seeing him, the man smiled and said, "I'm Claudio, how may we help you today, sir?"

"I'm looking for The Writers' Workshop. Could you direct me to it?"

"You can find the director up on the eighth floor," Claudio answered. "They have classrooms all over up there, but I don't know if they're in session or not. I'd say Lars Bergen is your best bet." He gave Richard the office number and watched him walk toward the elevators. How odd, the head waiter thought. This visitor looked exactly like the man he was looking for, certainly an uncanny coincidence.

Upstairs, Lars Bergen was in his office, eyes closed, his breathing fast and shallow. The Writers' Workshop was a disaster and getting worse every day. In years past, Lars had found amusements during individual feedback sessions. This year, not one female student had requested his one-on-one coaching. Never in his life had Lars worked harder, gotten less praise, and received more threats than this year. The year before had been a mess without Rika, damn her, but this year had been even worse. Lars was deep into feeling sorry for himself when he heard a knock on the door. In that moment, he imagined one of the prettier young writers might be coming by to ask for his assistance.

With that hope, he straightened himself and called, "Come in."

THE GHOST

Neither Jack nor his brother was present when the ghost of Lars Bergen came down from the eighth floor of The Cube to greet Chief Rossiter and all those attending the body of the deceased. The ghost was a younger version, dressed in crisp detail, his eyes large with the horror of what had just happened.

"I'm his son," the ghost reported, good soldier that he was. "I came to see him and he got very upset. He rushed at me. It all happened so fast."

Chief Rossiter straightened to greet him. The man looked the way Lars might have looked in his prime, she thought, though she was too young to remember Lars Bergen that way.

"I'm Richard Scott." He almost recited his rank and serial number as he would have done in a situation like this throughout his military career. But he did not. Instead he wept. Silently and without drama, he wept tears of loss for something he never had and now never would. "I can't believe what just happened. I only wanted to know the man."

"Would you like to tell us exactly what happened, Mr. Scott?" Subtly the chief had communicated to her officers to keep close to this man just in case. Lars Bergen had not just jumped eight stories to his death, of that she was certain. He had thought much too highly of himself to throw his life away.

"I knocked on the door and when he told me to come in, I did, but just inside the door. He was behind his desk in some angry state, it seemed to me. Maybe he was angry a lot. He was angry when I called him a few weeks back too."

"You called him? He knew you were coming?"

"I called him, but he didn't know I was coming. He hung up on me then. He told me never to call him again, so I didn't. But I decided to come anyway."

"And why was that?"

"He had a relationship with my mother and when she died, she told me I had a father who was a writer she'd met at a bookstore in Louisville. So I researched and I found him. I saw his picture and there he was, looking pretty much like me, I'd say."

Chief Rossiter nodded. She'd say that too. "And when you went into his office upstairs, then what?"

Richard strained to assemble the details. What had happened first and second, how it had so quickly become physical, Lars pushing him and Richard trying to hold ground, the open door to the balcony, the missed swing at him that propelled Lars to the edge and then over the edge, all a nightmare he could barely relate to the officers. "I shouldn't have come," Richard concluded. "He wanted me to leave him alone and that's what I should have done."

The security cameras in the building would confirm that Richard had gone to Lars Bergen's office just minutes before the accident, which is what the chief was now calling it. "But we will need to investigate further, of course," she said to this handsome, hapless ghost. "We'll need to hold you in custody while we do this." She said this gently for she liked the man. He was respectful and remorseful and very, very sad.

"I just thought I might have a father," he said, perhaps to Chief Rossiter, perhaps to himself.

Richard spent the rest of that day in a room at the neighborhood precinct while the police examined all the footage they had on the various cameras in The Cube. Because the worst of his encounter with his father had been just outside the office door in the open corridor overlooking the atrium, the detectives could see definitively the younger man's efforts to protect himself from Lars Bergen's rage. It was not the first time the police had seen minor incidents escalate quickly and end in tragedy. Clearly Richard Scott was not responsible for Lars Bergen's death and just before six that evening he was allowed to leave the station. Chief Rossiter herself drove him back to his car parked at The Cube.

“I’m sorry for your loss,” she said to him. “Do you mind if I say one thing to you off the record?”

Richard stood outside the police car looking in at her.

“Lars Bergen wasn’t such a nice man as you are, Mr. Scott. You’ll be okay without him.”

This was something for Richard to think about as he drove his old car back to his hotel and the turned-down bed the maid had left for him.

THE AFTERMATH

At the time of the accident Ellie Mae was in her yoga studio. Screams in the atrium drew her to the window where she stood watching the police surround a body lying on the concrete floor near the café. She could not see who it was, and by that time, her two sons had already been evacuated. So aside from her general compassion for her fellow humans, it didn't really concern her.

And then she saw Richard Scott walk across the atrium, a man so like her brother's younger self, the very sight of him drew her out of her studio and into the open area. She saw Richard approach the center of activity, but there were many people about in small clusters preventing her from seeing Lars's body. She caught what the bystanders were saying: Lars Bergen. Writers' Workshop. Suicide. And there was the younger version of Lars.

At this point Ellie Mae bounded through the crowd to see the twisted heap of her brother's body. She didn't scream and she didn't tell the police she was the man's sister. Her lifetime of struggles against Lars flooded her mind, the endless torments of childhood and his impossible stance on almost everything she loved, but also the loss for her mother, and the loneliness of being the last of her siblings alive. She returned to her studio, gathered her things, and left to tell her poor mother that her only son was now gone.

As she drove to Sunny and Susie's house, she found herself thinking of the man who looked like Lars and wondering what had happened. She knew her narcissistic brother would not jump to his own death and the young man she saw didn't look like anyone strange or violent. It didn't make sense. And that's what she would have to tell Sunny. That Lars was dead and that it didn't make any sense.

She pulled her car over a few blocks short of her mother's Kenwood home and called Andrew. His first instinct was to find more information and immediately logged on to every social media platform he knew. "The word is that police took a man into custody—he looks like Lars here in this picture."

"I saw him. It's remarkable, Andrew, the resemblance."

"Well, there's speculation that the two had some fight, but really, El, nobody knows."

"So that's what I tell my mom?"

"That's all we have to tell your mom."

No sooner had Andrew ended his call with Ellie Mae, than his daughters contacted him from Charlotte where they were in the process of filming the Republican candidate for president, making a live documentary called *I Alone Can Fix It*. They'd seen the images of the accident on Twitter. They wanted to know more, but Andrew could not tell them anymore.

"How's it going following Trump?" he asked them.

"Lots of red hats, Dad. He's revving up the troops," Sarah said, and her sister added, "He reminds me of early Hitler. Like history repeating itself. He's the one, you know? The only one who matters."

"It's troubling," Andrew told his daughters. "Keep on him." They parted agreeing to talk again as soon as Andrew had more information on Lars.

Talking to Andrew had helped Ellie Mae gather her wits and she continued to her mother's house. A midsized white rental car was parked in the driveway and when she came into the backyard garden, Jack was sitting next to Sunny who was holding on to Susie's hand. Both women were weeping.

Sunny looked at her daughter and saw at once that Ellie also knew of the tragedy. "Did you just come from The Cube too? Do you know what happened?" The question was no sooner out of Sunny's mouth when she wailed in pain and cried out, "My boy."

Ellie Mae knelt next to her mother and quietly met Jack's eyes. Softly he told her, "I was with Cameron having lunch when it happened, Mom, it was so horrible, that crash through the glass and the utter mayhem. Then they asked us to leave and we did and I came right here."

"How's your brother then?"

"He's pretty upset. He had high hopes for the meeting we were in." Jack shrugged. "Time for all that later."

Within two hours of Lars Bergen's death, his family had gathered at his mother's house to grieve and wonder at what had happened. Only Cameron III was not there. After the disaster at The Cube and the many gin and tonics on an empty stomach, Cameron had headed over to the apartment of the last girl he'd slept with to see if she might be interested in more of what they'd had before.

Neither Sunny Bergen nor Richard Scott slept that night. Although Susie had given her friend Tylenol PM, it wasn't enough to numb the wild thoughts in Sunny's mind. This son of hers, this only son, had always been such a star to her. His lawn business, his photographs of beautiful women, all that talent, the good report cards, his service to his country, and that book telling all about it. Her handsome, brilliant son.

The images just kept coming all night as the moon moved from west to east, and she just kept thinking. Why had Lars never married and left Sunny something of himself now that he was gone? Why would he have chosen to live alone all his life, someone like him? It didn't make any more sense than the fact that he was now gone. She couldn't recall that he'd had girlfriends. He'd seemed to stay apart or aloof, she kept thinking, though it was nothing she had considered before. When he was here to walk through her door now and then, she hadn't wondered why he was alone or why his friends had drifted away, why he and Andrew were no longer close and hadn't been for so many years.

Her son's views about the world had troubled her, but she had never wanted to dwell on that. What she'd heard him say about a civil war in the country, race riots, the Christian nation of Northern Europeans, his voice impassioned and unreasonable. She'd known it was his voice, but she hadn't asked him about it, didn't really want to know. But now she had to think, what was on her son's mind all the time? What kind of life was he living?

Maybe that's why he'd died. Maybe somebody didn't like his ideas. Andrew and Ellie Mae hadn't said anything about that. An accident, they'd said. No real reason, they'd told her. But she wasn't born yesterday. She knew that a genius like Lars, who stood over six feet tall, didn't just happen to drop over a ledge and crash through a ceiling to this horrible kind of death. So what had really happened? As she flipped from side to side, waiting for the glint of sunrise, Sunny decided she would ask Ellie Mae and Andrew to find out the truth. She needed to know the details. She needed that if she was ever going to sleep again.

Although Richard had been in wars and gone against military enemies, he had never caused a civilian death, never had such a thing on his head. He wasn't the kind of man who ran away from any problem. He stepped up, that's what he did. He didn't respect people who would cut and run and that surely wasn't him. He stared at the perforated ceiling tiles of his hotel room all night planning what he could do to make it right. The chief of police was a nice person. He would call her in the morning and tell her he needed to be in touch with the Bergen family to tell them he was sorry. If he hadn't come to Minneapolis to see Lars, this would not have happened, and Lars Bergen would still be alive. Maybe he had a wife who had now lost her husband. Other children who had been orphaned.

These thoughts were unbearable to Richard. In his honorable attempt to claim a father, he had somehow brought about the man's death. He'd always been more alone in the world than most people. He loved his mother and called the US Army his family, but right now, in August of 2016, it appeared that he had no one. All he had were his decency and pride. He needed to make this situation right.

By seven a.m. Sunny and Richard Scott had made the phone calls that would lead them toward one another.

FAMILY

It only took a day.

When Chief Penny Rossiter stopped by work briefly Sunday noon, she found messages waiting for her from both Sunny Bergen and Richard Scott. Sunny had told the desk sergeant that she wanted more information. "I didn't know what to tell her," the sergeant said when he gave Penny the message. "Don't seem like we know much either. Do we?" he added.

The message from Richard Scott was a request for contact information on the Bergen family.

"Guy says he wants to apologize," the desk sergeant said with a shrug. "What the hell is he apologizing for, we let him go, didn't we? I mean, he didn't kill the Bergen professor." He shook his head as though the whole situation was more than he cared to think about. But the whole situation was something Chief Rossiter welcomed. She immediately reached out with information to both parties. She told Sunny Bergen everything the police had uncovered about the accident, the video with its clear images of her son charging the newcomer ragefully, and the conclusion that this had been a terrible series of unintended events. Her son had not committed suicide, nor had anyone killed him. She let Sunny know that the visitor who was arguing with Lars wanted to meet her and talk with her about the event. Was she open to that?

Hungry for any morsel, any connection to her son, any small detail of his last minutes, Sunny said she wanted to meet this man as soon as possible. Penny Rossiter then called Richard at his hotel and gave him Sunny's number. "She's a pillar in this community, Richard, I want you to know that. Sunny Bergen and her best friend, Susie MacAlpine, are great friends of the disenfranchised here and what I would call pioneers in our city. She will be gracious. And I know you will be too."

Sunny told nobody except Susie. The two of them sat in their garden filled, by this time of the summer, with an abundance of roses, zinnias, lilies, and dahlias, ready to greet this man, whoever he was, whose presence had so upset her son. She was prepared to be disturbed. She knew this would not be an easy encounter. But neither Sunny nor Susie was prepared for the sight of Richard Scott, crisply dressed and groomed, coming up the walkway looking exactly like Lars had twenty years earlier. Sunny gasped and covered her mouth in shock. Susie, always wise and measured, stood up to welcome him to their home.

Richard sat across from the two women and leaned forward to say, "I'm so sorry about your son. I just wanted to meet him, not to have anything bad happen to him."

"Did you know Lars?" Susie asked.

Richard was not sure how to answer her question. He felt in some way that he had always known him, though of course that was not true. And he felt uncomfortable just then telling these women that he was Lars's illegitimate son, that he was certain this was true. He chose to say, "I only spoke to him on the phone a few weeks ago. Then I came here to introduce myself to him in person."

"Why did you phone him?" Sunny probed. She moved to the edge of her lawn chair in anticipation. "Were you in The Writers' Workshop?" She knew she was flailing.

"No, ma'am, I was not. Maybe I could tell you a story? About my mother."

Both women nodded, Sunny almost holding her breath.

"My mother's name was Rose Scott. She died just eight months ago, a terrible cancer. I was in the military then, Chief Warrant Officer in the Army, Fort Bragg. I came home for her last days and she told me, really just at the end, really at her end, that I had a father and he was a writer she'd met in Louisville right after she graduated from high school. So after she passed, I looked for him. I have no brothers or sisters and I never had a father that I knew about. My mother used to say he'd died in Vietnam."

"Lars was in Vietnam," Sunny put in. "He wrote a book about it, you know."

"Yes, Mrs. Bergen, I found that book and it led me here to your son. I thought maybe I could get to know him over time, but he seemed so upset by me, so angry at me and then there was this commotion between us and he fell against that low railing and went over. It should never have happened. I should have been able to pull him back and I wanted to pull him back, but everything happened so fast and I couldn't stop it and I've never been so sorry about anything in my life."

"You're his son, then," Susie concluded in her most peremptory voice. "He's your grandson, Sunny. You are," she repeated to Richard.

Sunny Bergen had had such a horrible and confusing twenty-four hours. She studied Richard like a rare specimen in her garden. "He's my grandson." She said this to no one and expected no answer. Then she looked directly at Richard. "I can see that. I can see that you are." Her eyes were not deceiving her. This Richard Scott seemed to her a gift from the God she had always trusted. He had a steadiness about him that Lars had not displayed for so many years, her poor son. Always on edge, always apart, never married, never part of the family the way she had wanted him to be. In that instant, Sunny decided that her son had caused his own death, had fueled his own demise. How much anger would it take to propel a six-foot man over a railing? This was the question that would haunt Sunny Bergen for the rest of her life. But it was not going to keep her from accepting Richard Scott as her grandson.

She and Susie peppered Richard with questions about his mother, his childhood, his life in the Army. Midafternoon Andrew and Ellie Mae arrived, as they always did on Sundays, to spend time with their mothers and eat a casual supper with others in the family. This time they expected to offer their shoulders to lean on and perhaps to plan a memorial for Lars. They were certainly not expecting to see their mothers with Richard Scott, relaxed and seemingly happy, telling the kinds of stories saved for reunions and major birthdays.

"Richard's an Army man, Andrew," Sunny said, as if this told him everything he needed to know.

INTESTATE

Andrew had known Lars Bergen best when they were young boys. Now, as a mature man nearing seventy, he'd seen how a person could drop all pretense of civilization and culture, live only for physical pleasure, measure everything by wayward impulse and become a beast.

Lars Bergen's personality had been created in a never-ending war between outward uber masculinity and internal poetical impulses. The older he got, the more disconnected he was from what was real. He was sincere in his belief that America had lost its way and needed to be brought back to its white Anglo-Saxon roots. And though his family all knew this, they had no idea he had written articles and books for years as the radical firebrand Thor Larsson.

Andrew had agreed to clean out Lars's office. He had the time and he wanted to protect Ellie Mae and the two older women from any unpleasant discoveries. Within minutes of being in his old friend's office, he saw exactly what Lars had been up to for so many years, shocked at how far Lars had gone in his right-wing, white supremacy delusions, his vitriol and determination to alter the nation's course. Here was his book entitled, *You Will Not Replace Us*, and another, *The Return of the White Man,* and folders of articles both published and unpublished, all of a genre that Andrew had monitored many of the years he worked for the State Department and CIA.

He was not sure what to do with it all. Should he warn Sunny and Susie to soften the blow if it should make the news—or should he assume that Lars's secret identity would remain just that.

He called a contact at the *Star Tribune* to poke around about what was known and not known. He searched online to find out what trail Lars might have left, and he called his favorite tech guy to come over and strip the computer. In the end, he decided that nobody in the family needed to know what Lars had become. In death, Andrew decided, Lars Bergen would be the man he could have been, not the one he was. All his right-wing books and files were shredded and incinerated for less than the cost of a weekend stay at a halfway decent hotel. And when there was nothing left in Lars's office at The Cube, nor at his home office on Lake of the

Isles, Andrew sat down to write a eulogy that would please the family.

Days later he told the small gathering of mourners that, "Lars Bergen was an unusually talented writer who left us both poems and books, as well as the legacy of The Writers' Workshop, which he started with his sister Lena Bergen, my late wife. Lars was a soldier, an educator, and an internationally known author." Andrew added a few more details then read from William Ernest Henley's poem "Invictus" –

It matters not how strait the gate,
How charged with punishments the scroll,
I am the master of my fate,
I am the captain of my soul.

Sunny and Ellie had selected the music, flowers to the family were in abundance, and they all had to say what a beautiful send-off they'd given to Lars. But almost nobody had cried. Even Sunny found herself more focused on the handsome grandson sitting next to her than on anything Andrew or the minister had said. Later she thought about that. Why she had not sobbed during the burial service for her only son. Maybe, she decided, she had cried too much already. Or maybe, she considered, she was choosing her future and not her past.

Richard Scott did not leave Sunny's side for one minute of the service or the socializing before and after. He was gentlemanly when she introduced him as Lars's son, smiled politely at the comments about their obvious resemblance, and took in the day with the amazement of one who has never been part of a family before. He knew that most of what Andrew had said about Lars was not really true, but he appreciated the display, the formality, like soldiers in dress uniform at events even when they don't want to be there. The Bergens and MacAlpines had already given him the carriage house behind Sunny and Susie's house to live for the time being and Andrew was networking on his behalf to find him work. How his mother would have loved to know this. And maybe she did.

In the mingling after the service, the family attorney Lewis Wright found a minute to pull Andrew aside and say, "You know he had no will."

"Lars had no will?" That, too, surprised Andrew though it should not have. Lars may have thought he would never die and would therefore need no such thing as a will.

"So what do we do?"

"When you die without a spouse and without a will, then everything goes to the children. Sunny says the look-alike is his son, is that right? So let's get the paternity work done and we go from there." He chuckled. "Looks like that son showed up at just the right time, doesn't it?"

But Andrew didn't answer. He was imagining all the possibilities that had opened up for Richard Scott simply because he had tried to find a father.

Over the next two weeks, Lewis handled everything. He assessed Lars's combined assets, including the remainder of his trust, his duplex on the lake, his book royalties, teaching pension, and investments, to be very close to five million. He coordinated the blood tests to confirm that Richard was, in fact, Lars Bergen's son. And then he called a meeting in his office for the Bergen family to inform them of his findings and to present his strategy for the court proceedings as the executor of the intestate estate. When he informed Richard that he would be inheriting several millions of dollars, the younger man gasped. He'd grown up in the Kentucky mountains where men who died might leave their families a burial policy and maybe work-earned life insurance totaling a few thousand. If they were lucky.

When the meeting was over, Richard found it difficult to leave the chair in the attorney's office. He wasn't sure his legs would hold him up.

MANO A MANO

The only one not happy about Richard's newfound place in the Bergen family was Cameron III who now had to deal with a stranger controlling all his uncle's money. At least Cameron always knew he could get a few thousand from Lars in return for introducing him to young women. But now what? The Writers' Workshop was done, Lars was gone, and some new guy held the purse strings.

Cameron III waited a polite three days after the memorial service and then drove over and parked his Corvette in his grandmothers' driveway, rang the bell to the carriage house, and marched up those steep stairs like his own kind of soldier. Man to man, that's what this conversation was going to be. Mano a mano.

"Heh, Richard," he started, wondering a little if he should try calling him Rick or Dick or Rich. "So what do your friends call you?" His new second cousin stood very tall—he was such a goddamned tall man—and answered "Scott."

"Oh sure. Nice. You got some coffee, by any chance?"

Richard said he did not drink coffee very often and offered Cameron a place to sit. "You got something on your mind?"

"Just thought we should get to know one another." Cameron put his sunglasses on top of his head. "Damn, you look a lot like my Uncle Lars, I mean, your dad. I guess that's what he was."

Richard waited patiently.

"You know your dad was a big supporter of my real estate enterprises. Course, it's a family business. My two grandfathers started it back in the fifties and then my dad took over and now I keep it going, trying to grow it in this new hyper-competitive field. It's hard to be as small as our company is in a field dominated by giants. You know, Wall Street eats up Main Street, you've heard all about that, right? So Andrew, Lars, and Jack—the women too—none of them cared too much for business, but maybe you do. I mean, they all liked teaching and spying and stuff like that. But anyway, I wanted you to know that I could use a guy like you to bolster up the business. You know, that our grandparents built."

Cameron noticed that Richard was actually listening, so he continued.

"So The Cube there where Lars, I mean your dad, had his school, I mean the school's gone now. Nobody seemed to want to keep it going so there's all that space. And an old building like that always needs refurbishing to compete, because you know there's all this new construction down along the river."

"What are you asking then, Cameron?"

"Oh, I was thinking maybe you could invest some of your inheritance into the business. Maybe be a consultant once in a while. Meet with people. You're a nice-looking guy. People like you. Right?"

"I don't know much about real estate. It's something to think about though. I appreciate you coming to talk to me about it, Cameron. Let's see how things go over the next year. It's all so new to me."

That's what Richard said as he watched this new relative fidgeting in the chair across from him, making his clumsy attempt to hustle a bit of money out of Richard's millions. He saw him coming from a mile away, as obvious as an Army recruit asking his sarge for a loan until the next payday.

Cameron struggled to find an urgent comeback, but he hadn't had enough coffee yet and this guy Richard or Scott, or whatever he called himself, looked too much like Lars for comfort. Cameron put his sunglasses back on his face. "Well, I can see you need time to think it over. How about I call you on Monday?" He left not registering Richard's answer.

It was hard for him to believe that he had so few resources in a family that had built an entire company and generations of wealth. Just because he had taken a calculated risk back in 2005, he was now left to struggle like some upstart schmoozer driving around town in a used Cadillac.

Why hadn't Lars left some of that money to Cameron, or all of it, for that matter.

What kind of guy doesn't have a will?

To hell with them all.

THE STORM GOD

They used to be the fringe, relegated to corner stories in tabloids like the *National Enquirer* alongside "Tattoo of Snake Climbs Up Man's Arm & Strangles Him to Death." But after four decades of watching their old world change, disaffected white men from Montana to Mississippi and from the neighborhoods in Detroit to the open ranges of Texas wanted to be heard.

Thor Larsson and his like had not created the anger of these men, they had observed it and then fueled it.

As the Storm God, Thor Larsson had spent his adulthood amplifying a dogmatic anti-government attitude and poisoning the public well with white-is-right rhetoric.

And now here was Donald Trump telling them, these men who didn't trust the government and didn't believe in their future, that he wanted to Make America Great Again. That's what the man said and all the followers at his rallies wore hats that said that too. MAGA. Donald Trump favored their point of view. They weren't on the fringe anymore, by God, they were ready to seize control.

"It's time for Americans to unite and take back our government," Trump said.

"Law and order must be restored," he said.

"It's a rigged system," he told them, which is what they had been thinking for years. A stupid, stupid rigged system. And so they rose to the surface. They attended Donald Trump's rallies. They bought MAGA hats and wore them proudly, gave him money, cheered his irreverence. They found one another on the web and their ranks grew stronger, went deeper, reached out like tentacles of power to anyone who believed what they believed. They had power again and they knew it.

One of their own was HE, always known as HE. Always capitalized in that way. HE and Thor Larsson were active on a far-right blog hosted on the dark web. HE was one of a very small group who knew they could send snail mail to a certain post office box in Minnesota and be certain that Thor, the Storm God, would receive it. And shortly after that, HE would receive mail in return. Then in the early fall of 2016 there was no return mail. HE had no way to know what had happened to the brilliant, prolific writer of fire and truth, and continued to send queries out to him, requests for information on what had happened to silence this wonder, this man they called Thor.

HE had no way to know that on a sultry Saturday, this Storm God had faced his son in rage when the younger man defied Thor's demand to be left alone. HE had no way to know that Thor had lashed out with a lifetime of hate boiling within him and had fallen to his death as a result. There were no obvious connections between Professor Lars Bergen of The Writers' Workshop and Thor Larsson. HE was left to roam the darkness on his own, reading again the many works of Thor along with other inspirations like David Duke's *My Awakening*. HE was left to fuel his own rage at the American government that had failed hard-working white men. But even without new word from the Storm God, HE marched forward in the knowledge that a new voice for the right and righteous would soon become president of the country and purge the ranks and build the walls. And all would be well again.

In Minneapolis, Andrew found a post office box stuffed with letters from all over the country. He read two of them and chose to share none of them. The night after this discovery, he built a fine fire in his library fireplace and tossed the letters in, watching the flames surge with each and every one.

ELECTION DAY

At the start of 2016 during the NFL playoffs, Vikings kicker Blair Walsh had missed a twenty-seven-yarder in the final seconds of a crushing 10-9 wild-card loss to the Seattle Seahawks. And the summer ended with the Twins setting a team record of 103 losses, the worst in the league. So Sunny and Susie were putting their bets on Hillary Rodham Clinton to break this losing streak.

Today was election day. The bruising campaign was over. Polling places were filled with Americans exercising their franchise, the most sacred element of a democratic republic. "Hillary could become the first woman president of the United States of America!!" Susie wrote this in her journal in her best Palmer Manuscript style and punctuated the sentence with two exclamation points.

Both she and Sunny were rested and ready for an eventful evening, wearing their favorite Hillary Clinton campaign button that read Madame President. "It's Hillary's time, don't you think?" Sunny asked, already knowing the answer.

"I just wish she hadn't called them a basket of deplorables. Civility and trust are what hold the country together."

Sunny nodded. "She did kind of sink down to his level with that comment."

They didn't turn on the television until the polls had closed in the East. They enjoyed a leisurely dinner and drank an extra glass of their favorite prosecco to toast Hillary Clinton, then cleaned up the kitchen and made themselves comfortable to watch history being made. It had been a day of good weather and high turnout and they knew in their hearts they were going to hear good news.

But immediately they saw that things were going in an unexpected direction. From the minute they turned on the television the bad news began and continued until it was clear that Hillary would not be the first. She had lost key states and the electoral college, and she would not be the first woman president of the country. Sunny and Susie sat numb and in tears as they watched her concession speech in the early hours of the next day.

They would not have been able to sleep even if they had gone to bed. Instead they turned off the television and sat silently together through the night.

Born in the late 1920s, Suzie and Sunny grew up with Roosevelt as their president. He gave the country confidence to face the enormous challenges of the Depression and World War II. "There is nothing to fear but fear itself," he had said. Susie and Sunny were not disillusioned or cynical when thing got difficult. Their entire lives had taught them that when people shared values and aspiration, they accomplished great things. They believed in the objectivity of truth and the complete equality of the sexes. They had worked shoulder to shoulder with their husbands to build a company that employed many good people and now they supported a foundation that helped many more good people. They knew that America was at its best when it strived for justice, truth, and freedom. They sat together, old friends who had been side by side for most of their lives, and they thought about the country they loved and the lives they had lived.

Near dawn Sunny turned to her best friend. "Is this the end of our democracy?"

But Susie had no answer.

GIVING THANKS

The next four years did nothing to assuage Susie and Sunny's concern about the state of their democracy. But they both had routines and grandchildren and each other, so life continued day by day. They had seen many of their friends pass away and also their reliable former employee Lucy Shea, who died early in the Covid pandemic. It was around that same time when Susie noticed her best friend's growing frailty, Sunny's shortness of breath and more frequent naps. So it should not have surprised her when, in the middle of watching the startling television coverage of the January sixth insurrection at the nation's Capitol, Sunny suddenly stopped speaking mid-sentence and was gone.

Sunny did not get to see Joe Biden sworn in, a president elected by eighty-one million voters, more than any other president in history. For Andrew, who at seventy-one campaigned energetically for Biden, this new presidency reinvigorated his interest in teaching his students that democracy is not inevitable, that the fight is always and ever alive. Andrew's daughters, Sarah and Angela, were his light of the future. The two were making political documentaries and writing Andrew about the despair and hope they saw in their travels, the rage and exhaustion across the country.

Andrew also heard from Ellie Mae's son Jack regularly, the two of them bonded by a point of view about the world and their love of country. To Andrew, Jack and Laura were real patriots doing the hard, day-to-day work of the government. They had their day jobs at the State Department and their undercover work as professional "listeners," seeking those who had important information on what was dangerous to the nation.

Although Ellie Mae didn't completely understand her younger son's work, she believed Andrew when he told her, "Jack is a hero," and she relished that thought and meditated on that possibility.

Cameron III, however, continued to break her heart. He had now lost the remaining family buildings, which sold for no more than the mortgage balances in the grim summer of 2020, leaving Cameron virtually penniless. He told her he was working at a firm helping buyers and sellers of single-family houses these days, rebranding himself as a hot success in local real estate. "Can't make money owning commercial property anymore, Mom. That ship has sailed," he repeated every time they talked, and Ellie Mae would nod as if she agreed, though she really never did.

The surprise of the family after the death of Lars turned out to be his son's comfortable role in the Bergen-MacAlpine circle. Richard Scott's life had changed dramatically the day he met Sunny and even more so the day he inherited his father's millions. His mother Rose Mary had loved him, but she had struggled and suffered so much and Richard had been apart from her most of his childhood. Everything now was new, the warmth of an extended family, the money to live well and do well, and the duplex left to him from his father's estate.

This home of his was another turning point for Richard. He had never felt so content or so safe, and within months of settling in, he knew he wanted others to have this too. He wanted to use his inheritance to provide homes for others. The day he asked Sunny and Susie if he could create low income housing through their foundation, and distribute his money through their non-profit, the two women sat late into the night marveling at this kind young man who had come to them under such troubling circumstances.

"Isn't it something how Richard looks so much like Harold, Susie? It's almost as if Harold is here again."

"He's got Harold's big heart, Sunny. Lars never did, we both know that, though who knows why. And now Richard's interested in housing the way Harold always was. Isn't that something?"

"Remember how Harold and Cam used to dream about building things after the war?"

"We all worked hard making that happen, didn't we?"

"And now here's Richard building much needed homes in a different way."

They vowed to help him in any way they could.

That was sometime in 2017, when Sunny still took an active role in the foundation and both women worked hard to combat the anger and polarization they were seeing bubble up in their country. Both women were pretty sure the trouble had started with the growing income inequality and workers not able to get ahead, unlike their union employees all those years.

After Sunny died, Susie and Richard spent more time together. Richard developed an appetite for knowledge and wisdom and Susie shared her insights and books from her ample library. Andrew also contributed ideas, books and magazines, and they spent many thought-provoking evenings together in Susie's living room.

Now in November of 2021, Susie sat alone at the head of the Thanksgiving table. When she raised her glass to toast all those the family had lost through the years—Sunny and Harold, her husband and elder son, Lena and Lars—she wanted to explain to the others what living meant to her. "I came from a large family, I had many sisters, and I've always seen the people around me as family too. I've been fortunate to live comfortably but that hasn't been my purpose. I feel that my love for others has been my legacy, those who have benefited from me and Sunny, Harold and Cameron. That's what has been key. I want you all to know that. Love is the key."

As Susie finished her Thanksgiving toast, Cameron III sized up the group to see who might be in the market for a bigger house.

"Hey, Andrew," he said to his uncle as he passed him the mashed potatoes, "maybe you and my mother could let me sell your houses and I'll find you a home on Lake Harriet where you can live together."

"That's an idea, Cam," Andrew said. Lately, he'd had that very same idea.

Made in United States
Orlando, FL
10 March 2022